CELIA C. PÉREZ

Kokila

Readers love *Strange Birds*!

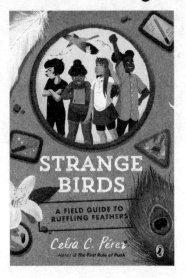

"*Strange Birds* respects its readers' intelligence and sophistication. Pérez's charming story explores what it means to belong to a community while being willing to stage small but significant revolutions, all the while reveling in the joy of childhood."

> —Erika L. Sánchez, *New York Times* bestselling author of the National Book Award finalist *I Am Not Your Perfect Mexican Daughter*

"An inspiring story about the power of truth, and of true friends."

> —Rebecca Stead, *New York Times* bestselling author of the Newbery Medal winner *When You Reach Me*

"Thought-provoking, timely, and laugh-out-loud funny."

> —Aisha Saeed, *New York Times* bestselling author of *Amal Unbound*

★ "Writing with wry restraint that's reminiscent of Kate DiCamillo . . . a beautiful tale."
—*Kirkus Reviews* (starred review)

★ "[An] engaging, well-plotted second novel from Pérez."
—*Publishers Weekly* (starred review)

★ "A perfect title for school and public libraries."
—*School Library Journal* (starred review)

★ "Perfect for preteens becoming aware that friendships can be complicated, and that the world is more so."
—*The Horn Book* (starred review)

A *Washington Post* Best Children's Book of 2019

A 2020 ALSC Notable Children's Book

A *Kirkus Reviews* Best Middle Grade Book of 2019

A Chicago Public Library Best of the Best Book of 2019

A Center for the Study of Multicultural Children's Literature Best Book of 2019

A 2020 Rise: A Feminist Book Project List Selection

A 2019 Middle Grade Fiction Nerdies Selection

A *CCBC Choices* 2020 Selection

A Bank Street College of Education Best Children's Book of the Year, 2020 Edition

Cheers for *The First Rule of Punk*!

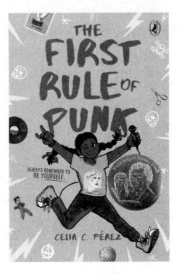

"Malú rocks!" —Victoria Jamieson, *New York Times* bestselling author and illustrator of the Newbery Honor winner *Roller Girl*

★ "Charming." —*Kirkus Reviews* (starred review)

★ "Vivacious." —*School Library Journal* (starred review)

★ "Exuberant." —*Publishers Weekly* (starred review)

A 2018 Pura Belpré Author Honor Book • A 2018 ALSC Notable Children's Book • A 2018 Tomás Rivera Mexican American Children's Book Award Winner • A 2017 ABA Indies Introduce Title •

A Kids' Indie Next List Pick • An E. B. White Read-Aloud Middle Reader Award Honor Book • A 2018 *Boston Globe–Horn Book* Fiction and Poetry Honor Book • An Amelia Bloomer List Book • A *CCBC Choices* 2018 Selection • A 2017 Nerdy Book Award Winner • A 2018 Judy Lopez Memorial Award for Children's Literature Honor Book • A *Publishers Weekly* Flying Start • A 2018 Américas Award Honorable Mention Title • An NPR Best Book of 2017 • A *Kirkus Reviews* Best Middle Grade Book of 2017 • A *School Library Journal* Best Book of 2017 • A *Horn Book* Fanfare Selection • A Center for the Study of Multicultural Children's Literature Best Book of 2017 • A NYPL Best Book for Kids 2017 • A Chicago Public Library Best of the Best Book 2017 • An Evanston Public Library 101 Great Book for Kids 2017 • A Seattle Public Library Top 10 Children's Chapter Book of 2017 • A UPenn Graduate School of Education Best Book of 2017 • A 2018–2019 Dorothy Canfield Fisher Children's Book Award Nominee • A 2018–2019 Sunshine State Young Readers Award Nominee • A 2018 Great Lakes, Great Reads Award Winner

KOKILA

An imprint of Penguin Random House LLC, New York

First published in the United States of America by Kokila,
an imprint of Penguin Random House LLC, 2022

Visit us online at penguinrandomhouse.com.

Library of Congress Cataloging-in-Publication Data
Names: Pérez, Celia C., author. | Title: Tumble / Celia C. Pérez.
Description: New York: Kokila, 2022. | Audience: Ages 9-12. | Audience: Grades 4-6. |
Summary: Before she decides whether to accept her stepfather's proposal of adoption, twelve-
year-old Adela Ramírez reaches out to her estranged biological father—who is in the midst
of a career comeback as a luchador—and the eccentric extended family of wrestlers she has
never met, bringing Adela closer to understanding the expansive definition of family.
Identifiers: LCCN 2022010149 (print) | LCCN 2022010150 (ebook) |
ISBN 9780593325179 (hardcover) | ISBN 9780593325193 (ebook) | Subjects: CYAC:
Wrestling—Fiction. | Families—Fiction. | Mexican Americans—Fiction. | New Mexico—Fiction. |
LCGFT: Novels. Classification: LCC PZ7.1.P44747 Tu 2022 (print) | LCC PZ7.1.P44747 (ebook) |
DDC [Fic]—dc23 LC record available at https://lccn.loc.gov/2022010149 | LC ebook record
available at https://lccn.loc.gov/2022010150

Book manufactured in Canada

ISBN 9780593325179

1 3 5 7 9 10 8 6 4 2
FRI

Design by Jasmin Rubero
Text set in Alkes

For Brett

★ CHAPTER 1 ★

I bit into a french fry, one of those tiny crunchy pieces that always make their way to the bottom of the pile, just as Apollo slammed a folding chair across The Eagle's back. The small TV on the shelf behind the counter was muted, and while I couldn't hear the whack of metal against muscle, it startled me anyway. I flinched and jabbed myself with a shard of potato so hard that my eyes watered.

"Uyyyy," Alex said. He peered up at the TV from the flat-top grill and let out a slow whistle. "El Águila is getting his butt kicked again, eh, Adelita?"

"Yeah," I said. I ran my tongue over the fresh cut on the roof of my mouth. *"Again."*

"Maybe he'll win this one, right?" Alex winked at me and cracked an egg into a bowl.

I watched as he attacked the egg with a fork. Alex said the key to making a good scrambled egg was to keep the heat low and to beat the egg before pouring it into the pan. In general, I found the idea of eating eggs gross, but even I had to admit that Alex made a fine scrambled egg. Still, when he caught my eye and motioned to the runny glob he was cooking, I shook my head.

Bacon grease popped and snapped on the grill as Apollo smacked the palm of his hand across The Eagle's chest. A sizzle and the scrape of a spatula accompanied The Eagle bouncing off the ropes, zipping across the ring, and attempting a failed clothesline. My insides jumped as if the mat, which vibrated with each impact, were sitting in the middle of my stomach.

On-screen, The Eagle showed no signs of winning this one. He struggled to get up, only to be met with the toe of Apollo's golden boot. He didn't stand a chance.

"Why does The Eagle always have to lose?" I asked.

"Because he's a jobber," Alex said, not looking up from the grill.

"What's a *jobber*?"

"A jobber puts over the other wrestler," Alex explained as The Eagle tried to untangle himself from the ropes.

"Plain English, please."

"It means his job is to lose and make the other guy look good," Alex said. "He's not a heel nor a face. Not a bad guy and not a good guy. Just—"

"—a jobber," I finished.

Unlike Apollo, who was definitely the good guy. He's the one you're supposed to want to win. But Apollo had enough people cheering for him already, so I found myself going for the masked luchador. Mom says someone has to root for the underdog. That someone is me.

While The Eagle slowly got up and rolled back into the ring, Apollo climbed to the top turnbuckle and waited like *he* was the bird of prey. I knew what was coming next. Wrestling might look like chaos, just a couple of people brawling, but it's a ballet. And anyone who was a fan would know that the final curtain was about to drop.

Sure enough, when The Eagle stood and turned, Apollo pushed off like his boots had springs, flying through the air in his signature closing move, the Sunset.

"And that's liiiiights OUT!" Alex yelled, just like the ringside announcer did every time Apollo finished off an opponent. He slashed his spatula through the air for dramatic effect.

"Hey," I said with a frown. "Whose side are you on anyway?"

"Yours, Adelita." He pointed at me with the spatula. "Always."

I rolled my eyes. Alex was my stepfather. He was supposed to say mushy stuff like that.

Alex lifted his Albuquerque Isotopes baseball cap, revealing the shiny bald spot that had expanded over the years, the area of hair on his head shrinking like a polar glacier. He wiped his forehead with the back of his hand before pulling the cap on.

"Order up!" he yelled, smashing the bell on the counter.

On the TV screen, The Eagle lay motionless in the ring. *Get up get up get up.* I thought the words so hard, I was giving myself a headache.

The referee dropped down next to the wrestlers and started the count.

"One!" He slapped his hand against the mat.

Get up.

"Two!" The crowd was counting along with him now.

Get. Up.

"Three!"

The bell rang, signaling the end of the match. Apollo stood and pumped his fists in victory while the audience cheered and whistled in appreciation.

In the grainy image, I could see The Eagle's belly rise and fall with each heavy breath, like a ball of unbaked dough. He rolled over on his side, and the camera zoomed in on him. His spotted gold-and-brown mask was slightly twisted. Something about the way the mouth and eye holes didn't line up with his face made me feel sad for him. He looked like a helpless little kid who needed an adult to fix his costume. I wanted to reach through the TV and straighten him out.

I slumped on my stool, feeling like I'd lost too. I looked away from the screen and pushed my fries around on the plate, making a french fry face on what was left of my pancake syrup.

The door to the kitchen swung open, and Mom came

out of the back, pulling her curly dark hair up into a messy ponytail. Her T-shirt rose a bit, exposing her stomach, the tight skin like a big brown balloon ready to pop.

"Mom," I whispered.

"What?" she whispered back.

I widened my eyes in the direction of her midsection.

"Oh." She laughed and pulled down on her shirt. "I thought I felt a draft."

"Not funny," I said.

"Ay ay ay." Mom groaned and made a face at the TV, where The Pounding Fathers rode in on horseback while "The Star-Spangled Banner" played. "They could at least be historically accurate," she said. "The Founding Fathers came before 'The Star-Spangled Banner.'"

"It's not supposed to be historically accurate," I said. "They're *zombies*."

"And the zombies come *after* the apocalypse," Alex added. "Everyone knows that."

Mom and I looked at each other and shook our heads.

"Does this have to be on all the time?" Mom asked, reaching across the counter and switching off the TV.

"It does," Alex said. "This is wrasslin' country, lady."

And it was. Roswell had its aliens. Albuquerque had its hot-air balloons. We had wrestling. Lots of people came into Esperanza, one town over, for Cactus Wrestling League matches at the arena. The diner stayed open later on the weekends to feed hungry fans after the matches.

The menu was even separated into two sections: The Undercard—breakfast and lunch—and The Main Event, which was dinner, of course.

Alex had grown up a wrestling fan. The wall across from the counter was decorated with lucha libre masks he picked up at events in Esperanza and on trips to Mexico. His old wrestling action figures sat on the shelves behind the counter, flexing their muscles between big jars of homemade salsa and pickled peppers and plastic tubs of spices. His most prized possession was a signed and framed black-and-white photo of André the Giant that was propped up on a shelf above the flat top. Next to it was a color photo of Alex as a little boy standing next to the seven-foot-four wrestler, who had visited the diner after an event in Esperanza. On the other side of the signed photo was an André the Giant action figure. The whole thing was a shrine to his favorite wrestler.

It was hard not to be a wrestling fan in the Dos Pueblos area—the neighboring towns of Thorne, where we live, and Esperanza, where Cactus Wrestling happens. I wasn't a fanatic like Alex, but I liked the characters and the costumes and the stories. Wrestling was a lot like mythology, and I loved mythology.

"It's too early for body slams," Mom said. Mom was definitely *not* a fan. "And it's giving me indigestion."

"You sure it isn't you-know-who?" I pointed to her pregnant belly.

"That's possible," Mom said. She looked at my plate. "Speaking of indigestion, the last time I checked, french fries were not a breakfast food."

"Says who?" I asked.

"I tried to give her some hope," Marlene called over from the table she was wiping off. She laughed at her own joke.

There were a lot of things about the Four Sisters Diner that hadn't changed since Alex's grandfather opened it in 1963. Marlene Rosado was one of them. Marlene was the closest thing I had to a grandma. She was tiny and ancient, with a cap of tight black curls that made her look like she wore a blackberry on her head. Despite her age, she moved around quicker than most of the younger servers. She always said that when she stopped moving, she'd know it was time for her to go. "And by go, I mean *GO*," she'd say, and look down toward the ground in case people weren't sure what she meant.

Marlene liked to holler out orders in diner lingo. She said things like "moo and wrap" for beef enchiladas and "don't cry over it" for no onions. She said diner lingo was a dying language.

"These young people today speak in mojitos," she said one day.

I told her the word was *emojis*.

"Mojitos, emojis, whatever it is, there's no poetry in it," Marlene complained.

Anyway, *hope* is diner lingo for oatmeal, which is funny because oatmeal seems about as hopeless a breakfast as I can imagine.

"Oatmeal is cringe," I said. Even more than eggs. "Besides, french fries are practically hash browns. *And* I had a piece of French toast too."

"Ooh la la." Alex twisted an imaginary mustache. "French fries *and* French toast. Oui, oui, mademoiselle."

"You are reaching dangerous levels of corniness," Mom said, but she laughed anyway as she bent down to pull something from behind the counter.

"Look what I remembered." She placed a white poster board in front of me. "What are you doing with this again?"

"I told you already," I said. "Like, three times."

"Fourth time?" Mom gave me an apologetic look. "Please?"

"It's for the mythology assignment," Alex said, walking to our end of the counter while Carlos took over the flat top.

"See? *He* remembers."

"And what's that supposed to mean?" Alex pouted.

I didn't say anything, but what it meant was that stepfathers don't have to remember.

"I knew that." Mom tapped her forehead.

Between getting ready for the baby and helping with the diner and her real job at the museum, Mom said she didn't have room for one more thing in her brain. That one more thing was me, I guess. She said it was good that I was old enough to take care of a lot on my own. I thought it was pretty convenient how I was old enough to handle the stuff she couldn't remember or make time for but not old enough for everything else.

"Your mom has a lot on her plate right now," Alex said. He looked at his watch. "Don't leave. Let me grab your lunches."

Mom came out from behind the counter and put an arm around my shoulder. She gave me a little squeeze. Mom wasn't a hugger, and awkward hugs from Mom usually meant one thing.

"How are you feeling?" she asked, tucking a strand of hair behind her ear.

Mom wasn't very good at showing her feelings. I think expressing herself made her uncomfortable, like I feel when I see people kiss in movies.

"I'm fine," I said, shimmying out from under her arm.

Alex came out of the kitchen with two brown paper bags that he set on the counter in front of us.

"Sardine-and-horseradish sandwiches." He let out a maniacal laugh and went back to the flat top.

Mom and I both scrunched up our faces.

"You're always fine," Mom said with a sigh. "I wish you would tell me how you're feeling. You're just like me."

"Why do you always do that?" I asked, opening my lunch bag and sniffing. Just in case.

"Do what?"

"'Just like me,'" I mimicked and sighed. "Who else would I be like?"

The question wedged itself between us like when we have to squeeze three people into one seat on the school bus for field trips.

"We haven't really talked about the adoption," Mom said. She looked at me and then over at Alex.

We have these old ornaments that we put up on the diner's Christmas tree every year. The glass is so thin that they shatter easily, and then they're impossible to clean up—little flecks everywhere. Sometimes, talking with Mom felt like putting up those decorations. Each word, each feeling, was a delicate glass ornament that could break if it wasn't handled carefully. The adoption was one glass ornament. My biological father was another. Sometimes it was just easier to not talk.

"I'm fine," I said again. I took a sip of milk. The raw spot on the roof of my mouth hurt. "And I have to go to school. Unless . . ."

"No unless," Mom said. "We'll talk later." But she seemed relieved to not have to continue her attempt at a conversation. "Don't forget this."

She nudged the poster board toward me, then tugged on her shirt again before collecting my plate. When she turned away to scrape the french fry face into the trash, I grabbed my lunch bag and the poster board and hopped off the stool so fast, I almost tripped on my own feet.

I pushed open the diner door with my sneaker, ignoring Alex's *Enjoy your sardines and horseradish*, ignoring Mom's *Have a good day*, ignoring Marlene's wave at the window. I threw the brown bag in my bike basket and pedaled away.

★ CHAPTER 2 ★

There's a poster of the pantheon from *D'Aulaires' Book of Greek Myths* hanging in Mrs. Murry's classroom. It looks like an outtake from a family photo session. Hera is smiling, and Zeus looks like the serious patriarch. They stare at the camera. They're ready to have their photo taken, but the rest of the family isn't. Aphrodite's head tilts down, her eyes closed. Poseidon looks to his left, like someone outside the frame called to him. Hermes appears to be up to no good. By the way Ares stares at him, he knows this too. Demeter fusses with baby Persephone on her lap. Hades couldn't even be bothered to show up. He's too much of a rebel for something like a family portrait.

I imagined the Greek gods and goddesses wearing matching funky Christmas sweaters and standing for a photo in front of the tumbleweed snowman on Route 13 just like Mom and I do every year. One year, we wore gray sweaters that had reindeer with bright red plastic noses that squeaked when you squeezed them. Another year, we wore chunky green sweaters with sparkly silver tinsel. One of my favorites was the sweater with the fireplace pattern and real stockings hanging off the front.

Mom hung each year's photo on the same wall in the living room. She used a ruler to make sure the photos were even and then had me stand back with her to check that nothing needed adjusting. We had a tumbleweed snowman photo on the wall for every Christmas. Or at least that's what I'd always assumed.

Until one day, a few years ago, when I was in the third grade. I was working on a math assignment where we had to count groups of things in our home. I counted the snowman photos, and then I counted the age I was in each one. That's when I realized that my first Christmas was missing from the wall.

"There was never a photo for that year," Mom said when I asked her about it.

The next time I asked, she said it must have gotten lost. That's when I learned that adults sometimes lie.

When I lied, it was usually because I was afraid of getting in trouble. Because I knew I'd done something I shouldn't have done. Like the time I ate half the lemon buttercream frosting Alex had made for Marlene's birthday cake. But what reason did Mom have for not telling the truth? I didn't know. What I *did* know was that the wall suddenly felt . . . incomplete. Just like the pantheon illustration without Hades. Just like I did. I also knew the truth usually had a way of coming out. Like it did when I threw up the lemon buttercream all over the diner floor.

Mrs. Murry started each class by reading from the big

mythology book. Even though we were in the seventh grade, no one complained about being read to. She let us spread out and get comfortable. It was the one time in the school day when it almost felt like we weren't in school, and we could just be. It was the one time when everyone paid attention—even Brandon Rivera.

Today Mrs. Murry read to us about Cronus swallowing his sons because he was afraid one of them would grow up to be more powerful than him. When she finished, she let us spend the rest of class brainstorming for our mythology projects.

Cy dragged her desk over so that it touched mine.

"What are you going to do?" she asked, plopping down in her seat.

"Your hair!" I glanced at Mrs. Murry, afraid I'd been too loud. I unrolled my poster board, but my eyes were back on Cy's new hairdo.

"Do you like it?" she said, posing. "I asked the lady who does my mom's hair to make me look like Cleopatra in that old movie."

Cy's head was covered in tiny braids that hung to her shoulders and ended in gold beads that made little clicking sounds when she moved. Her bangs were straightened and cut bluntly across her forehead as if someone had trimmed along the edge of a bowl. Cy shook her head, and the beads grazed her brown cheeks.

"It looks very you." I smiled at my best friend.

A lot of people found it hard to believe that Cyaandi Fernández and I were best friends, because we seemed like opposites. She was the kind of kid who would come to school wearing mismatched high-tops—one purple and one black—green tights, a shiny gold dress, and a totally new hairstyle without feeling awkward at all. Which was admirable because sometimes seventh grade was nothing but awkward.

I had never cut my hair shorter than the middle of my back. Today, I wore one of Mom's button-down shirts over a T-shirt, rolled jeans, and checkered slip-on sneakers. Cy said I dressed like I wanted a cloak of invisibility, which was exactly the point. My style was *please don't notice me* chic.

But Cy wasn't just my best friend. She was more like a sister. We'd known each other since kindergarten, and while we were different in a lot of ways, at our core we were the same. We looked out for each other. That's what made us best friends.

"So"—Cy nudged her head toward my poster board—"what's the plan?"

"There is no plan yet." I shrugged. "This isn't due for a while anyway. Why is she having us work on it already?"

"I'm making oracle cards," Cy said, holding up a stack of purple index cards. "I'm going to draw the gods and goddesses and characters from mythology on them. Maybe

15

I'll do readings. I'll be like the oracle at Delphi without the wacky gases."

"That's a good idea," I said, wishing I had a plan too.

"Brandon gets the Medusa card." Cy frowned at the boy who was shooting balls of paper into the garbage can, the spell from Mrs. Murry's read aloud broken.

"Can I ask you something?" I said, staring at my blank poster board. It was like an oversize oracle card that revealed nothing.

"Listening." Cy leaned over an unlined index card and began drawing.

"If you were an adult and you wanted to hide something from your kid, where would you hide it?"

"Interesting question," Cy said. I waited while she drew. She was quiet for so long that I thought she might've forgotten I asked her a question. Finally, she spoke. "It depends."

"On what?"

"Well, if it's a boy, I would definitely put whatever I was hiding in a place I knew he wouldn't look," she said.

"Obviously," I said. "But like where?"

"Like in a box of maxi pads," Cy said. She laughed but didn't look up from her drawing.

"Yeah," I said, thinking. "That's a good spot. But what if it's a girl?"

"If it's a girl," Cy said, "that's trickier."

"Why?"

"Because girls are way more curious and wouldn't be scared off by something like maxi pads," she said.

"I don't know if that's true," I said.

Until recently, *I'd* never even been curious enough to seek out anything about my biological father.

She looked up at me. "Is this about the adoption?"

"Maybe," I said.

"You're searching for something." Cy put down her pencil and eyed at me suspiciously. "What is it? I want to know."

"I'm not sure . . ." I hesitated.

"Well, in that case, you're never going to find it," Cy said and turned back to her index cards, her braids sliding off her shoulders.

I stared at my blank poster board. What if Mom had been telling the truth? What if there never was a first photo? But then why would she lie and say it was lost? Deep down, I knew exactly what I was looking for.

"You're right," I said with certainty. "I am looking for something, and I think I know what it is. Wanna help?"

★ ★ ★

Mom and Alex had sprung the adoption surprise on my birthday. I should've known something was up, because they seemed distracted all day. Even during dinner at my favorite Korean BBQ restaurant, Mom didn't talk about fossils or say something weird, like how the baby was sitting on her bladder. And Alex wasn't workshopping new diner menu ideas. They seemed to be only half listening to anything I said.

After I'd opened gifts and we'd had the best homemade chocoflan, while I played around with the little powder-blue instant camera I'd gotten, Mom announced that Alex had one more gift.

"Adopt me?" I asked after Alex told me that he loved me and would be honored to be my dad and wanted to know what I thought about him adopting me. It seemed that our definitions of *gift* were not the same.

"I know it's probably confusing and a little strange, maybe," he said.

"A little," I agreed.

"Do you have any questions?" Mom asked. "We know it's a lot to think about."

"A lot," I repeated.

Questions exploded inside my head like balls in a bingo blower. Finally, one rose to the surface.

"Why now?" I asked. "I mean, we live together. And you're married to Mom, and you're already my stepdad."

"That's a great one to start with." Alex laughed nervously.

I looked over at Mom, who was chewing on a nail. Her other hand rested on her stomach. She looked back at me and smiled.

"Well, it's kind of like why I married your mom," Alex said. "Because I love you, of course. I feel like I am your dad, but I'm not *legally* your dad. And like marriage, adoption makes our relationship legally binding. You know what that means?"

"Like a contract?" I said.

"Yeah, like a contract." Alex nodded. "It means that in the eyes of the law, we have a relationship that makes me responsible for you."

"Aren't you responsible for me anyway?" I said, confused. "Why does it have to be legal?"

"Well, yes, and it'd be nice if it was as simple as saying that because I love you and think of you as my daughter, it should be enough," Alex said. He furrowed his brow. "And it is. In some ways. The emotional piece has been there for a long time and is always going to be there. I'm committed to you and your mom, with or without a contract. But other pieces—financial, medical, things like that—those get a little trickier without a legal document."

"So without a piece of paper you wouldn't be responsible for me?" I asked. Sometimes the world of adults made no sense.

"Of course I would," Alex said quickly. "A piece of paper doesn't change how I feel about you or my responsibility to you."

"But?"

"Well, this would make everything legal, official," Alex

said. "I can make decisions on your behalf while you're a minor. And it's just something I've felt like I wanted to do for a long time."

Alex glanced at Mom. I tried to read the look between them, but Alex turned back to me quickly.

"Think about it, okay? It doesn't have to be something you decide right away," he said, taking my hand and giving it a squeeze. "Or at all. My feelings won't be hurt."

I hadn't even considered the possibility of hurting Alex's feelings. I liked to imagine that having hurt feelings was one of those things you outgrew, like a pair of shoes or playing with toys. The idea that you could be a full-grown adult and someone could still hurt your feelings was just too much.

I did think of Alex as my dad. And maybe that should have been enough for me to say yes right then. But I knew there was something missing, even if Mom and Alex didn't acknowledge it: my father. My biological father.

Mom looked like an unassuming science nerd on the outside, but she was full of secrets. My father was one of them. Mom said there was no point in dwelling on the past. Which was ironic because her job at the museum was all about the past. Maybe my father was her past, something she was done with. But he wasn't *my* past. He wasn't anything. The past, my father, they didn't matter to her, but they mattered to me.

At that moment, while Mom and Alex looked at me with hope, all I could think about was the missing Christmas photo. Was it a coincidence that there was no tumbleweed snowman photo for my first Christmas? I didn't know. But I was sure there had to be a connection between my father and the photo, and I intended to figure it out.

★ CHAPTER 3 ★

"Where do we start?" Cy asked.

We biked to my house after school. Usually, Cy and I would eat a snack, do our homework, and watch our favorite telenovela, *Mundo raro*, before she had to go. But today we had other plans. With Mom at the museum and Alex still at the diner, we had at least an hour before anyone came home.

"And what exactly are we looking for anyway?" Cy looked around, hands on her hips and gold beads clicking, as if whatever we were looking for might be in view. "A birth certificate?"

"A birth certificate," I repeated. I hadn't even thought of that. And now, as we stood in the living room, I had cold feet. "Maybe this wasn't such a good idea."

I grabbed the remote control and turned on the TV.

"What are you talking about?" Cy took the remote out of my hand and clicked off the television.

I sat down on the couch and pressed a pillow to my face.

"I don't want Mom to get mad," I said into the pillow. "And I'm probably wrong anyway. And . . ." I tossed the pillow.

"And what?" Cy said, sitting down next to me.

"I guess I'm a little scared," I said. "I never really thought about finding my bio father. But now it feels like I have to."

"You mean because of the adoption," Cy said.

"Of course," I said. "How do Mom and Alex think they can just throw this at me and not talk about him at all? What if I don't ever find out the truth about him? What if I find him and he's awful?"

"Well, you're never going to know anything if you don't at least try," Cy said, standing up. "Come on. Let's find . . ." She grabbed my hand and pulled me off the couch.

"We're looking for photos," I said. "*A* photo."

"Does your mom keep any photo albums?" Cy asked. She walked over to the bookshelves.

"Yeah," I said. "But that would be too obvious if she was hiding photos, don't you think?"

"Maxi pad box?" Cy asked and raised her eyebrows.

I shrugged, and we headed to the bathroom Mom and Alex shared. I hardly ever went into Mom's bedroom. Adult spaces seemed boring. When we stepped into the room, I felt like I was the disobedient Pandora. But unlike her, I wasn't just being nosy. This was important.

"I feel weird poking around in my mom's things," I said.

"Want me to do it?" Cy asked, following me into the bathroom.

"Thanks." I knelt in front of the vanity. "But I can do it."

I opened the bottom cabinet and peered in. Everything

was neatly organized, medicines and a first aid kit, bars of soap, a few extra rolls of toilet paper. I reached in and pulled out a small blue box.

"Tampons," I said, shaking it. I opened the box, just in case, and found nothing but a few paper-wrapped tubes. "What now?"

"Closet? Under the bed? In the dresser?" Cy rattled off possible hiding locations. "I once watched this show where someone hid stuff inside a plastic bag in the toilet tank."

We both looked at the toilet.

"I'll check the closet," I said, walking back into the bedroom.

I could hear the porcelain lid of the toilet tank rattle.

"Ouch," Cy yelped. She came out of the bathroom holding her thumb. "That thing weighs a ton. Nothing but water in there."

She tapped on the trunk at the foot of the bed.

"How about this thing?" The top was piled with clothes, a stack of magazines that threatened to topple over, and an empty coffee-stained mug.

"Sure," I said.

While Cy checked the trunk, I looked in the closet, being careful to place everything back where I found it. Someone who used a ruler to line up picture frames would probably notice if things had been moved around.

I pushed hangers from one end of the rod to the other, checking the space at either end.

"Look at this tiny dress," Cy cooed from where she knelt over the trunk. She held up a blue corduroy dress with yellow flowers. "Is this all your baby stuff in here?"

"I guess," I said, shoving an empty suitcase back into a corner of the closet.

"Ha! Look at this," Cy said. She held up a small red-and-black box of toddler-sized sneakers. There was a 50 percent off sticker on its side. "Can you believe you ever fit in shoes this small?" She looked at the box and then at my current size-eight feet.

"Let me see those," I said. It was the same brand of shoes I still wore. Maybe I *did* need a wardrobe update.

Cy placed the box on the floor and pushed it toward me. I pulled open the lid.

Inside the box, I peeled away layers of brown tissue paper and found that instead of the checkered shoes with Velcro straps pictured on the label, there were photos underneath. I picked up the top one. It was of a younger Mom with Nana, her grandmother who had raised her. I knew that Nana came from a small town just across the border with Mexico, and that she raised Mom when her parents died. I had no memory of her—my bisabuela died when I was still a baby—but she was the only person from Mom's past that Mom *did* talk about.

"Just a bunch of old baby stuff and *a lot* of Christmas sweaters," Cy said, riffling through the contents of the trunk once more before closing the top. "Your mom could open her own Christmas sweater shop."

She crawled over to me. I pulled the photos out of the box and spread them out on the floor.

"Is this what you were looking for?" Cy asked, excited. She knelt over the photographs, her braids dangling so that she looked like a chandelier.

"I'm not sure," I said. "Maybe."

Whoever had taken the photos was a terrible photographer. Some of them were off center or unfocused. Definitely not the stuff you'd put on social media for your friends to see. I knew they hadn't been taken recently. I was born when Mom had just turned twenty, and I wasn't in any of them, so she had to be younger than that. Alex wasn't in any of them, either, and I didn't recognize the places.

Mom didn't have a lot of friends. To be honest, she really didn't hang out with anyone who wasn't Alex or the folks from the diner or the people at the museum. But these photos were filled with people who looked like friends. Maybe even family. Whoever they were, I could tell they were important to her, or at least had been. I wondered if my father was one of the faces that stared back at me.

It felt strange not knowing what Mom's life was like before I was born. Even if she didn't mention my father, you'd think she would at least have a back-in-my-day story like all adults do. Mom had always guarded the information about her life before me. I imagined that maybe she was an undercover government spy, or a secret agent, or even someone in a witness protection program. But the old photos scattered in front of me seemed, well, normal.

I pulled a Polaroid from the stack. It looked like it had been taken through a filter of spun sugar or tulle, everything in the frame soft and dreamy. In it was a teenage Mom—the same Mom as in the other photos—with a boy about her age. She wore jeans, and he wore dark sweatpants. They both had on matching ugly shaggy green sweaters with ornaments embroidered all over the front. Behind them was a curtain of desert oranges and browns. And a tumbleweed snowman.

I almost missed something in the photo because it was so tiny. But there, peeking out from the crook of the boy's right elbow, was a little face. It was me, bundled up in my own ugly shaggy green sweater, one that blended in with the boy's.

I jumped to my feet.

"Where are you going?" Cy asked, scrambling up after me. "What'd you find?"

I hurried into the living room, my legs trembling like flan, to the wall where our annual tumbleweed snowman photos hung. In the space just to the left of the first frame,

I held the white plastic-like border of the photo against the wall with my thumb and forefinger. I had found it. It was our first tumbleweed snowman photo—the missing photo.

Cy looked from me to the wall. She moved in to get a closer look.

"Is that him?"

"I think so," I said. "I'm pretty sure."

"Wow." Cy's eyes widened. "He looks familiar, right?"

"It would be a little strange if he didn't, don't you think?" I said, pointing to my face.

"I guess. What are you going to do? Are you going to tell your mom?"

"I don't know," I said. I walked back to the bedroom, Cy following. We sat down next to the pile of photos. I looked through to see if I could find any others with the same boy.

"Why do you think she never talks about him?" Cy studied the photo.

"All she ever says about my father is that he was someone she'd once known and then she didn't," I said. "Who knows what goes on in my mom's brain."

"She's a complicated lady with a mysterious past," Cy said.

I rolled my eyes. "We need to put all of this away before Mom and Alex get home."

We collected the photographs, and I stacked them

neatly into the shoebox and covered them with the tissue paper. The small container suddenly felt heavier than it looked as I placed it back where Cy had found it.

"Don't forget this," Cy said, holding out the tumble-weed snowman photo.

I took the little square and studied the three faces one more time, focusing on the teenage boy. He had an expression that I couldn't make out. A half smile and something else. I opened the trunk and started to tuck the photo inside the box with the others. But then instead of putting it back, I closed the lid of the trunk and slid the photo into the pocket of my hoodie. If Mom could keep secrets, so could I.

★ CHAPTER 4 ★

Mom is a fossil preparator, which is a kind of paleontologist. She works on fossils in a lab, carefully removing them from the rocks where they've lived for thousands of years. But she also goes on digs, which means she gets to be part of those moments when someone finds something important. She says it's like Christmas morning, except maybe ten times more exciting. I always found it hard to believe that anything could be more exciting than Christmas morning. But in my bedroom that night, I held the photograph and imagined that this was what it felt like.

I looked around the room, thinking of where I could hide the photo for safekeeping. A cork bulletin board hung on the wall over my desk. The surface was covered with keepsakes. There were photos and a tumbleweed snowman postcard Mom gave me and a ticket stub from the Atlantic Wrestling Federation's Fourth of July Destruction in the Desert that I'd gone to with Alex last summer. There were science fair ribbons and Mom and Alex's wedding announcement from a few years ago—a photo of us dressed as Fred, Wilma, and Pebbles Flintstone taken at the museum. But even with so much pinned to the board,

I knew there was a good chance Mom would notice the photograph.

I scanned the bookshelf lined with paperbacks and graphic novels and Alex's old childhood encyclopedia set and some of Mom's plastic dinosaurs and geodes. Hiding it inside a book might work. But I imagined accidentally giving it away and decided against that.

I recalled Cy's toilet tank hiding place and shuddered. And then I remembered being in Mom's room and thought of the perfect hiding spot.

I opened the closet door and pushed aside dresses and shirts and jackets like I was drawing apart curtains. It was only September, but this year's Christmas sweater already hung in the middle. Mom liked to buy our sweaters when all the Christmas stuff went on sale. She said if it was still on the rack after Christmas that meant that it was really ugly, which got bonus points from her.

She always bought a sweater for me, one for her, one for Alex, and one for Marlene. Sometimes she even bought extras. I thought she was just being weird when she'd come home with more sweaters than we needed, most of which, apparently, ended up in the trunk in her room. But Mom was a "just-in-caser" and a "you-never-knower."

"If you or Addie invite someone else to join us in the photo, they can wear their own sweater," Alex insisted. "You don't have to control everything."

But like with the framed tumbleweed snowman photos

on our wall, if Mom could control, she would. And that meant everyone wore the same sweater even if it was too big or too tight. Mom said she wasn't a control freak. She liked things "just so."

This year's sweater was red, with a cactus covered in LED lights. At the top, inside a hole in the cactus, was a star that lit up too. In a metallic-gold cursive font that looked like a lasso was the message MERRY SOUTHWEST CHRISTMAS, PARDNER! It wasn't the ugliest sweater Mom had ever found, but it was the brightest.

I flicked the tiny switch on the battery box, then grabbed a roll of tape from my desk. I tore off a small piece, pulled the photo out of my pocket, and secured it to the wall at the back of the closet.

I moved a few shoes and sat down just inside the doorway. The Christmas lights flashed on the sweater, red, blue, green, one by one, to the yellow star at the top, reflecting on the shiny surface of the photograph.

When I was younger, Mom would make up stories whenever I asked about my father. "I found you in a cholla," she would say. "Like a little wren." When she was being even sillier, she'd tell me I was an alien baby she picked up on a trip to Roswell. I used to hope that one was true.

But since the adoption came up, not knowing who my father was had become like an itch I couldn't scratch.

When we were learning about genetics, Ms. Gaudet told

us about a study done on mice. It found that their brains were more like their fathers' brains than their mothers'. In the same study, scientists discovered that more than half the genes of mice were copied from the father. The researchers thought this might be the case for people too. If that was true, it meant that I was more than 50 percent like some guy I didn't even know.

Which of my traits did I get from my biological father? Was he tall like me? Did he have big feet like I did? Were his arms hairy too? Was he picky about who he was friends with? Did he hate being late?

I had learned early on that bringing up this unnamed ghost was something that put Mom in a strange mood. I didn't like seeing her that way. She'd pretend everything was normal, but she'd get quiet and distracted and irritated if I mentioned him. Mom's silence taught me that I wasn't supposed to ask questions, at least not about him.

Still, I had questions. Why didn't he want to know me? Why was it so upsetting for Mom to talk about him?

Sometimes when I looked at myself in the mirror, I felt like there was a stranger looking back at me. I had a face that was half someone I had never met. These were things I couldn't say to Mom.

"Adelita," Alex's voice called from the other side of my bedroom door. A knock followed.

"What is it?" I said, scrambling to my feet. I switched off the sweater lights.

"Can I come in?" he asked.

"Sure," I said. I closed the closet door and threw myself on my bed. I grabbed a library book from my bedside table and opened it to a random page just as Alex walked in carrying a tall glass.

"No homework?"

I shook my head.

"I need your tastebuds, then," he said and wiggled his eyebrows conspiratorially.

"You can't have them." I slapped my hands over my mouth.

"Fine," Alex said, holding out the glass. "Keep them but try this. Thinking of adding it to the menu."

Alex took over the diner when his grandfather retired. He'd pretty much grown up there and knew everything there was to know about the place. Mom worked there, too, waiting tables while in college. That's how she and Alex met. They were friends for a long time before they got married. Alex was a little older than Mom, but Mom said she liked that he was mature. I think she meant mature in age, because he acted like a kid sometimes. When Mom was in grad school, after Nana died, I spent a lot of time at the diner, since Mom had no one to leave me with. You could say I'd pretty much grown up there too.

"What is it?" I asked, sniffing.

"What does it taste like?"

I took a sip.

"There's cinnamon," I said, closing my eyes and savoring the familiar flavors.

"That's right," Alex confirmed.

"It tastes like Christmas," I said, realizing what the shake reminded me of. "Like biscochitos. I can taste the anise."

"Ding! Ding! Ding!" Alex said. "You got it. That's why I come to you first. You're a supertaster."

"Not really," I said. "A supertaster is someone with a lot of taste buds. They're sensitive to flavors. We did an experiment in science class, and I'm just an average taster."

"Okay, then," Alex said, dropping into the furry bean-bag chair that was propped against a corner. "You're just super."

I shook my head but smiled.

"I'm thinking of calling it the Posadas Shake," he said.

"And maybe you can serve it with a cookie on the side too."

"Good idea," Alex said. "I'll surprise your mom. You know how she loves Christmas."

He folded his hands behind his head. He did that whenever he had something on his mind. I waited.

"I didn't just come to have you taste the new shake," he finally said.

"I didn't think so." I took another sip.

"I wanted to talk to you about the adoption."

"What about it?"

"I just want you to know that you can ask me anything about the whole process, okay?" Alex offered. "We're in this together."

"Anything?" I said, raising an eyebrow.

"Of course."

If Mom wouldn't talk to me about my father, maybe Alex would.

"What do you know about my father?"

"Your father?" Alex asked. His eyes widened.

"You said I could ask you *anything*."

"I did," Alex confirmed. "But you know that's a topic that only your mom can address."

"She never wants to talk about him," I said. "You must know something. Tell me. Please? Is he even alive?"

I imagined that maybe he had been an astronaut who went up into space and never returned. Or maybe he had died saving children and puppies from a burning building. Maybe it was too hard and too sad for Mom to tell me these stories. The father in my imagination was always a hero who wasn't with me because he couldn't be, not because he didn't want to be. But now I panicked at the realization that he might not be alive. What if I never got to know him? What would that mean for me? I felt like I'd been dropped in the middle of an ocean with nothing under my feet but the darkness below.

Everyone around me seemed to have some idea of where they came from. Alex's family had been in Thorne for generations, long before it was Thorne. Like a lot of people in the area, he was a mix of Mexican and the Navajo who had lived on the land forever and the Spanish who colonized it. Cy called herself Blaxican because her mom was Black from Philadelphia and her dad was Mexican American from Albuquerque. I wanted to know, too—more about my mom and something, anything, about my father.

"I'm sorry, Addie," Alex said, shaking his head. "I wish I could."

"Does he know Mom wants you to adopt me?" I asked. I was hoping to trick Alex with a yes or a no that might give me some information.

"This wasn't your mom's idea," Alex said, avoiding the question. "I didn't mean to put either of you in an uncomfortable position."

"It's not fair," I said. "None of this is fair."

"Yeah, I suppose it isn't," Alex agreed and leaned back into the beanbag, staring up at the ceiling from under the bill of his baseball cap. "Your mom might be more willing to share now, so talk to her."

"Why now?" I asked.

"Well, with the adoption," he said, "she has to."

"She has to," I repeated. "What do you mean?"

"Just . . . just talk to her," Alex said.

"Why can't she talk to me?" I asked, anger bubbling inside me. "She's the grown-up."

"I think . . . I think this is hard for her too," Alex said, running his hand along the beanbag's surface. "Maybe she's a little scared."

"Grown-ups don't get scared." I frowned.

"You'd be surprised," Alex said. "I'll tell you one thing I'm scared of. Being stuck in this thing forever. I'll trade you another milkshake for help getting out of this chair."

He held up his arms, wiggling his fingers, and reached out to me. He looked so ridiculous that even though I was angry, I had to laugh.

After I helped Alex up and he left the room, I opened the closet door again and grabbed the photo from where I'd taped it. I didn't believe that Mom would tell me anything. Not if she could help it. I was going to have to find information about the boy in the photo on my own.

★ CHAPTER 5 ★

The lights in the auditorium came on, and I blinked as my eyes adjusted.

"All I have to say is that if Mrs. González makes me a snowflake, there will be trouble," Cy whispered. "There's *snow way* I'm playing a flake."

She poked me with her copy of *The Nutcracker and the Mouse King.* Mrs. González always made the seventh graders read the story before production on the annual show began.

"Good one," I said, though I was too distracted to appreciate the joke.

"Is there a problem, girls?" Mrs. González asked. She stopped where we were blocking the aisle and looked from me to Cy. Her cat-eye glasses made her eyes appear bigger than they were. "Adela? Cyaandi?"

Mrs. González had been the drama teacher at Thorne Middle School, home of the Fighting Long-Nosed Bats, since forever. And she'd been running the seventh-grade production of *The Nutcracker* for just as long. She had been Alex's teacher, and he was forty-something, which was practically as ancient as the fossils Mom handled.

The seventh-grade production of *The Nutcracker* was a tradition in Thorne. The flyers that went up all over town, an open invitation to the community, were as much a sign of the holidays as the tumbleweed snowman. What everyone especially looked forward to was the surprise twist each year's class would put on the show. Once, it was a musical. Another year, it was a shadow puppet show. And after a bat infestation in the auditorium one year, all the characters were bats.

I knew Cy wanted to be the director this year. She had been talking about it for months.

"No problem, Mrs. González," Cy said cheerfully. "I was just saying that I hope you remember that I'm not a snow-flake kind of gal and that my talents would be better used elsewhere." She did a little at-your-service bow. Today, Cy was dressed in yellow corduroy overalls, a white blouse with black polka dots, red-and-orange-striped socks, and black platform shoes.

"Cyaandi, you are certainly unique," Mrs. González agreed. "Just like a snowflake. Remember, no two snow-flakes are alike." She flashed a smile, her lips a bright traffic-cone orange, and squeezed past us toward the exit.

Cy's eyes widened in horror.

"What do you think she meant by that?" she asked.

I shook my head and collected my things. Normally, I might have been excited about the show, but this year was different. How could I think about something like a school production when I had so much else on my mind?

"It's like you don't even care about the show," Cy said, shaking me by the arm. "It's our year to shine, sister."

"Sorry," I said. "I was just—"

"Thinking about the photo," Cy finished for me. "Why don't you ask your mom about it already?"

"Because I can't," I said. I pulled the photo out of my bag, where I'd tucked it into a folder.

"What's the worst that could happen?" Cy said, shoving her book into her backpack.

"I don't know," I said, waving the photo. "My mom will be super angry that I found this."

The auditorium door slammed behind us, and we headed toward the cafeteria.

"Okay, and?" Cy asked. "She'll either tell you what you want to know, or she won't and nothing will be different."

"I did some research online last night," I said. "Did you know that my father has to give up his parental rights for me to be adopted?"

"Hmph. So the person who hasn't been around to be your dad wouldn't legally be your dad anymore."

When she said it aloud it seemed silly to be upset about it. Why should this person get to be my father? Why should he be able to make decisions about my life when he didn't even want to?

"But if he has to give up his rights," I said, "it means that maybe Mom has spoken to him about it. And—"

"And he doesn't seem to be rushing over to meet you," Cy said.

It wasn't what I was going to say, but it fit just as well.

"I'm sorry." Cy gave me a sympathetic look. "This must be really hard for you."

"Yeah," I said. It *was* hard. I looked at the photo again. "Hey, can you make out what that says on his sweatpants?" I shoved the photo in front of her face as she pulled open the door to the cafeteria. Cy let the door go and grabbed the photo.

"It looks like one of those things you see on flags and government buildings," she said, squinting. "Like the Thorne Middle School thingy. It's a seal. Right?"

"A seal, yeah."

The cafeteria door swung open, and Gus Gutiérrez almost ran into us.

"Watch it," he said.

"You watch it yourself," Cy retorted.

"Hi, Gus," I greeted him.

Gus grunted and stepped around us.

"What's his story?" Cy asked.

I turned to glance at Gus as he walked away. He wore the hood of his big brown zip-up jacket over his head while the rest of it hung down his back. His black messenger bag bumped against his hip.

Of all the kids in our grade, I was probably the one that knew anything about Gus's story, and that was next to nothing. We shared a homeroom, and when he appeared on the Friday of the first week of school, Mr. Tanaka had asked me to be his buddy for the day.

Thorne was a small enough place that most of us had gone to school together our entire lives. So there was a buzz of excitement as kids tried to figure out this new person. I was happy to see him at school for my own personal reason: He was the only kid in the seventh grade who was taller than me.

But after a day of asking him questions, all I knew was that he was new to Thorne and that he didn't want to talk. And weeks into the school year, he was still a mystery. I only ever saw Gus alone. He hadn't attached himself to any group of kids. It was like he *wanted* to be alone. He was like a white hole in space where nothing gets in. But I couldn't help feeling bad for him. He never looked lonely, but he seemed angry. So whenever I saw him, I said hello. Even if he didn't respond.

"I don't know," I said, grabbing the photo from her. "But I have another mystery for us to solve."

"Now?" Cy asked. She looked toward the cafeteria and sniffed the air dramatically.

"Yes, now," I said. "I need a magnifying glass. Where can we find one?"

"You know I love a mystery," Cy said. "But I'm hungry. Can we look for a magnifying glass after lunch?"

"Really? I'm looking for my father, and you're thinking

about lunch? Here, you can have mine." I held out the brown bag Alex had packed.

"Library?" she proposed, opening the bag and peering in. "I hope there's something good in here."

"No, let's see if Ms. Gaudet is in her room."

We caught the science teacher as she was leaving the science lab, a bag of microwave popcorn and a stack of papers in her arms. A sad-looking spotted banana stuck out of her lab coat pocket.

"Ms. Gaudet, wait," I called to her.

"Hey there," she said. "I'm on my way to a meeting, and you should be at lunch. What's the emergency?"

"We need a magnifying glass," Cy said. She made a circle with her fingers and peered through it.

"Check the supply closet," Ms. Gaudet said, holding the door open. "There should be some in there. But please make sure the door to the room locks behind you when you're done. Someone took all the earthworms we were going to dissect next week."

"Eww," Cy said, sticking out her tongue. "Why would anyone do that?"

"I'm not sure, but they left a manifesto of sorts," Ms. Gaudet said and shook her head.

"A what?" Cy asked, pulling a plastic baggie of grapes out of my lunch bag.

"A manifesto," Ms. Gaudet repeated. "A statement on the liberation of lab creatures. Something like that."

"Right on," Cy said, raising a fist. "Free the worms."

"We'll be sure to lock up," I said, pulling Cy into the classroom. "Thank you."

"What do you think they did?" Cy asked as we dug through plastic bins in the supply closet.

"What do you mean?"

"With the worms," she said, wrinkling her nose.

"Focus, Cy."

After digging through a few bins, we finally found a box of small magnifying glasses with plastic handles. I held one over the photo and looked, excited about what I might find, like when we studied drops of water collected from the Rio Grande or wet moss to see if there were bdelloid rotifers.

"What is it?" Cy asked. She sat on one of the lab tables, dangling her legs and popping grapes into her mouth.

"It *is* a seal," I said. "It's from Esperanza High School."

I had always assumed Mom had met my father in Albuquerque, where she went to college and where I was born, not in Esperanza, where she'd grown up. I moved the magnifying glass over the photo, looking for other clues. I stopped at the tiny baby face and tried to make out my features.

"So now you know he went to Esperanza High School," Cy said thoughtfully.

"I was born when Mom had just turned twenty; that was twelve years ago," I said, moving the glass to the boy's face. "She would have graduated from high school when she was eighteen. So they would have been at Esperanza High thirteen or fourteen years ago."

"But even if your mom went to Esperanza, you don't know that he did," Cy said. "Although, why else would he be wearing those pants if he didn't go to Esperanza, right?"

"Where can we find yearbooks from Esperanza High?" I asked, thinking aloud.

"At Esperanza High?" Cy offered.

That wasn't the answer I wanted.

"How in the world am I supposed to get into the school?" I said, frustrated.

"Yeah, that's a problem." Cy unwrapped my sandwich. "Why do science classrooms always smell funky?"

"Come on," I said, stuffing the magnifying glass in a pocket of my backpack.

"Where are we going?" Cy asked. She hopped off the table and followed me. I checked that the door was locked behind us and hurried down the hall.

I pushed open the door to the library and went straight to the circulation desk, where Ms. Baig, the librarian, sat. She turned to look at us from her book cart and then glanced at the clock.

"If you're returning books, leave them in the bin," she said. "The bell's about to ring, so come back later to check out."

"We're not," I said quickly. "I have a question."

"Give me one second," the librarian said, collecting a stack of books from the counter and placing them on the cart.

"Vivisection?" Cy said, holding up a book with a caged rabbit on the cover.

"It means testing on live animals," Ms. Baig said, taking the book from Cy. "These are for a display on animal cruelty."

"The more you know, right?" Cy said and gave the librarian a tight-lipped smile. "Poor things."

"What can I help you with?" Ms. Baig said.

"Where can I find old yearbooks?" I asked.

"For Thorne?"

"No," I said. "For Esperanza."

"Well, they'd probably have copies at the high school, but—"

"But what?" Cy said before Ms. Baig could continue.

"Let me check with the public library," she said. The bell signaling the end of lunch rang. "Come back after school, and I'll let you know what I find out."

★ ★ ★

The afternoon dragged as I waited for the last bell of the day to ring. When it finally did, I grabbed my backpack, notebook, and pencil case and rushed out of the classroom. Cy was already waiting for me in the library.

"I've been thinking," she said. "If you have to go to Esperanza for the yearbook, we can ask Kobie to help us."

Kobie was Cy's older brother. He was a junior at Thorne High School. "He can drive, and since he runs cross-country he sometimes goes to Esperanza High for meets. We can just hitch a ride with him."

"Thanks, Cy," I said. I hated to think about having to wait until whenever Cy's brother had a meet in Esperanza. "Let's see what Ms. Baig says first."

Ms. Baig was checking out books to a few students, so we waited nearby. I drummed my fingers on the circulation desk until the librarian gave me a *please stop* look.

"Guess what," Ms. Baig said when she was done. She grabbed a sheet of paper from her desk.

"The public library has them?" I asked hopefully.

"Nope," she said. "But the historical society does. They collect yearbooks and other ephemera from the two high schools in the area. They have the full run of the Esperanza High School yearbook."

"Yes!" Cy squealed and jumped up and down.

"When are they open?" I asked.

"Here's some information about their hours," Ms. Baig said, handing me the sheet of paper.

"They're open until five today," I said, reading over the sheet.

"Plenty of—" Cy started.

The door to the library opened, and Gus walked in. He looked from me to Cy but didn't say anything.

I waved.

"Hi, Gus," Ms. Baig said. "How about finishing up what you were working on yesterday? Here are the books you wanted for the display."

Gus walked behind the desk and rolled the cart away, ignoring us.

"Are you having detention, Ms. Baig?" Cy asked, looking in Gus's direction.

"What? Oh, no." The librarian laughed. "Why would you assume that? Gus volunteers with me after school."

"Let's go," I said, folding the sheet of paper.

"To the historical society?" Cy asked.

"Where else? If we bike over now, we should have time to find what we need."

"What are you looking for in an old Esperanza High yearbook?" Ms. Baig asked.

"She's looking for . . ." Cy glanced at me. I gave my head a subtle shake.

"Fossils," I said. I grabbed Cy by the arm and pulled her out the door.

★ CHAPTER 6 ★

The Dos Pueblos Historical Society was in a big adobe building that looked like someone had draped it with a sheet of burnt-orange fondant. I ran my hand along the smooth wall until I reached the door. I waited for Cy, who was struggling with her bike lock.

"Come on," I said. "We don't have all afternoon."

I told Mom we were staying after school to help in the library. Despite having a mom who was full of secrets, I didn't feel great when I sent the text message with the emoji of stacked books at the end. I knew she would be upset if she found out I was poking around. Even though it was her fault I had to resort to sneaking, I didn't want to disappoint her.

"Okay, let's go," Cy said, jogging up to the door.

We stepped inside the quiet space. It was cavernous but cozy at the same time. The sun was shining in at an angle through western-facing windows, and the room seemed to glow.

"Can I help you, kids?" an older man with white shoulder-length hair and a white beard and mustache greeted us from the information desk. He wore a blue denim shirt with a bolo tie that had a clasp shaped like a silver moon and a name tag that read RUDY.

"Um, yes," I said, walking up to the front desk. "We're looking for old yearbooks. From Esperanza High School."

"Sure, we've got those," he said. "How far back are you looking?"

"Fourteen years ago?"

The man let out a chuckle that made the ends of his tie dance.

"I thought you said *old* yearbooks," he said. "Fourteen years ago was just yesterday."

I looked at Cy, who shrugged. That was the kind of thing Mom might say after a day at the museum. She would say this moment was just a tiny speck in time.

"Follow me," Rudy said, motioning to us.

The place was empty except for a woman who sat at a large wooden table, bent over a book. She looked up at us with sleepy eyes when we walked past.

We followed Rudy into a room with rows of metal shelves. Each one had what looked like a steering wheel at the end. Rudy surveyed the labels on each shelf as he moved along and then finally stopped. He turned the wheel, and the shelves shifted, opening an aisle for us to enter.

"Whoa," Cy said, stepping into the open space. "It's like magic."

"Abracadabra," Rudy said. "Pretty magical, eh?"

He placed one hand on a shelf to the left of him and one on the right. "Now, we've got the old yearbooks on this side and the ancient ones on that side. All chronological. If you need to scan anything, let me know. Sound good?"

"Yes, sir," Cy and I said in unison.

As soon as Rudy left us alone, I turned to the shelves.

"Here," Cy said, immediately zeroing in on and pulling a volume with a maroon cover. "The Esperanza High School Rocket from fourteen years ago. Your mom would've been a senior, right?"

"Yeah." I grabbed the book she handed me and the one from the year before too.

We carried them out to one of the tables next to where the woman was reading. I opened the more recent one and started at the beginning.

"What if they're not in here?" Cy asked.

I glared at Cy and kept turning page after page of teacher photos and candid lunchtime snapshots taken by student photographers.

"Here we go," I said. I'd gotten to the senior portraits and ran my finger down the alphabetical last names on the left margin of the page. "And there she is. There's my mom. Third photo."

"Aww, look at your mommy," Cy said. "Wow, she's even wearing makeup. You go, Ms. Ramírez."

Mom wore the same black top all the girls had on for the

senior portrait. The way she'd done her hair and makeup was unfamiliar, but she had that same smile. She never showed her teeth in photos, like it embarrassed her to do so, and her eyes crinkled at the corners. Underneath their photos, all the seniors had quotes. Mom's read: *"Never lose your curiosity about everything in the universe—it can take you places you never thought possible!"* —*Sue Hendrickson.*

"Who's Sue Hendrickson?" Cy asked.

"She's the paleontologist that found SUE in South Dakota," I said. "SUE's the biggest and most complete *Tyrannosaurus rex* skeleton ever found."

"That's cool," Cy said. "Hey, look at that." She tapped Mom's photo. "That doesn't say Lourdes."

The Mom I knew never wore jewelry, much less a necklace with her own name. I looked closely at the nameplate that lay between her collarbones.

"'Lulu,'" I read the gold cursive script. "That must've been her nickname."

"Oh, never mind, then," Cy said, disappointed. "I thought it was a clue."

"Wait. Look at *that*." I placed my finger next to the nameplate on the necklace, where half a gold heart rested.

"I wonder who has the other half," Cy said.

"How do you know there's another half?"

Cy looked at me and tilted her head.

"It's a heart," she said. "There's *always* another half."

I pulled my language arts notebook from my bag and dug the Polaroid out of the pocket. I studied the teenage boy in the photo. He had long hair and a mustache, but it was hard to really make out the details of his face. If either of them wore necklaces with half hearts, they weren't visible in this print.

"I don't see any boys with long hair," Cy said, scanning the pages of the yearbook.

"This was taken more than a year later," I said, holding up the Polaroid. "At least."

"So it could be anyone," she said, running her thumb along the edges of the pages. "Great."

"Yeah." I sighed, flipping back to the beginning of the senior portraits. I propped my elbows on the table and looked from one face to the next. "None of these boys are wearing—"

"An earring!" Cy yelled.

She pressed her fingertip against a little square photo on the second page. I grabbed her arm and squeezed, holding my breath.

"I think that's him!" I gasped. "He's wearing the other half as an earring!"

The woman looked up from her book again and stared at us. Rudy cleared his throat at his desk.

"Research can be exciting, eh?" he said.

"Indeed," the sleepy reader replied and went back to her book.

"'There's no crying in wrestling,'" Cy read the quote under the boy's photo. "Okaaaay."

I counted back to the names on the margin and ran my finger down the list until I found his.

"Bravo, Emmanuel," I read.

I stared at his clean-cut face. He had a pointy chin. I had a pointy chin too. His dark hair was short on the sides and spiked up at the top. In the Polaroid, his hair was long, but I could tell it was the same face. And unlike Mom, he had a big smile, a crooked smile that showed his teeth and his dimples. He had one on each cheek, just like I did. He looked like someone who was fun to be around. He looked happy. And he wore the other half of the heart in a little hoop in his right ear.

"Let's see if there are more photos," I said, placing my finger between the pages to hold my place.

For the next few minutes, we flipped through the rest of the yearbook. I found Mom in the Future Scientists Club and in the Esperanza Trivia Team, and Emmanuel Bravo was on the wrestling team. He stood in the front row in his Esperanza High School wrestling singlet. I could tell that he was tall too. I looked down at my size-eight feet.

"Your dad was a wrestler." Cy giggled.

"My *father* was a wrestler," I corrected.

When we were almost to the end of the yearbook, and I didn't think there would be any more photos of them, we came to the two-page spread featuring the home-coming court.

"Ohhhh," Cy gasped, looking from the yearbook to me and back to the yearbook.

"Is this for real?" I whispered. "Am I seeing things?"

In the photo, Emmanuel wore a black tuxedo and Mom wore a pretty green sleeveless dress. They both had sashes across their chests and crowns on their heads. I could imagine Mom in a lot of scenarios but never this one. A strange feeling washed over me. The girl in the yearbook was someone who looked like my mom but who people called Lulu and voted homecoming queen. It was like looking at someone I didn't know. For the first time, I realized how much had been kept from me.

"You okay?" Cy asked, looking in my eyes.

"Yeah," I said, blinking. "Let's get a copy of this."

As if he could hear us from where he sat, Rudy stood.

"You girls find what you need?"

"Yes," I said, carrying the yearbook over to him. "Where can I scan this?"

"Come on this way," Rudy said. "I'll help you with that. We use a special book scanner so that we don't break the spines."

"Definitely don't want to do that," Cy agreed. "I myself avoid stepping on cracks for the sake of my mom's back." Her beads clicked in agreement.

Rudy looked amused.

"All right," he said, holding out his hands. "Let me see what you've got."

I passed the yearbook over to him. He looked closely at the homecoming court photo.

"Doing research on Manny Bravo?" he asked, pressing a button on the scanner and placing the book facedown on the glass.

"Who?" Cy asked.

"Manny Bravo," the man repeated.

"You mean Emmanuel Bravo?" I asked. "You know who he is?"

The machine whirred as it scanned the page.

"Not a wrestling fan, eh?" he said, smiling. "Or maybe he's too ancient for you to be familiar with."

Cy and I looked at each other. I imagined the confusion on her face mirrored my own.

"Well, this guy here is Manny 'The Mountain' Bravo," Rudy said, pointing to the photo. "Of the Bravo family."

"The Mountain?" I repeated. "Bravo family?"

"Oh yeah, his father was one of the biggest wrestlers to come out of Cactus back in the day." He handed the book to me. "Anything else you need scanned?"

I found the senior portraits and pointed to Mom's and Emmanuel's.

"And the wrestling team photo too," I said.

"Tell us more about Manny," Cy said as Rudy turned back to the scanner. "And the Bravos."

"I haven't kept up with them in a while," he said. "But there's Manny, the youngest. And Mateo and Speedy. And, of course, their dad, Francisco, El Terremoto."

"The Earthquake," I whispered. I imagined a grandfather I'd never met holding my world up like Atlas and shaking it.

"I believe even their mother might've wrestled in her younger days too," Rudy said. "Want me to email these to you or print them out?"

"Print, please," I said. I watched in a daze as Rudy pressed buttons.

"If you're doing research on the Bravos, we have some wrestling stuff here," Rudy continued. "The Cactus Wrestling League donated their archives to us not too long ago."

"Can we see whatever you have on Emmanuel?" I asked. "And the Bravos?"

"Sure," Rudy said. "But you'll have to come back tomorrow. We're closing soon."

The sleepy reader stood, stretched, and closed her book. She collected a few other books from her table and carried them over to Rudy's desk. The woman wore a long black skirt, a flowy black top, and a big silver-and-turquoise necklace. Her dark hair was threaded with silver.

"You think she's a bruja?" Cy whispered.

"Cy!" I hissed, hoping neither the woman nor Rudy had heard.

"Hasta mañana, Rudolfo," the woman called. Rudy

waved and then motioned for us to follow him toward the door.

"Can I check out something before we leave?" I asked. "Anything from the Bravo collection?"

"Sorry, but that's not how archives work," Rudy said. "You can't take any of this home."

"I thought this was like a library," Cy said.

"It's a kind of library," Rudy replied. "But these things"—he spread his arms out and looked around the space—"these are memories and histories. Everything here is unique. Either one of a kind or one of a few in the world. Researchers like you can come here to use them, but they stay here so that everyone has a chance to use them too."

"We'd bring it back," Cy said. "Scout's honor."

"Sorry, Cleopatra." Rudy winked. "Come back tomorrow."

"Fine," Cy said. "We'll be back tomorrow, right?" She nudged me.

"Right," I said. "Tomorrow. And I'd like to see the Bravo collection. Everything you have, please."

"You got it," Rudy said, gently ushering us outside and closing the door behind us.

The faint click of the lock echoed in my ears. It felt final. Like tomorrow would never come.

★ CHAPTER 7 ★

"You look like you could use a cup of mud."

Marlene's voice drifted from what seemed like somewhere very far away.

"No coffee for her," Alex said from behind the counter. Then he turned to me. "But you do look really tired."

"I'm fine," I snapped.

Alex appeared startled.

"Wanna see who's tumbling on the wrestling channel?" He motioned to the TV with his head. "Might help wake us up."

"No," I said.

Alex slid a sandwich off the flat top and wrapped it in a square of paper-lined foil. He placed it inside a brown bag.

"What's going on?" he asked, putting the lunch sack in front of me.

"Nothing is going on," I said, rubbing my eyes. "I'm just tired." That Alex even had to ask what was going on made me feel crankier.

"I hear you," he said. "I think we're all pretty tired today. Your hermanito was moving around a lot last night, which means your mom was having a hard time sleeping, which means *I* was having a hard time sleeping." He laughed. "He might've been doing some dropkicks in there."

Alex waited for me to say something. He let out a big yawn. It was only seven thirty, but his apron was already smudged with grease and his baseball cap stained with sweat. He always wore his abuelo's old watch, and Monday through Friday he opened the diner at six on the dot according to that timepiece, no matter what any other clock said. "Never been a minute off," he claimed.

"I made you grilled PB&J," he offered. "Hope it's not too soggy by lunchtime."

He waited.

"Thanks," I said, afraid he would never leave.

He patted my head, and as soon as he returned to his workstation, I climbed off the stool and moved to a booth.

I wasn't supposed to keep my phone in my room at bedtime, but last night I couldn't fall asleep. So after Mom and Alex went to bed, I quietly made my way to the kitchen and grabbed it from the counter where I left it every night. Back in my room, I opened the browser to the page I'd been looking at since I got home from the historical society that afternoon.

The Cactus Wrestling League's website had an entry for every wrestler in its history. I went through the list of names and clicked on the link for Manny Bravo. There, I scrolled through photos of Manny "The Mountain" pinning opponents and flexing his muscles for the camera.

I found a few videos of matches where Manny placed opponents across his shoulders in the 3B, the Bravo Back Breaker. He could pick up full-grown men in one swift, graceful motion. He looked confident and sure of himself.

I thought about how in the tumbleweed snowman photo he held me like I was a loaf of hot bread, fresh out of the oven, and he was afraid of burning himself. I realized that the look on his face in the photo, the one I couldn't quite figure out, was fear.

A short biography told me some things I'd already learned about him, like that he wrestled in high school. It listed his father and brothers, my grandfather and uncles, all their names with links to their own pages. Of course, my name didn't appear anywhere. How much did Manny know about me? Did any of the Bravos care that I existed? Had they ever tried to meet me? What would my life be like, what might I be like, if these strangers had been a part of it?

I was disappointed in Alex. Mom had kept the truth from me, but so had he. Alex, who always had his ridiculously small TV tuned in to the wrestling channel, all the time dangling a clue under my nose. Once, when The X Factor turned on Cohete Cortez, his friend and tag-team partner, Alex explained to me what it meant to double-cross someone. I felt double-crossed, too, betrayed by every adult in my life.

Marlene placed a bowl of cornflakes in front of me.

"And a little blond with sand," she whispered, setting a mug of coffee with cream and sugar next to the bowl. "Don't worry, it's mostly milk."

She touched my forehead with the back of her hand.

"You feel okay on the outside," she said. "Wanna talk?"

I smashed the cornflakes into the milk, pretending I was smashing all the grown-ups.

"What's the point?" I grumbled. "No one wants to talk about what *I* want to talk about."

"Pobrecita," Marlene said. She set the coffeepot on the table and sat down. "What do you want to talk about?"

I took a sip of the milky coffee. It was warm and sweet.

"My father." I eyed her expectantly.

"What about him?" Marlene asked, glancing over at Alex.

"Not Alex," I said. "My *father* father."

I chewed on a spoonful of cereal that tasted like wet cardboard.

"Okay, what about the jerk?" Marlene asked.

I coughed, and cornflakes flew out of my mouth. I stared at Marlene, shocked.

"What?" she said, making a face at the specks of cereal that had landed in front of her. "I don't know anything about him, but my guess is he's a jerk."

"Why would you call him that?"

"I don't know," she said, wiping cereal from the table with a napkin. "Maybe because I assume that anyone who abandons their kid with no good reason is a jerk."

"*Abandons*? So you do know stuff about him," I said suspiciously.

"Nah," she said. "I got nothing that's going to be helpful to you. All I know is you have it pretty good here to be wasting time thinking about a j—"

"Marlene, stop it!" I said, but something about the way she shot out the insult made me want to laugh.

"I assume you've asked your mom."

"Mom doesn't want to talk about him."

"Good for her," Marlene said.

"She says when I'm older she'll tell me more," I continued. "How much older do I have to be? As old as *you*?"

"Hey, don't take this out on me," Marlene said and cackled. She let out a big huff and pushed herself up to her feet.

"I'm sorry," I mumbled.

"Alrighty, you need to get going, and I have to get back to work." Marlene straightened her apron. "Came in early today because I'm doing a set tonight."

Marlene did stand-up comedy and hosted a talent night once a month at the Thorne Senior Center.

I sighed and pushed my bowl away. I took one last gulp of coffee and grabbed my lunch bag.

"Addie"—Marlene followed me to the door and held it open—"I know it's hard. And I wish it wasn't. But maybe it's for the best."

She gave me a sympathetic look.

For the best was the worst consolation. Didn't adults know that? I could feel a burning behind my eyes, like something threatened to break. I squeezed them shut and took a deep breath. *There's no crying in wrestling,* I said to myself as I slid past Marlene.

★ CHAPTER 8 ★

As soon as the last bell rang, Cy and I pedaled as fast as our legs could take us until we were back at the Dos Pueblos Historical Society.

The sleepy reader was a familiar sight at her table. There were books spread out around her again. She looked up. Cy waved to her like they were old friends.

"You came back," Rudy said as we approached.

"Reading all day, huh?" Cy asked, motioning to the book on his desk. "This is a pretty sweet gig."

"It *is* a pretty sweet gig," Rudy agreed. "But believe it or not, I don't just read all day."

He stood up and motioned for us to follow him into another room.

"It's freezing in here," I said.

"We keep everything temperature controlled so it doesn't—"

"Melt?" Cy finished, shivering exaggeratedly.

"In a way," Rudy said, leading us past rows of identical gray boxes with labels on their sides. "We don't want anything to decompose or grow mold, so we keep it nice and cold."

"Do you leave your lunch in here?" Cy asked. "This place would make a great refrigerator."

"Not a bad idea," Rudy said. "Except we don't allow food."

He stopped in front of a shelf with several boxes marked CACTUS WRESTLING LEAGUE.

"So this stuff just stays here?" I asked. "In boxes? Like a storage space?"

"Sort of," Rudy said. "Sounds like a storage space, but it's better for these things to live here than in someone's attic or garage, where they aren't available to the public and where bugs and rain or heat or other things can ruin them, don't you think?"

"Yeah," I said, imagining the boxes with information about the Bravos tucked away in someone's office, where I couldn't get to them. "Can we look inside?"

Rudy lifted the lid off a box, and the three of us peered in. It looked like a bunch of papers.

"How are we supposed to find anything in there?" Cy asked. "Do all the boxes look like this?"

"Someone on staff goes through each one and organizes the contents and then creates a finding aid so that researchers like you can easily locate what they're looking for," Rudy explained. "Right now, this is all Cactus League lumped together. We haven't had time to go through these boxes yet. But if someone was looking for something specific, a finding aid would be helpful to have."

"We don't have a lot of time," I said. "How are we supposed to find stuff about the Bravos in here?"

"I set aside what I could find on first inspection," he said. "Over here."

We followed him to a table where another box sat. Another Pandora's box, I thought.

"Working on a research project for school?" Rudy asked, opening the box.

"Kind of," I said.

"A history project," Cy added matter-of-factly.

"All right, well, I'll leave you to it," he said. "Handle everything carefully. No drinking or eating, okay? And let me know if you need help or have any questions."

"Thanks," Cy said. "We will."

I didn't notice Rudy leave, because I was busy lifting things carefully out of the box.

"These are just old contracts," Cy said, looking at some of the papers I pulled out. "Between CWL and Francisco Bravo, CWL and Sebastián Bravo, CWL and Mateo Bravo. And here's a CWL and Emmanuel Bravo." She set the papers aside.

"There are some photos in here," I said.

I sat down to go through the series of promotional eight-by-tens. Each one had a name printed at the bottom and a signature in bold black marker. I pulled the photo of Francisco, my grandfather, from the pile. He was stocky and muscular, with jet-black hair, a boyish face, and flared nostrils. His face was set in a stony expression, like he couldn't let his guard down, not even for the camera. He wore dark wrestling trunks and boots. Around his waist was a championship belt that covered most of his stomach. An engraved metal plate in the center read ATLANTIC WRESTLING FEDERATION. Jewels were embedded above and below the plate, spelling the words WORLD CHAMPION. The photo was signed Francisco "El Terremoto" Bravo.

"World champion," Cy said, staring at the photo. "Wow."

I worked my way through the photographs, studying the faces, all different but similar, like family. Sebastián—also known as Speedy—Mateo, and Manny. In his photo, Manny's hair was longer. He looked more like he did in the Polaroid with me and Mom than in his yearbook picture. He wasn't wearing the earring, and he wasn't smiling. He held his arms out in a stance that made him look like he was ready to grapple. The last photo was of the four of them together, sons on either side of Francisco, with THE BRAVOS OF ESPERANZA, NEW MEXICO printed at the bottom.

"I can see the resemblance," Cy said, looking from the photos in my hand to my face.

"Really?"

"Sure," she said. "You have the same intense eyes. And when you get mad, you do that nose-flaring thing." She pointed to Francisco in the photo.

I flared my nostrils at her, and she giggled.

"Just like that," she said.

We looked through the other items in the box, which included flyers and programs from shows, nothing especially recent, and some script notes.

"There's not a lot in here," I said with a frustrated sigh. "I mean, there is, but nothing that really tells me much about Manny outside of wrestling." I used my phone to take pictures of the promotional photograph of Manny and the one of him with his brothers and father.

"What about this?" Cy asked.

She held up a paperback. I took the book from her. It was a Bravo family biography published by the Cactus Wrestling League. The back cover listed other biographies in the series. The book was short, only about ninety yellowed pages, with a section of black-and-white photos in the middle. The summary on the back promised to tell the reader "everything you ever wanted to know about the Bravos of Esperanza!"

I held on to the book. We placed everything neatly back in the box and walked out to Rudy's desk.

"Done so soon?" he asked.

"Is that all there is?" I said.

"I haven't gone through all the boxes with a fine-tooth comb yet, so there might be more," he said. "I have a student from the university who's going to be helping me organize the collection. Is there anything in particular that you're looking for?"

I considered his question for a moment. I wasn't sure what I hoped to find in the boxes. Maybe something that connected me to Manny. Maybe something that told me what he was really like. Maybe something that explained why he disappeared from my life.

"Not really," I said. "Is there any way I can borrow this?" I held up the book. "Just for tonight?"

"Ah, I'm really sorry," Rudy said. "Like I said before, nothing here can be checked out. It's possible I can scan some pages for you if there's something specific you want to read. Though that book looks a little beat up. I'm afraid it might fall apart if I crack it open, even with our special scanners."

"Oh," I said, disappointed. "Okay, I'll return it."

I walked back to the other room and opened the box. I placed the book on top of the papers and started to close it. I looked over to where Cy was talking animatedly with Rudy about something. Without thinking twice, I grabbed the book and stuck it in the pocket of my hoodie, making sure it was secure, before walking back to the desk.

"The Bravos of Esperanza, New Mexico," Cy exclaimed in a booming voice as if announcing their arrival in the wrestling ring.

Rudy raised an eyebrow, and I looked over at Sleepy Reading Lady, who looked back at me.

"That's what it says on the photo," Cy said. "Are they still? From Esperanza? *In* Esperanza?"

I gave Cy a *what-are-you-doing* look, and she smiled at me.

"As far as I know," Rudy said. "Been there a long time. I believe they own a big plot of land out there."

"What if someone wanted to get in touch with them?" I asked. "Can you find their address online?"

"I doubt that's public," Rudy said.

He turned to his computer and typed in something, clicking his mouse and scrolling. He tried a few different searches, then shook his head.

"Not finding an address," he said. "Let me look up one more thing."

He typed in another search and printed the results.

"Here's an email address for the Bravo Fan Club," he offered. He handed me the sheet of paper. "If you're trying to get in touch with one of them, this might be a good place to start."

I looked at the printout with the contact information.

"Esperanza isn't that far," Cy said. "And it isn't that big, right? How hard could it be to find them? Could someone bike there?"

"Planning on taking a ride?" Rudy laughed.

"Yeah," I said, raising an eyebrow. "*Are* you planning on taking a ride?"

"Nah," Cy said, shaking her head. "I was just thinking out loud. Sorry. My mom says I have no filter."

"It's probably not a good idea to show up at a stranger's house unannounced anyway," Rudy said.

I wanted to ask how someone who was your father could be a stranger. It didn't make sense. And yet, I knew Rudy was right. The Bravos, including Manny, were strangers to me. And I was a stranger to them.

"We should go," I said. "Thank you. You've been a big help."

"All right," Rudy said. "You come back here anytime. Maybe we'll have sorted out the boxes by then."

He returned to the room where we'd been looking through the Bravo collection, and I pulled Cy toward the door.

"We have to go," I said. "Now."

"Psst," Sleepy Reading Lady called to us before we could reach the door. "Come."

Cy looked at me. I looked at her. We both moved toward the table where the woman sat. She was dressed in black again. From up close, I could see that her eyes were different colors. One was green and one was brown, and it felt like looking at two different people.

Eye color is a polygenic trait. That means that several genes are involved in determining what eye color someone will have. So it's not as simple to determine as Mendel's peas might have you believe. But having two different color eyes is very rare. No one could ever predict that. Both of my eyes seemed to be the same shade of brown, but maybe they weren't. Maybe we're all like the woman—two halves that look the same from far away but on closer inspection are different.

"You most certainly can bike to Esperanza," she said. "I do it all the time. Just make sure you've got plenty of water to drink and plenty of air in your bike tires. And . . ."

The woman looked toward the doorway Rudy had gone through as if to check that he wasn't listening.

"And what?" Cy and I said at the same time.

The woman stood and leaned over the table toward us.

"Watch out for La Llorona," she said, widening her eyes. "She often walks along the road, looking to hitch a ride, crying, *¿Dónde están mis hijos?* Whatever you do, don't pick her up on your handlebars." The woman winked her green eye.

And just like that, she sat back in her chair and returned to her book as if we weren't even there.

★ ★ ★

By dinnertime, I was falling asleep at the table. I wanted to eat fast so that I could get to my room and start reading the book I'd borrowed—fine, *taken*—from the historical society. A yawn escaped my mouth.

"Looks like someone needs to go to bed early tonight," Mom said, standing. "Long day at the office?"

"She didn't sleep well," Alex offered before I could say anything.

"I'm okay," I added.

"Well, you're not getting out of cleaning up," Mom said. "But how about I make you a té de manzanilla to help you sleep?"

"Sure," I said. It had been hard to sit with Mom and Alex that night and not say anything about what I knew. Suddenly, everything that came out of their mouths seemed like a made-up story.

We went about our routine quietly. Usually, Mom washes, I dry, and Alex puts away. But now that Mom was pregnant, it was mostly just me and Alex cleaning up. Tonight, Alex and I worked while Mom boiled water for tea. She dropped a tea bag filled with the little dried white and yellow chamomile flowers into each mug and poured hot water over them.

"Here you go," she said, handing me a mug. "And no more screens tonight."

"Okay," I said. "G'night."

"Sleep tight," Alex said.

They settled into the couch with their cups of tea and a show, and I went to my room.

I changed into my pajamas and grabbed the Bravo biography out of my backpack. I felt guilty for taking it from the historical society, and I planned to return it. But right then, I just wanted to read it and learn more about Manny and his family. *My* family.

I opened the closet and pushed aside hangers to reveal the back wall where I'd taped the printouts from the historical society. The Christmas sweater and my bedside lamp gave just enough light to read. I took a sip of my tea and inhaled the sweet, delicate smell of chamomile. Té de manzanilla was Mom's go-to remedio for everything—an upset stomach, insomnia, nervousness, the blues. I knew it couldn't cure what ailed me, but it felt like a just-in-case as I curled up on the floor with the book.

Despite being sleepy, I read for hours. The little yellowed paperback told the story of Francisco Bravo, my grandfather, born in Mexico and raised in Esperanza, who fell in love with a Mexican woman named Rosa Terrones. They had three sons, who followed in their father's footsteps. A "dynasty," the book called it. The four of them battled giants and monsters around the world, from Esperanza to Seattle, from Mexico City to Tokyo. They came back from the brink of defeat, and even when they lost, they weren't down for long. They were betrayed by friends and befriended by enemies. People loved them. Other wrestlers wanted to be them. And through it all, they always had one another.

I read until the very last word, just like I'd devoured *D'Aulaires' Book of Greek Myths*. I learned that the Bravos were mythical too. They were earthquakes and mountains. But the book left me wanting more of the story. The biography had been published ten years earlier, when I was only two. I had changed a lot since I was two. What had happened to the Bravos in those ten years? Why weren't they all over the internet? I had more information about them, but I still felt like I didn't know anything.

I turned off the sweater lights and pushed clothes back into place. I wrapped the book in a plastic bag and nestled it carefully inside my backpack, where I noticed the printout Rudy had given me. I pulled out the sheet of paper. It was the contact information page for the Bravo Fan Club. There was an email address under a post office box address in Esperanza.

I opened my bedroom door quietly and peeked out into the hallway. The door to Mom's room was closed, and the light was off. I made my way to the kitchen, where my phone lay on the counter. I unlocked it and started a new email. I wrote. And I deleted.

Dear Emmanuel Bravo,

Dear Mr. Emmanuel Bravo,

Dear Mr. Manny Bravo,

Dear Manny Bravo,

Dear Mr. Manny "The Mountain" Bravo,

Dear Manny the Mountain,

Dear Mr. Emmanuel "The Mountain" Bravo,

Dear Mr. The Mountain,

Dear Mr. Bravo,

Nothing seemed right. I typed again, my thumbs moving quickly over the tiny letters.

Dear Dad,

Definitely not.

Dear Biological Father,

Even I had to laugh at that greeting. I clicked CANCEL and deleted the draft. I stared at the screen for a few minutes more before typing again:

Dear Manny,

You don't know me. My name is Adela Ramírez. I'm twelve years old, I live in Thorne, and I'm your daughter.

CHAPTER 9

Cy and I sat in the cafeteria as the chatter and laughter and clanging all around us was interrupted by the PA system crackling to life.

Attention, Thorne Bats. Principal Tuñón is offering a snack credit to anyone who provides information leading to the whereabouts of the science lab earthworms, which were reported missing recently. If you know anything, please see either Ms. Gaudet or Principal Tuñón. Thank you for your cooperation.

"Tempting," Cy said, wiggling her eyebrows. "But no."

"Not even for one entire snack credit?" I asked. "Think of the possibilities."

"Why don't *you* think of a question?" she said, fanning her oracle cards at me. "Then pick one."

I looked at the index cards.

"Are you thinking of a question?" she asked.

"I'm thinking of the worms. And the snack credit."

"Come on," she said. "Concentrate, okay?" Cy motioned toward the cards with her chin.

I pulled one and held it out to her.

"Artemis," Cy said, looking at the card. "Interesting."

She ran her fingers through her braids, thinking.

"What's so interesting about it?" I asked.

Across the cafeteria, I could see Brandon Rivera wielding a rolled-up notebook like a sword.

"Artemis was the daughter of Zeus and Leto," Cy said. "She was associated with wildlife and was also the goddess of hunting. She carried a silver bow and arrow."

"Okay," I said, peeling my orange. "And?"

"Artemis wanted to remain a maiden, a girl, forever," Cy said. "But it wasn't possible."

"You're not making any sense," I said. "What does that mean?"

"It means that you have to grow up," she said matter-of-factly. "There might be something in your immediate past, present, or future that will change the way you look at things. A maturing, if you will."

"Give me a break." I laughed. Cy could be so dramatic. I bit into a section of orange, and juice squirted across the table, landing on the card.

"Do you want to hear more or not?" Cy asked, wiping off the juice with her napkin.

"Fine," I said. "What else?" I pulled off another section of orange and placed it on Cy's tray. She ate it while staring at the index card.

"Artemis was a twin," Cy said. "You have a twin too."

"A twin?" I laughed. "Okay, I know you're making stuff up, but now you're being ridiculous."

"Not literally, of course," she said and rolled her eyes. "Unless there's something else your mom isn't telling you."

A chill went through me. I imagined all the things Mom hadn't told me. Would a twin be so far-fetched? And then I thought, yes, yes, it would be. Even for Mom. Still, I couldn't help thinking that I would have to inspect the photo I found more closely. Just in case.

"More like a symbolic twin," Cy said. "Maybe, like, a dual nature."

"A symbolic twin? A dual nature?" I repeated. "I don't think you understand how much I'm dealing with right now."

"Of course I do," Cy said. "A twin could be anything. Someone who is like you. Someone you share something with. Maybe even another side of yourself. It's not a bad thing. The cards are all about how you interpret them."

She took the index card, a regular school supply with the name Artemis on it and a sketch of a girl with antlers holding a bow and arrow, and stuck it back into her deck. All I had wanted to know from the card was if Manny would respond to my message.

"You really emailed Manny, huh?" Cy asked as if reading my mind.

"Yeah," I said. I rolled a piece of orange peel between my fingers.

"What if he does write back? What will you do?"

"*If?*" I said. "You mean you didn't see that in your cards?"

"Well, it's kinda hard to tell. He doesn't exactly have the best record, does he?" Cy gave me a sympathetic look.

"He has to write back."

I knew Cy was trying to keep me from getting my hopes up, but she was sounding just like Mom. I looked toward the food stations in time to see Gus grab a banana and a chocolate milk.

I waved as he passed us, but he didn't see me, or pretended not to, and hurried out of the cafeteria.

"Why are you always so nice to him?" Cy asked.

"I don't know," I said. "He seems lonely. Wouldn't you be lonely if you spent your entire school day *alone*?"

"If he was lonely, don't you think he'd wave back or say hello?" Cy said. "He doesn't seem lonely to me. He seems like a grumpy snob."

"Do you have any ideas for the show?" I asked, changing the subject. Maybe Cy was right about Gus.

"Not yet," she said, smiling. "But I asked the cards if Mrs. González would pick me as her director."

"And?" I said. "What did the wise cards reveal?"

"I pulled the cyclops," she said, covering one eye.

"What does that mean?"

"Depends," Cy said. "It could mean she'll only have an eye for me. Or that she won't notice me at all."

We both laughed.

★ ★ ★

When the last bell of the school day rang, I pulled out my phone and checked if there was a response to my email. But there was nothing new. I told Cy I had some things to do and biked alone to the historical society to return the book. I probably could've gotten away with keeping the book if I just never went back, but I felt bad about taking it. Maybe this was what Cy's Artemis card meant about maturing. I had to take responsibility.

When I opened the door to the building, Sleepy Reading Lady was at her usual table. I noticed that she had the same books, set out in the same pattern. I wondered if she ever actually read any of them or if she sat there pretending to read but really just watched people who came in. She looked up at me, staring as I walked to Rudy's desk as if she knew I was guilty of something.

"Well, hello there," Rudy said, sitting back in his chair. He wore blue suspenders over a plaid shirt tucked into his jeans, and his long white hair was in a ponytail. "To what do I owe this pleasure? And where's your friend today?"

"I'm here alone," I said. My heart raced as I pulled the book out of my bag and placed it on the counter. "I just wanted to read it. I took good care of it. I even put it in this plastic bag so it wouldn't get messed up in my backpack."

Rudy looked at the book and then at me.

"What's your name, young lady?" he asked.

"Adela."

"Well, Adela," Rudy said, "I appreciate you bringing

this back and taking care of it, but that doesn't make it okay."

"I know," I said. "I'm sorry." I was regretting returning to the historical society. What if Rudy called Mom?

"How am I supposed to leave you and your friend unsupervised with the collections if I'm afraid you might take something?" he went on.

"Cy didn't have anything to do with this," I said. "I took it."

"Hmm," Rudy said. "I appreciate your honesty. When things walk out of here, they usually don't come back."

Was that what happened with Manny? Did he just walk out and never come back?

"Promise not to take anything without permission again?" Rudy asked. "There's a level of trust that has to happen here, you know? People trust us to care for these things. And we have to be able to trust the public when they use them."

I nodded to let him know I understood. Even though I'd just met him, I felt like I needed him to know that he could count on me.

"I promise," I said.

"Good," Rudy responded. "All right, then, what can I help you with today? More Bravo information?"

"Is there more?" I asked hopefully.

"Not yet," Rudy said. "But I'll let you know if I find more in the boxes. Here." He handed me a clipboard and a pen. "You're welcome to sign up for our newsletter," he said.

"It's a good way to get updates. Make sure you use a parent's email."

"Okay," I said.

I looked at the sign-up sheet on the clipboard. Would this be the only way I would ever get information about the Bravos? Digging around in dusty boxes at the historical society or searching online, hoping for something new? I wasn't sure, but right then it was all I had, so I added my name to the list.

CHAPTER 10

"George Washington with a white blanket on wheels," Marlene said, setting down a plate with some cherries and a plain toasted bagel with melted Muenster cheese. "I made that one up."

Sunday was a day when we were all at the diner at the same time. After the breakfast rush, when things were quiet again, Mom and Alex did paperwork and checked inventory and placed orders for the week. I was expected to help out if I wanted an allowance, so today I was putting up decorations.

It was the first of October, which meant Halloween decorations were officially allowed to go up, according to Alex's rules. He wouldn't allow them before the first, even if Phipps's Pharmacy next door had been selling candy corn and costumes since August.

"Everything is on fast-forward these days," he said, setting the box of decorations he'd brought from storage on the floor next to me. "Can't we enjoy anything in its own season anymore?"

He looked at me as if expecting an answer. I pulled a black cat made of cardboard out of the box.

"Meow," I said on behalf of the cat.

A couple of weeks had passed since I'd sent the email, and no one had written back. It was probably one of those accounts where messages just disappeared into a void. Maybe no one even bothered checking it. After all, from my research online, it seemed that none of the Bravos wrestled anymore. Francisco was too old and Speedy died years ago and Mateo retired and Manny . . . Manny had disappeared.

There was a loser-leaves-town match a few years back, and then nothing. I read some articles that speculated that Manny was wrestling as un enmascarado in Mexico. Some said he'd retired and left New Mexico. One even claimed he was working as an elementary school PE coach, under an assumed name, in Montana. Wherever he was, I felt a little better knowing I wasn't the only one Manny had pulled a disappearing act on.

Still, I was mad. Mostly at myself for getting my hopes up and for letting myself feel disappointed when no one responded to my email. Alex and Mom hadn't brought up the adoption recently, but I knew they were both waiting for me. Maybe Mom had been right all along in not telling me anything about Manny.

I finished unfolding the black cat's limbs, then walked over to the counter TV, where Raging Rocco Pantaleo was pounding George "The Bruiser" Thorpe's forehead with his bare knuckles. I turned it off.

"Hey, I was watching that," Alex said in an exaggerated whine. "Doesn't anyone ask before they turn off *my* TV?"

"How about watching *that* instead?" Mom said. She pointed her pen at Alex's knife.

Alex turned on the radio and began to whistle along to a song. He chopped carrots, and Mom went back to working on her shopping list. Both of them going about their day as if everything was normal.

"Two hockey pucks, one dry, one painted yellow, one Atlanta, and a number forty-one," Marlene said as she placed burgers and drinks in front of a couple at the counter. Then she turned in my direction. She sat down in the booth across from me and grabbed an owl.

"No wrestling on the TV," she said, tearing a piece of tape and sticking the owl to the glass window. "And you haven't touched your bagel. Still in a funk?"

"I'm not in a funk," I said. I opened a black-and-orange honeycomb pumpkin and listened to the crackle of tissue paper as it unfolded. It was a satisfying sound. It made me think of what it felt like when I took a deep breath. I refolded the pumpkin and unfolded it again.

"How long have I known you?" Marlene asked.

"My whole life," I said, opening another pumpkin. It crinkled and crunched.

"Then you know that I can read you like I can read my own handwriting, right?"

"You can never read your own handwriting," I said,

rolling my eyes. "You're always asking me to try to make out the chicken scratch on your order pad."

"Beside the point," Marlene said, waving her hand at me. She pulled on an old plastic witch mask, setting the elastic band gently on her dark curls. "So? What's going on? You can fool those two, but you can't fool these old eyes. Is it still the j—"

"Marlene," I warned.

The witch wore a pointy black hat with yellow moons and stars. Her red mouth snarled, revealing sharp, crooked teeth.

"You're still pouting about him, huh?" she asked.

I could see Marlene's dark eyes studying me through the eye holes of the mask.

"Tell me about Man—" I stopped myself before the name slipped out, but I glanced over at Mom and Alex to see if either of them heard.

"Wait a minute," Marlene whispered. "I thought you didn't . . . How did you . . . ?"

I couldn't see her expression behind the mask, but she sounded surprised. And it was hard to surprise Marlene.

"Know?" I finished for her.

I felt a little nervous but also victorious. Like I finally knew what the adults didn't want me to know.

The bell above the front door chimed, and we both looked over. Gus Gutiérrez skulked in. His face wasn't visible, but I recognized him because he was wearing the same oversize brown sweatshirt he wore at school, the hood pulled over his head so that he looked like a Jawa.

Marlene stood and took off the mask. She patted her hair.

"You know what I'm going to say," she said before heading toward Gus. "Might as well, now that the cat's out of the bag."

Talk to your mom. I wanted to yell the words I'd heard so many times. Didn't any of these people know that trying to get information out of Mom was like trying to get into Buckingham Palace without an invitation? I looked from Mom to Marlene to Alex. How was it fair that everyone knew except me?

I listened to Gus order a burger with red and green chiles and a root beer to go. He pulled a few bills out of his messenger bag to pay, then sat down at a booth to wait.

I put on the mask Marlene had left on the table and walked over, my bravery fueled by the anger I felt toward Mom and Alex and Marlene. I sat down across from him and got right to the point.

"Why don't you ever say hi back?"

"Do I know you?" Gus mumbled, looking up from his phone.

"Funny," I said. "I'm just trying to be friendly, you know?"

"What makes you think I want friends?"

"Because everyone wants friends," I said. And then, as if doubting myself, I added, "Right?"

Gus stared at me from the shadow of his hood.

"What's your problem?" I said.

"Nosy people are my problem," he replied, crossing his arms.

"Are you calling me nosy? I'm not nosy."

I stood up to leave, embarrassed and wishing I'd never walked over.

"Who's the wrestling fan?" Gus asked. He motioned toward the André the Giant shrine.

"Oh, that's my stepdad," I said. "Do you watch wrestling too?"

"Sure." Gus nodded. "I've been to the Cactus League matches a few times. What else is there to do in this boring town?"

"Thorne isn't boring," I said defensively. "What exciting place did you move from anyway?"

"Las Cruces," he said. "It's way better there."

"I'm sure," I said, making a face behind the mask.

Gus pulled the drawstrings on his hood tight so that only the lower half of his face was visible.

"I guess you don't like it here, huh?"

"I don't," he said. "The people are weird."

I stared, speechless. What was weird about *me*? I was about to tell him that I'd had enough of his insults and that I wouldn't bother him anymore when Marlene came over with a bag of food.

"Here you go, fella," she said. "One dead cow on

Christmas and a number fifty-five." She placed the bag on the table and spun on her heels.

"Okay, fine," I said. "Maybe a little weird."

"Weird *and* morbid," Gus said, picking up his bag of food. "Nice mask, by the way. Assuming that's a mask."

I reached up to touch the plastic witch face that covered my own. I'd almost forgotten I had it on. I pulled it off, the plastic band getting tangled in my hair. But before I could think of a good comeback, Gus was gone.

I went back to my booth and started wiping down a ceramic jack-o'-lantern, thinking of all the things I could've said. Marlene came out of the kitchen, followed by Mom, who was zipping up her jacket. Mom stopped to whisper something to Alex before heading toward my booth.

"Let's walk," she said, putting a hand on my shoulder.

"I'm not done." I motioned to the decorations strewn around me. "Not even close."

"Leave that," she said. "You can finish later."

I put down the jack-o'-lantern and followed her outside. We walked past Phipps's Pharmacy, where a little kid rode the mechanical horse while his parents looked on like it was the most fun thing in the world. Mom smiled at them, and I felt relieved. If she was smiling, then the reason for the walk couldn't be bad.

"Where are we going?" I asked.

Mom didn't say anything. After a minute, I knew we were walking toward the park.

I had lived in Thorne my whole life, at least my whole life that I could remember. I could walk through it with my eyes closed. It was a small town, and just like at school, where new kids rarely appeared, a lot of the businesses in Thorne had been around for a long time.

We walked past Venus Hair and Beauty, where alien heads made of green Styrofoam wore fancy hairdos. Their black almond-shaped eyes stared at us from the front window. The business next to it didn't have a name, but the palm of a hand outlined in yellow halogen lights signaled that it was Maria the palm reader's place. The head, heart, and life lines glowed even in the daytime. Once we crossed at the end of the street, we passed the new kid in town, the coffee place that Alex called "Corporate Coffee" because it was a national chain. The air smelled like burnt coffee beans.

"How did you find out?" Mom asked. She stopped walking and turned to me.

"Find out what?" I replied, my stomach twisting like a pretzel.

Dogs barked and howled inside the Pooch Spa. There was a big glass window where you could see them being bathed and blow-dried from the sidewalk. I always imagined they were cussing up a storm at the indignity of being treated like entertainment.

"I know that you know, Addie," Mom said. "About your father."

"Oh." I stared at her belly to avoid looking at her face.

"How?" she asked again.

If I'd had Cy with me, she might've been able to think quick on her feet and come up with something other than the truth.

"I found the photo," I admitted. "In the shoebox in the trunk in your room."

I knew I didn't have to say which photo. It was *the* photo.

"You were snooping," Mom said. She still didn't sound mad, and now I was worried.

"I guess," I said. "Yes?"

"How would you feel if I did that to you?" Mom asked. "Invaded your privacy? Went through your room?"

"I'm not hiding anything," I said, thinking of the wall in my closet. "And he's my father. Why can't I know about him?"

"So you decided that sneaking around and digging through my things was okay?"

"You act like he doesn't exist," I said. I wished I still had the witch mask on so that I could hide from Mom's outraged stare.

"Addie, I was going to talk to you about him," Mom said with a sigh.

"When?" I asked. "After you ask him to give me up?"

"Give you up?" Mom repeated, a puzzled look on her face.

The dogs' howls had reached a crescendo. Mom glared

at the poor pups in the window before pulling me away.

"Does he even know?" I asked. "About the adoption?"

"Of course," Mom said.

"He *does*?" I yelled. I couldn't believe what I was hearing. "You mean all this time you knew how to get in touch with him? You'd been talking to him? And never told me?"

"There's a lot that's hard to explain," she said. "I needed to figure out how to talk to you about him. Some things you're just not old enough to understand."

"How do you know?" I countered. "So I'm not old enough for you to tell me about him, but I am old enough to make a decision about him not being my father anymore."

"When you put it that way, it doesn't make sense, does it?"

"No," I said, throwing my hands up in frustration. "It doesn't."

"I'm just trying to do what I think is best for you," Mom said.

But it didn't feel that way to me. And I suddenly knew what I had expected when I sent the email. I expected Manny or someone from the family to reach out to me, to want to meet me. And they hadn't. But that didn't change how I felt.

"I want to meet him," I whispered. And then, like my voice grew wings and took flight, I said it again, louder. "I want to meet him."

Mom stopped walking.

"It's not a good idea," she said.

"Why?" I asked.

"Because he travels a lot," she said. "He has no home."

"I emailed him."

"You *what*?!" Mom yelled.

"Not him exactly," I said, wincing. "I emailed his fan club. Don't worry, no one wrote back."

"Oh, jeez," Mom said. "Of course you would look him up online."

"What about Esperanza?" I asked.

"What about it?" Mom said.

"That's still home, isn't it? For the Bravos?"

"The Bravos," Mom repeated. "I need to sit."

We had entered the park, and she sat down on a bench under the shade of a ponderosa pine. "This is not how I expected to have this conversation."

"Why did you leave Esperanza?" Now that it was all out, I figured I might as well ask.

"Because I had to," Mom said. She looked tired. She unzipped her jacket and rubbed her belly, smoothing out her *Paleontology Rocks!* T-shirt.

"You had to . . ." My eyes widened at the possibilities of what that meant. "Were you in trouble with the law?"

"No," Mom said, rolling her eyes. "Not like that."

"Then why?"

"Here's the thing," Mom started. "The town is called Esperanza, but it felt hopeless to me. It felt like there was no place for me to go if I stayed there. I had plans for my own life. And then you came along, and I had to be the one to make plans for the both of us. Believe me, you growing up without your father was definitely not part of those plans."

"But I did," I said. "And now I want to meet him."

"I don't know, Addie." Mom shook her head.

"You've been in touch with him," I said. "You said so yourself. You talked about the adoption. What did he say? Doesn't he want to know me?"

Mom looked up as if pleading for an answer to appear in the early-afternoon sky.

"We can't just pick up like the past twelve years didn't happen," Mom said. "That's not how things work."

"Why not?" I asked.

I ran my fingers along the bark of the pine and inhaled its butterscotch smell. I knew the tree had to be at least a hundred years old, because that's when its bark peels, like it's shedding skin. It takes on a different appearance, and it starts to smell like cookies. It's like the tree starts a new phase of life. Maybe I could, too, I thought as I waited for Mom to answer. Maybe I could shed the me that had never known her father. I would leave the scent of cinnamon behind, and people would sniff the air and say: *Do you smell that? It smells like someone starting a new phase of life.*

I put my arms around the trunk and placed my ear next

to it, listening for something, just like Mom had looked to the sky for her answer. When I finally pulled away, I knew.

"I don't care how things work in your grown-up world. I'm not making a decision about the adoption until I meet Manny."

I crossed my arms and stood firm, like the pine tree, letting Mom know that my decision was final.

★ CHAPTER 11 ★

The days that followed were filled with whispered phone conversations between Mom and whoever was on the other end of the line and between Mom and Alex behind the closed door of their bedroom. Finally, she talked to *me*.

"Your father, Manny," she said as if I wouldn't know who she was talking about, "invited you to Esperanza on Saturday. How do you feel about going?"

"Really?" I nearly jumped out of my skin, shedding like a ponderosa. "I'm going to Esperanza? *This* Saturday? Will you come too?"

"I'd rather not," Mom said. "And it's fine if you don't want to go."

"I want to go," I said quickly before she changed her mind. "I can go by myself."

The look on Mom's face said she wished I'd answered differently.

"Your grandparents will be there," she said. "It won't just be you and Manny. It'll be . . ."

"What?" I said, eager for more. "It'll be *what*?"

"Interesting, at the very least," she finished. She looked like she wanted to say something else. I held my breath. "Manny will pick you up on Saturday morning."

★ ★ ★

As I waited for Manny outside the diner, I knew not only the stuff I'd read on the internet and in the old biography—basic things like his height (six foot four), eye color (both brown), and nickname (The Mountain)—but also something that people who weren't in his life probably didn't know: that he was not punctual. He was supposed to pick me up at ten in the morning. Ten had come and gone, and I was still waiting.

I scanned the diner parking lot, not sure what kind of vehicle I was looking for. Mom had insisted on being with me, but I didn't want the first time I met my father to involve a moody Mom. I told her and Alex that I wanted to wait by myself. But I wished that I'd at least agreed to Cy's offer on Friday after school.

"I can hang out until he comes," she had said, pulling her index card oracle from her bag.

"Thanks, but I think I'd rather wait alone."

"Are you sure? What if he—" She looked down quickly at her cards, not completing her thought, but I knew what she was thinking, because I'd been thinking it too.

"He'll come," I told her, trying to convince myself.

Cy stood to brush off the seat of her purple jeans.

"Pick a card," she said, holding out her deck. I pulled out a card and handed it to her.

"Persephone?" I said when we both looked at the card. "Really?"

"Daughter of Demeter, bride of Hades," Cy confirmed.

"Kidnapped," I replied. "*Unwilling* bride."

"True. But she travels between worlds. That's what's significant here."

"And she's miserable in one of those worlds," I said. "This sounds like a bad omen."

"Have you ever noticed that Greek mythology is really messed up?" Cy asked. "There are a lot of awful dudes in it. But remember that one good thing that came from the story of Persephone is that even though it was winter on Earth when she was in the underworld, Demeter gave humans the gift of agriculture. They made something good out of a bad situation."

"Uh, okay," I said, shaking my head. "This is not making me feel better."

"I know, sorry," Cy said, putting away her cards. "I hope you have a good visit with Manny."

"Me too."

The last thing Cy said to me was "Whatever you do, don't eat any pomegranates. I want you to come back."

But as I pulled my phone from my pocket, I didn't think she'd have anything to worry about. Manny was twenty-four minutes late and counting. *I* was worried. I tugged on my hoodie and pulled the drawstrings tight.

Mom had added Manny's contact information to my

phone. I stared at his name on my screen for a minute. All these years, he didn't exist to me, and suddenly he was a name on my list of contacts. I took a deep breath and called his number. It rang once, twice, a third time. I hung up at the fifth ring. No one answers after the fifth ring. When I looked at my screen, there was a text from Mom.

On the road? Everything okay?

I knew I couldn't call her. If I called her and told her Manny was late, she would leave whatever she was doing and come pick me up. My chances of going to Esperanza and meeting him would vanish. But if I didn't respond, she'd be worried.

Yes, I typed and hit the send arrow.

There was only one thing to do. I scrolled through my phone until I got to the number I needed. I took a deep breath and called.

★ ★ ★

By the time Alex arrived, Manny was almost an hour late. Alex climbed out of his truck and walked over to where I sat on the curb.

"I'm sorry this happened, Adelita," he said. "I'm sure your mom can work out whatever the mix-up was, and you can just go another time."

"No way," I said, surprising myself at the forcefulness of my voice. "If she finds out Manny didn't come, she won't let me go. Ever."

"So what exactly do you want me to do?" Alex asked.

I stared down at his sneakers. "Can't you just drop me off?"

"And not tell your mom?" He raised an eyebrow. "Nope. Besides, it's a long drive and I'm supposed to be at the diner this afternoon. How do I explain that to her?"

"I can talk to her," I said. "*After* you drop me off?"

Alex stared out at the parking lot and slowly shook his head.

"Please," I said.

A minute passed before he pulled out his phone. I knew he was calling Mom's number. He held the phone to his ear as he walked back toward the truck.

He paced, circling the vehicle. He ran his fingers across his forehead, squeezing his eyes closed as if he had a headache. My insides flip-flopped. I wished I could read lips. The longer the conversation went on, the more worried I felt. I didn't want to have to talk to Mom and hear her say *I told you so.*

It was a relief when Alex finally pulled the phone away from his ear and looked at the darkened screen. He waved me over to the truck.

"Okey dokey, then," he said, climbing back into the driver's seat. "Off to Esperanza we go."

"Really?" I asked. "Was she mad?"

Alex didn't answer. He opened the GPS app and pulled out of the parking lot. Of course Mom was mad.

"I know it's not easy to understand where your mom is coming from," Alex said. "But know that no matter what, you're her top priority. And even though she's not wild about you going to Esperanza, she does want it to go well. She just doesn't want you to get hurt."

"What does she think will go wrong?" I asked, watching his phone screen, where we were just a little dot cruising along a green line.

I had a father who couldn't even bother to show up to meet me for the first time. I had a mom who pretended my father didn't exist. I tried to imagine what else could go wrong.

"Nothing," Alex said after a few seconds. "She just wants you to . . . to not be disappointed."

"Well," I said, thinking. "If things don't go okay, I don't have to see him again, right? And it can just be like it's always been. Right?"

I glanced at Alex, waiting for him to reassure me.

"No matter what this visit is like, things are never going to be the same," Alex said. "Once you know something, you can't unknow it."

"What does that mean?"

"It means welcome to life, kid," Alex said and gave me a sad smile. The way he said *welcome to life* made me think that maybe he'd had his share of welcome-to-life moments.

As we passed the Dos Pueblos Historical Society before merging onto the highway, I tapped my window, a little hello to Rudy and Sleepy Reading Lady. And then we said goodbye to Thorne and were on Route 13, the road that led to Esperanza, with only the sound of Alex's favorite country music station on low.

The familiar scenery zipped past us—cacti and tumbleweeds and mountains reaching up toward the bluest October sky. Around here, it was always mountains and sky. A constant backdrop. But I knew that the next time I drove down this road, something major would have happened. It was strange how a person's life could change in such a big way while the world just kept on being. Always mountains and sky, no matter what.

Was this all a big mistake? Would it be so terrible if I never met Manny? For a moment, I thought about telling Alex to turn the truck around. But I pushed down that feeling and stared out the window. Maybe I would catch a glimpse of La Llorona hitching a ride.

I dozed off and woke up as Alex pulled off Route 13. A sign welcoming visitors to Esperanza declared it "The Hope of New Mexico!"

"Good snooze?" Alex asked, pausing at a stop sign.

"Okay snooze," I said and yawned.

We passed a herd of cattle grazing behind a fence near the side of the road. They chewed slowly, and one looked up as we drove by. Two women sat outside a gas station called the Flying Saucer. They had a big blue-and-white cooler between them with a handmade sign that advertised dos tamales for five dollars. My stomach growled, and I realized I'd been too nervous to eat breakfast.

Alex followed the instructions from the map lady on his phone, who told him in her British accent where to turn. We drove past the elementary school, the middle school, and Esperanza High School, the place where Mom had gone to science club meetings and Manny had wrestled. The buildings stood side by side like the Three Bears. The public library was a little blue house someone once lived in; a flag flapped in the wind near the entrance. We drove through downtown Esperanza, where a few shops and restaurants and a post office lined an open plaza.

Esperanza didn't look that different from Thorne. They were both small, quiet towns. But I thought of how Mom had said that there was nowhere for her to go, and it made the place feel smaller somehow.

Alex pulled off the paved street and onto a gravelly road. He followed this until the British map lady said, "You. Have. Arrived." As if each word was its own announcement.

Alex stopped the truck in front of a wooden gate framed by a tall sign that had LOS BRAVOS painted on it in bright green letters. Bundles of tumbleweed seemed to stand guard at either side of the entrance.

"This must be the place, eh?" Alex said, looking at me and then beyond the passenger-side window. He opened his door. "Wait here."

"Why?" I asked, my fingers on the door handle, ready to hop out too.

"Just wait," he said. "Please." He gave me a look that said he was serious before climbing out of the truck. Alex opened the gate and walked through with no challenge from the tumbleweed sentinels. Past the entrance, I could see a path that led to a sprawling house the color of mud. Alex rang the doorbell and waited until someone answered. I imagined what he might be saying to whoever stood at the door. *I've got your kid in my truck. I'm your kid's stepdad. You forgot to pick up your kid.* A couple of minutes later, he was walking back down the path toward me. A woman and a dog trailed behind.

Alex knocked on the passenger-side window and motioned for me to come out. I opened the door and hopped down from the truck, then clenched my fists inside the front pocket of my sweatshirt. I followed Alex to where the woman and the dog waited at the gate. When we reached them, Alex pulled me forward.

"Adela," he said, "this is Rosie. Your abuela."

★ CHAPTER 12 ★

Alex had driven off, back to my other life in Thorne, and now I was standing alone with Rosie, my grandmother, and the dog, a white pooch with a big brown spot that covered its rump. The dog wouldn't stop circling me and wagging its tail.

"Mira nomás," Rosie said, motioning to the dog with her head. She looked happy to see me.

Rosie reminded me of Alex's wrestling action figures—small and muscular. She looked like a grandma you did not want to mess with. She had a broad, tan face that had spent a lot of time out in the sun and chin-length wavy gray hair. She wore a flowered top, red shorts, and orange waterproof gardening shoes. A touch of pink lipstick brightened her face.

"Don't worry, he won't bite," Rosie said. Her voice was comforting and reassuring. "Hijo knows family when he sees it. Or when he *smells* it."

"His name is Hijo?"

"His pa's name was El Santo, like el luchador," Rosie explained. "So this is Hijo."

"I know about El Santo," I said.

"Everyone does," Rosie said, waving me closer. "Pero ven aquí."

I walked toward her, and when I was within reach, she grabbed me and pulled me into a hug. It felt like she'd been saving it for me. When she released me, I didn't know what to do, so I patted Hijo's head nervously and stared at the toes of her orange shoes, which made her look like she had duck feet.

"We had a little schedule confusion, eh?" she said. "Manny thought he was picking you up tonight for dinner."

"He's not here?" I asked, looking past the woman toward the door of the house as if Manny might suddenly appear and yell *Surprise!*

I wasn't sure what I had expected to find when I arrived. A parade? Balloons? A great big welcome banner? A father who was happy to see me? At the very least I was expecting Manny to be around.

"He's working," Rosie said. "But don't worry. He'll be here later. Everyone will, and they're all excited to see you again."

"Again?"

"Pues sí," she said. "It's been a long time. No te preocupes. Come on, then, let's get inside."

I felt like my feet were glued to the ground. Before I could make my legs take a step toward the house, the front door was flung open, and two girls practically tumbled out, stopping next to Rosie.

"Oh. My. God," one of the girls said.

"Don't use the Lord's name in vain," the other one said, shoving the first.

"Fine," the first girl said. "Oh. My. Dog."

The two girls laughed. I couldn't help smiling too.

They were identical twins and looked a little older than me, maybe thirteen or fourteen. They were small and wiry. Both wore black leggings, black shin-high wrestling boots, and gold satin jackets embroidered with small black skulls and stars. Their long dark tangled hair was streaked with gold. They wore black lipstick, and their eyes were lined with gold eyeliner and shimmery blue shadow. They were like a couple of teenage Medusas—the most terrifyingly beautiful girls I had ever seen.

"Niñas," Rosie said, putting an arm around me. "This is your prima Adela."

The identical faces stared at me. I thought about Cy's Artemis card. Maybe these were the twins she was talking about.

"Adela," Rosie said. "This is Eva, and that's Maggie." Rosie pointed to each girl. I studied them, trying to find something that would help tell them apart.

"Hi," I said nervously.

"You look just like Uncle Manny," one of the twins said. "Doesn't she?" The two girls circled me as if inspecting a piece of art in a museum.

"Are you gonna call Manny *Dad*?" one twin asked.

"Have you ever even met him?" the other twin said.

I shook my head. And then shook it again.

"Shoo, you two," Rosie said, nudging the girls aside. "Are you hungry?" she said to me.

"A little," I replied. My stomach growled as if countering with *a lot*.

The twins and Hijo followed us inside to the kitchen, where an older man stood at the sink, staring out the window. The faucet was running, and water spilled out of the overflowing glass he held. The twins sat down at a large wooden table in the center of the kitchen. I stayed in the doorway as Rosie hurried over to the man.

"Ay, Pancho." She sighed and turned off the faucet. She took the glass and poured out some water. The man didn't seem to notice we were there. "Pancho, look who's here."

"Hi, Abuelo," the twins called to him.

"Not you two," Rosie said, waving them away.

The man looked at Rosie, at the twins, and then at me. He was barrel chested, with gray hair that matched Rosie's, and a white mustache. He was tall but not as tall as he looked in the photos I'd seen. I had imagined Francisco Bravo a Titan and was surprised that he was only about my height.

"Pancho," Rosie repeated. "Tu nieta Adela. Manny's girl is here."

"Eh?" the man said, confused. "Manny?"

"Tu hijo," Rosie whispered.

His eyebrows raised, and he gave a look of recognition. "¿Manny tiene una hija?" he asked, taking the glass Rosie held out to him.

"You know this," Rosie said reassuringly. "Adela, this is your grandfather Pancho."

I wasn't sure how to greet the man who seemed to be in his own world, where neither I nor Manny existed. I waved. To my surprise, he waved too.

"I'll be right back," Rosie said, leading my grandfather out of the kitchen by the arm.

"Abuelo is sick," one of the twins explained. I noticed she had braces. She pulled out the chair next to her, and I sat down.

"What kind of sick?" I asked.

"He forgets stuff," she said. "And he gets bad headaches sometimes."

Just like Zeus, I thought.

"Don't take it personally if he doesn't remember you," the other twin said. "He sees us all the time and sometimes forgets who we are."

"Our mom says it's from all the years of wrestling," the twin with the braces added.

They talked in turns. One, then the other. Just like twins in books, like sisters, like a tag team, like people who knew the same story.

"Oh," I said, unsure how to respond. "That's too bad."

"Yeah," the twins said in unison.

Nothing on the internet had told me that my grandfather couldn't remember things anymore. I wondered how much Mom—Mom! I still hadn't sent her a message.

I pulled my phone out of my pocket and typed all good. I almost sent it without punctuation but added an exclamation mark because it bugs Mom when I send texts without punctuation. All good! The exclamation mark would indicate excitement and enthusiasm and not the feeling I had that maybe this was a mistake. I hit the send arrow.

"Okay, what should I make?" Rosie asked, returning from wherever she'd dropped off Pancho as if he'd never been in the kitchen. "What do you like to eat, Adela?"

"Anything is fine," I said.

"Waffles!" Maggie and Eva yelled.

"Qué waffles ni qué waffles," Rosie said. "It's lunchtime."

"Please, Abuelita," one of the twins begged. "We never have waffles. I bet Adela likes waffles, right?"

Rosie and the twins turned to me. I felt like I was looking into a three-way mirror, seeing myself for the first time. The twins both gave me a cool stare that communicated that the correct answer to the waffle question was yes. I nodded.

"Bueno," Rosie said, "waffles for lunch it is."

I imagined Marlene yelling an order for checkerboards at the diner.

The twins did a little dance in their seats. One twin got

up and went to the refrigerator. She pulled out a gallon of chocolate milk and shook it.

"Dangit, Maggie, you intentionally took the last of the chocolate milk." The twin with the braces, Eva, smacked her sister on the head with the empty container.

"Ow," Maggie yelped, rubbing her head. "Did you see that? She just hit me."

"Don't say *dangit*, Eva," Rosie called from the counter where she'd pulled out a waffle iron and was mixing ingredients.

"You say *dangit* all the time," the twins replied.

"And *dangit* isn't a bad word anyway," Eva said.

"Right," Maggie added, pouring milk from her glass into her sister's. "Damnit is bad. And dogdamnit is worse."

"Magdalena," Rosie said in a warning tone.

"I said *dog*," Maggie said. The girls grinned at each other.

When Rosie set a plate of waffles on the table, the twins attacked it with their forks. Hijo ran over and planted himself between the sisters.

"¿El burro primero, eh?" Rosie said, frowning at Eva and Maggie, who ignored her. "Guests first, girls."

"She's not a guest," Eva said. "She's family."

"Better get in there," Rosie said. "These two will leave you with nothing but migas if you aren't careful."

I speared a waffle onto my plate. Hearing Eva call me family made me feel like my insides were the pat of butter melting on my warm waffle.

"Stop feeding him people food, Eva," Maggie yelled. "Every time you do that, he gets the farts."

"He's hungry," Eva said. "Look at that sad face." She gave Hijo another piece of waffle, which he snapped out of her fingers.

"He's sleeping on your bed, then," Maggie said.

"Do you live here?" I asked, looking from one girl to the other.

"No," Maggie said. "We spend the weekends here, though."

I wanted to ask about their parents, which uncle was their dad, but I wasn't sure how.

"Dangit," Rosie said. "Do you know what I just realized?"

I shook my head in case she was talking to me. For a moment, I worried that Rosie was going to say that Manny wouldn't be back today. That he wouldn't be coming at all and that I'd traveled to Esperanza for nothing. Could I just go home, back to my old life, like I'd never met my wacky cousins and my sick grandfather and my abuela? Something inside me told me that Alex was right.

"I just realized that I don't know what you know," Rosie went on. "About us."

"Don't worry, Abuelita," Eva said, picking something out of her braces. "I'll draw her a map of the family."

"When you girls are done, you can show your prima around," Rosie said. "Take her to see Mateo. I'll show you my workshop later, okay? This is your house, too, so don't be shy."

I felt terribly shy. I wanted to ask Rosie what *they* knew about *me*. How they could just welcome me so easily, as if they'd always known me. Didn't they have questions? Didn't they wonder about me?

The twins pushed back their chairs. Maggie picked up the last waffle. She looked at me, then at the waffle she held between her fingers.

"You can have it," I said. "I'm full."

"Meet us in the squared circle when you're done," Maggie said. "You know what that is, right?"

I had done some geometry in math class, but I had never heard of a squared circle. Clearly, I was missing something. But Eva and Maggie stared at me expectantly. Was it a test? Now wasn't the time to show my ignorance.

"Of course," I said confidently. "I'll see you there. At the squared circle."

Maggie stuck the waffle in her mouth, gave me a thumbs-up, and followed her sister.

"The squared circle is the ring," Rosie said when the twins were gone, as if that made things clear. "In the backyard."

"Right," I said. "Thank you for breakfast. I mean lunch. Brunch?"

Rosie scraped waffle bits into the trash.

"Lourdes taught you manners," she said. "She was always a sweet girl."

It was strange hearing Rosie talk about Mom as a girl, a Mom I didn't know.

"Hazme un favorcito," Rosie said. "Tell Abuelo his lunch is ready. He might be sitting out front. Or he might be in the family room watching TV. And if he's smoking, tell him to put it out right now or else."

Hijo followed me out of the kitchen and to the front door. I poked my head outside, making sure not to let the dog out, but there was no sign of Pancho. I closed the door behind me and wondered where to look next. I hesitated, not wanting to wander around this strange house. But I didn't have to wander, because I heard his voice calling for Hijo. The dog trotted off, and I followed him into the family room.

My grandfather stood next to an open window, his arm half dangling out of it, holding on to a fat cigar whose smoke curled away from him, slithering out into the afternoon air like a garter snake.

"Hello," he said when he saw me. "Are you a friend of the twins?"

"I'm Adela," I said. "Manny's, um . . . daughter?"

"Manny has a daughter?" the man asked just like he had earlier. And for a moment, I wasn't sure if it was true. Did Manny have a daughter? Where *was* Manny?

"Yes," I said. "Me."

My grandfather took a puff of his cigar and blew the smoke out the window.

"Well, in that case, don't tell your abuela." He held up the cigar. "She doesn't like it when I smoke. Thinks she's la jefa."

He flicked ashes and stubbed the cigar on the side of the house. He pulled his arm back in and closed the window.

"Rosie said lunch is ready."

"¿Ya comiste?" he asked.

"Sí," I answered.

"Good," he said. "You can't grow up to be strong like me if you don't eat."

He flexed an arm muscle, and for a few seconds, beneath the old man in shorts and a T-shirt and plaid wool slippers, who couldn't remember someone he'd known forever, I saw a flicker of El Terremoto, the world champion.

★ CHAPTER 13 ★

I squinted into the backyard, my eyes adjusting to the bright afternoon sun, and took in the view. There were the familiar piñon trees and a couple of wooden picnic tables. A brown pickup truck with a bed full of tumbleweeds was parked next to an old barn. A few square-foot garden boxes filled with things I couldn't identify sat side by side with little flagstone paths between them and rain barrels nearby. And smack in the middle of it all was a full-size, honest-to-goodness, real-life wrestling ring. For a moment, I thought I was hallucinating. And then it made sense. A squared circle.

While I stood in the doorway with my mouth hanging open, Hijo pushed against me and out the door. He took off past the ring where the twins sat and disappeared up a trail. The property seemed to have no end. Something shone in the distance, in the direction the dog had gone. I thought it might be a UFO, which, to be honest, would have been an only slightly stranger thing to find in the yard.

"The dog got out," I called to my cousins. I pointed to where Hijo had run off.

"He's okay," one of the twins said. "Get over here."

I closed the door behind me and made my way to the ring, imagining I was a wrestler and my entrance song was playing.

"Climb up," Maggie said when I stood at the edge. "There's no door."

The twins laughed.

The ring was about twenty feet long on each side and a good eight feet tall from the ground to the top rope. It had three red ropes that created a frame. These connected at black-padded turnbuckles in the corners. A dark green skirt hanging off the edges of the mat hid the space underneath the structure. The ring looked worn, like it had seen some action over the years.

There were no steps, and the mat was about three feet or so off the ground, so I rested my forearms on it and pushed myself up. I heaved a leg onto the surface and rolled under the ropes. I always assumed the mat in a ring was like a trampoline, but it was hard, solid wood with a layer of canvas-covered padding.

"You're a natural," Eva said and clapped.

She patted the mat next to her, and I sat down obediently.

"What's with all the tumbleweeds?" I asked, pointing to the truck.

"That's Abuela's workshop over there," Maggie said.

"What does she make?"

Maggie and Eva looked at each other.

"Jeez," Eva said. "You really don't know anything, do you?"

I blushed, embarrassed at my ignorance.

"Abuela makes tumbleweed statues," Maggie explained. "She makes the snowman."

"*The* snowman?" I gasped.

Maggie looked at me like it was no big deal.

All these years, Mom had us taking photos with the tumbleweed snowman and never bothered to tell me my own grandmother made them. I felt a sharp pang in my chest, the now-too-familiar feeling of betrayal. I looked over at the barn. What was it like inside? What other secrets had Mom kept that I had yet to uncover?

"We're brainstorming wrestling moves," Eva said. "Wanna help?"

"Moves?" I asked, looking at the notebook that lay between the girls. "For who?"

"For us," Eva said. "The tzitzimime."

"The what?"

"The tzitzimime," Eva repeated. She sounded like a snake hissing.

"Sisimemeh?" I said, trying to replicate the sounds I heard.

"You say it like you're shooting sparks from between your teeth. Tz! Tz!"

I imagined Eva shooting real sparks from her mouth instead of drops of spit.

"Tzi-tzi-me-meh," I tried again.

"Better," Maggie said.

"What is it?" I asked. "What's a tzitzimime?"

"It's not a what, it's a who," Maggie said. "*We're* the tzitzimime." She pointed to herself and then to her sister.

"They're star goddesses," Eva explained. "In Aztec mythology."

"Oh," I said, thinking. "Like the Pleiades?"

"I don't think so," Maggie said. "But I'm not sure."

"Do you really wrestle?" I asked. Aside from their costumes, the twins didn't look like they could do much damage to anything except maybe a plate of waffles.

Maggie didn't answer. She stared at the page in deep concentration, chewing on a nail. Suddenly, something fell out of her mouth. A tooth attached to what looked like a piece of pink chewed-up bubble gum landed on the notebook. Maggie looked up, revealing a hole in her mouth. I gasped.

"What happened to your tooth?" I asked, trying not to look as shocked as I felt.

"I knocked it out," Eva said with a hint of pride. "It was an accident, though. Elbow to the face gone wrong." She said this as if there were a right way to get an elbow to the face.

"Was it, really?" Maggie asked, looking at her sister suspiciously. "An accident?"

Eva picked up the tooth and its pink plastic retainer. "Of

course it was." She smirked. She held it out for Maggie, but when her sister tried to grab it, Eva pulled it out of reach.

"Give it back," Maggie said.

"Come get it," Eva taunted. She stood and stretched, holding the tooth up in the air.

Maggie got to her feet and pushed her sister. Eva stumbled, and the tooth fell out of her hand and bounced to the edge of the mat. The twins scrambled for the tooth. Next thing I knew, Maggie was on Eva's back. Eva rolled her off and jumped to her feet.

"The tooth won't help you," Eva taunted. "Everyone knows you're the ugly one."

I wanted to point out that this didn't make sense because they were identical, but there was no time for making sense, because soon, Maggie was on her feet too and headed toward her sister.

The twins locked arms, their long, skinny fingers gripping each other's in a test of strength. Maggie broke free and grabbed Eva by the hair. Eva shrieked, holding on to Maggie's wrist.

"Let go of me, chimuela," Eva yelled.

Maggie laughed maniacally, like she was possessed. She pulled her sister halfway across the ring before releasing her with a shove that sent her sprawling. The mat shook under the impact of Eva's body.

Maggie grabbed Eva by the calf and dragged her like a mop across a floor.

"Help me, prima!" Eva cried, holding her hand out to me.

I looked behind me to see if there was another cousin around, but only saw Hijo wandering the yard, sniffing at dirt and plants. He lifted his leg to pee on one of the truck's tires. Meanwhile, Maggie had sat down on Eva's back, holding on to her hair so that she looked like Ares riding his war chariot.

"Don't listen to her," Maggie grunted. "Get my tooth before she does."

I knew I couldn't help Eva get out of her sister's clutches, and by the look on Maggie's face, I didn't really want to get in the middle of their fight. But I could save Maggie's tooth. I crawled toward the apron of the mat, where the tooth lay on the edge. A loud groan froze me in my tracks. I turned to see that Eva now had her sister's arm twisted behind her back. I wanted to run inside to get Rosie but was afraid to leave the twins alone with each other.

I turned again to grab the tooth, but the mat was now empty. I crawled to the edge and under the bottom rope to see where it had fallen. There was no sign of it on the ground.

"What should I do to this chimuela, prima?" Eva yelled. "Toss her over the top rope? Body slam?"

"You're asking me?" The question came out a strangled squeak as I crawled back into the ring. "Can both of you just stop? I can't find Maggie's tooth. Maybe we should all look for it."

"Help me, Adela," Maggie said, shaking the hand she reached out to me.

"Well," Eva said, pulling at her sister like she was a rag doll. "Doesn't look like anyone's gonna save you, hermana."

Eva shoved Maggie into a corner. Maggie grabbed the ropes, holding on so that when her twin came for her, she couldn't pull her away. Instead, Eva fell back. Then she did the coolest roll and popped up onto her feet. She turned and motioned me over. I shook my head.

"Look out!" I yelled as Maggie came up behind her. Maggie hooked her sister's left arm. She turned so that their backs touched and hooked Eva's other arm. Back to back, elbows locked, they looked like Janus, the Roman god of beginnings. Though from where I stood, this seemed more like an ending for someone.

"The Bravo Back Breaker is for the old men," Maggie sneered. "I call this move I'm about to do the Supernova!"

She lifted her sister off her feet. Maggie was a lot stronger than she looked. Hijo barked. I glanced back at the house, where there was no sign of help. Eva let out a howl. I took a deep breath, my heart pounding, and lowered my head. Then I charged at Maggie and gave her the hardest push I could. She stumbled, releasing her hold on Eva, and both of them tumbled to the mat.

"I'm so sorry," I said, staring at the pile of hair and limbs. "Are you okay?" I crouched down and could see they were both breathing—heavily, but still. "Can you move? Should I get Rosie?"

The twins slowly unraveled. Maggie flopped over from where she'd landed on top of her sister. Beneath her, Eva lay giggling. Maggie joined in, laughing. The space where her tooth was missing looked like a little doorway.

"I was wondering how long we'd have to wrestle before you jumped in to help one of us," Maggie said, sitting up. She pushed strands of hair out of her face.

"Yeah," Eva added, wiping away tears of laughter. "I was afraid Maggie was going to run out of moves and try something we hadn't practiced yet."

"What are you talking about?" I asked, confused. "I thought you were really fighting."

"Well, she did knock out my tooth," Maggie said.

"It was an *ac-ci-dent*," Eva said, shaking her fists.

For a second, I was afraid they would start fighting again. This time I wasn't getting involved.

"You should've seen the look on your face," Eva said.

"I can't believe you can really do all that," I said. "How?"

"We train," Maggie replied. "It takes a lot of practice so that you know how to not get hurt and how not to hurt someone else."

"Where did you learn?"

"What do you mean?" Eva asked. "Here." She waved her arms around.

"And it's in our blood," Maggie added. "Yours too."

"No way. Not me," I said, shaking my head. "Besides, I'm not really a Bravo."

"Of course you're a Bravo," Eva said, gently shoving my shoulder. "That's why you jumped in to save me. I mean, it took a while, but you did."

"We're going pro when we're eighteen," Maggie announced proudly. "Just like Speedy."

"Speedy is your dad," I said. One more piece of the puzzle fell into place.

"We're going to be big," she added. "Bigger than Abuelo. Bigger than all of them." She motioned toward the house.

"*You're* going to be big," Eva said to her sister. They looked at each other. Maggie rolled her eyes.

"Your mom doesn't mind?" I asked. "My mom would flip out if I came home and said I was going to wrestle."

I wasn't sure what I wanted to be when I grew up. Maybe some kind of scientist. I certainly didn't have a plan like the twins, and I never imagined wrestling as a possibility.

"She doesn't love it," Eva said. "But she likes for us to stay connected to Speedy."

"I wish my mom felt the same way," I whispered as if she might be somewhere nearby, listening.

"Oh, hey," Maggie said. "If you want to visit Uncle Mateo, he's up that way." She pointed toward the silver object I'd spotted when I walked outside.

"Yeah, maybe I'll go over there now," I said, standing up.

"You'll like Uncle Mat," Eva said. "He's cool. He made these jackets for us."

She slipped on her gold satin jacket and ran her fingertips along an arm, tracing stars and skulls.

I rolled under the bottom rope and brushed off my jeans, leaving the twins spread out on the mat with their notebook. As I walked toward the trail, I heard Maggie yell from the ring: "Has anyone seen my tooth?"

★ CHAPTER 14 ★

The shining object in the distance wasn't a UFO after all. Off the main path, like a giant silver Hostess Twinkie, sat an Airstream trailer.

White curtains hung from the windows, and a bunting made from scraps of different fabrics was strung along the side of the camper. A blue-and-white-striped canopy opened out over a green metal table and matching chairs. An old typewriter that had faded from red to a shade of dusty pink was set up on a tree stump next to the door. Instead of stories, lavender branches grew out of it. I bent down and sniffed the flowers. The little trailer looked bright and magical, like something you'd find in a forest in a picture book.

I could hear music playing inside. The wind carried it through the curtains and past the towering fir that cast its shadow over part of the trailer. Hijo nosed the door open from inside. It swung and hit the wooden wind chimes next to it, and they clack-clack-clacked in response.

"Who's out there, Hijo?" a man's voice called. But Hijo was busy digging in the dirt, pulling up the wildflowers that grew nearby. He looked like he was on a mission.

The person who appeared in the doorway wore a white T-shirt, striped pajama bottoms, and a long satin robe with a colorful yellow-orange-and-black floral pattern. He had short, curly dark hair.

"Are you Mateo?"

"Who's asking?" the man said, his brows furrowed.

"Me?" I said. "I'm Adela. Manny's—"

"I'm kidding," he said, breaking into a big smile. He had the same round face as Rosie, like a smiling terra-cotta sun. "Of course I know who you are! Get over here and give your uncle a hug."

When he opened his arms, the robe spread out and flowed behind him so that he looked like a swallowtail. I felt a little self-conscious, but I walked to my uncle and let him enfold me in the soft fabric.

"Come on inside," Uncle Mateo said, holding me at arm's length.

He turned and walked back into the trailer. Hijo had finished whatever he was doing in the yard and followed him, tracking dirt inside.

"Do you want something to drink?" Uncle Mateo asked. "Some tea?"

"Okay," I said. "Thank you."

I knew that this uncle was the middle brother. An article on the Pro Wrestling Today website said he retired a few years ago to the disappointment of many.

"Sit at the table," Uncle Mateo said, motioning toward

the surface. "Just push those things aside. But careful with loose pins."

The inside of the trailer was as colorful as the outside. The sun glinted off the green sequins on an emerald feathered robe that hung on a dress form like a life-size bird. I recognized it as the robe the wrestler Guapo García, a heel, wore to the ring. A big, bright pink beehive wig perched on a wig stand. Plants hung from the ceiling in glass globes and cascaded over the sides of ceramic pots. An old stereo sat on the counter, playing classical violin music that sounded like a swarm of frenzied bumblebees. Uncle Mateo's trailer felt like the kind of place someone goes to disappear from the outside world. Like when I went into my closet to look at my pictures of Manny.

I sat down, careful not to move anything. The table was covered in swatches of fabric like the ones on the bunting outside. There were long laces and wrestling masks in different states of completion. A sewing machine with its light still on seemed to peer at us from the corner, as if waiting for my uncle to return. Next to it was a pair of golden scissors.

My uncle poured hot water from a teakettle into two mugs. He placed one in front of me and sat down across the table. A little metal tea ball floated in the water. The steam that rose had the familiar smell of manzanilla.

"When Ma said you were coming, I couldn't believe it," he said. His eyes shone with excitement. "There was

no way I ever imagined Lulu would allow it. Not after—"
He stopped himself. "Anyway, I want to know everything about you." He tapped my hand.

I wrapped my fingers around the warm mug, thinking, *I want to know everything about me too.*

"Have you seen your dad?" he asked.

"Manny?" I said. "No. He's not here yet, I guess."

"Oh." Uncle Mateo made a face. "How old are you now? Thirteen?"

"Twelve," I answered.

"Right." He sat back and began fiddling with a black shoelace. "A couple of years younger than the twins. I saw you a few times. Before."

"You did?" I said. "I don't remember you."

"Of course you don't, silly," he said. "You were just a little peluda. Very cute and very hairy."

I knew he wasn't making fun of me. Still, I blushed, and even though I was wearing my sweatshirt, I crossed my arms because that's what I did when I wanted to hide them.

"You need something to go with that tea," my uncle said, getting up. He went back to the tiny kitchen and pulled a tin of shortbread cookies out of the cabinet. "Here you go."

I opened the box. Inside, there were spools of thread and a silver thimble.

"Whoops," he said. "Wrong one." He left and returned with shortbread.

"What's all this stuff?" I asked, looking over at what appeared to be an unfinished sewing project.

"Máscaras," he answered. "I have a few special orders that I've been working on." He held up a mask. "This one is for The Scorpion. You need one?"

I laughed and picked up a shiny red mask with orange flames on the sides.

"That one is for The Deming Devil," he said. "El Diablo de Deming."

"You really make these?"

"I do," he said proudly. "You're looking at the most in-demand mask-maker in the Southwest, thank you very much. I've been working on a few robes and costumes too. Take a look at this."

He turned a dress form around for me to see.

"Guess what this is going to be," he said.

I recognized the style of the jacket. "Is that for one of The Pounding Fathers?" I asked. I ran my hands along the soft brown velvet fabric.

"Nice, right?"

One of my favorite matches of Manny's was the one between him and a wrestler named John Addams. It was a classic battle of good versus evil. John Addams, as in the Addams Family, was part of a group called The Pounding Fathers that included Alexander Slamilton, George Bashington, and Thomas Pain. They dressed like the Founding Fathers, with powdered wigs and knickerbockers and fancy velvet coats with brass buttons and tails. But they were the Founding Fathers as zombie ghouls, with powdered faces and dark circles around their eyes. I wanted to hate The Pounding Fathers, especially after one had pounded on my own father, but the truth was that I liked them.

I had played the match over and over, so many times that I knew exactly when John Addams would put his foot on the bottom rope for leverage—an illegal move—and when he would blow wig powder—an illegal substance—in Manny's face.

The zombie had almost finished Manny with a brainbuster. A brainbuster is a banned move where one wrestler picks up another one, lifts them upside down, and drops them on their head. It's as dangerous as it sounds. John Addams would've been disqualified for doing a brainbuster, but he didn't get a chance to anyway because Manny managed to break out of his hold and lift him in a Bravo Back Breaker until the zombie went limp. Then he dropped him to the mat and rolled him up for the threesecond count.

"You don't wrestle anymore?"

"Nope," Uncle Mateo replied.

"I read an article online that said you retired under mysterious conditions."

"Mysterious conditions? Oooh," Uncle Mateo said. "The internet is full of nonsense. Just makes for a more exciting story than telling the truth. That I'm right here sewing."

"You stopped wrestling so that you could do this?" I asked.

"Yep."

"The story said you could've been a world champion," I added. "Like your dad."

"Maybe," Uncle Mateo said. "But I wanted other things. I'm happy doing what I'm doing."

Uncle Mateo gave me the kind of smile adults give when they're holding back. I'd seen it on Mom's face plenty of times.

"You're supposed to be telling me about you," he said. "So? Who is Adela Bravo?"

"Ramírez," I corrected.

"That's a start," he said. He flipped open a sketchpad and held it out to me. "Here's what the jacket will look like when it's done. Keep talking."

I stared at the drawing and thought about all the things that made me who I was. Like not knowing my father. If I'd grown up with Manny, what kind of person would I be? How would I describe myself to someone I just met?

"I'm in the seventh grade," I said, turning the pages of the pad to see more of my uncle's designs. "My best friend's name is Cy. She's cool. She'd love this place. And I have a stepdad, Alex. And I'm going to have a baby brother soon."

"A baby brother! That's great," he said. "And how is your mom? Lulu was one of my favorite people."

"She's always busy," I said. "She works at a museum. She's a fossil preparator. That's the person who—"

"I know, prepares the fossils, cleans them up. She was always talking about that when we were kids. She was a regular Indiana Jones." He laughed. "She was like a kid who never outgrew dinosaurs."

Of course Uncle Mateo knew that about Mom. I knew she liked dinosaurs, but I didn't know that she had always been obsessed with fossils. Rosie, Uncle Mateo, probably all the Bravos, knew more about Mom than I did. I felt like I only knew the hard things from before I was born. That she grew up with no parents. That she had gotten pregnant with me young and had to work her way through college.

"Why do you think she doesn't like to talk about Esperanza?" I asked.

Uncle Mateo placed a section of mask on the bed of the sewing machine.

"I don't know. I can't speak for your mom," he said. "I'm sure she has a lot of feelings about this place. I know that sometimes places hurt you. It's kind of like . . ." Uncle Mateo paused, thinking. "Like going to the dentist. You have a bad experience, and then you're afraid to go back."

"Mom isn't afraid of Esperanza," I said. "I think she just hates it."

Uncle Mateo laughed. "Sometimes hate and fear are just two sides of the same coin," he said. "Anyway, I'm happy for her. That she's following her dream. Away from here."

"She says there was nowhere for her to go in Esperanza," I said, quoting my mom. "What does that mean?"

"Sometimes people have dreams that are too big to fit in a small place," he said. "Don't get me wrong, I love Esperanza. But I had to learn how to make my own place here. That's not easy for everyone. And sometimes you realize that it's not possible, so you go."

"I'd never thought of Mom as someone with big dreams," I said, mesmerized by the needle as it went up and down, leaving a road of tiny black stitches in its path. "What else can you tell me?"

"About what?"

"About *me*," I said. Uncle Mateo seemed like someone who was honest and whom I could ask anything. "About Mom and Manny."

Uncle Mateo lifted his foot from the pedal, causing the machine to fall silent. "Look, Adela," he said. "I'm in no position to judge other people. We all make mistakes. People are complicated. You're here now, right? I encourage you to ask Manny all the questions you want to ask. Only Manny knows his truth."

But how much did Manny's truth match Mom's? I sighed and stood up.

"Leaving already?" Uncle Mateo asked. "You can stay as long as you want. Finish your tea, at least."

"Thank you for the tea, but I should go," I said. "Will I see you tonight?"

"Of course," he said, tilting his head. "Wouldn't miss it."

"Okay." I reached for the door. "Good." I liked my uncle already. He reminded me a little of Cy. He was kind, and he spoke his mind. And he had a strong personal style too.

"Oh, wait! Take a look at this," he said, grabbing something from a pile of fabric. "You recognize this one?" He held up a gold mask with black spots and black-lined eyeholes.

"Yeah," I said. "That's The Eagle, right?" I thought back to the crooked mask on the defeated wrestler. "He always loses."

Uncle Mateo studied my face for a few seconds. He looked like he wanted to say something, and I waited in anticipation.

"Yeah, I guess he does," Uncle Mateo said, returning the mask to its pile. "But in wrestling, a character's story is never set in stone. It can always change."

He pressed the pedal and went back to work. I closed the door carefully, leaving the symphony of sewing machine and violins behind me.

CHAPTER 15

When Manny finally showed up that evening, it felt like someone hit the PAUSE button on a movie. One minute, I was sitting in the ring, trying not to laugh as Eva and Maggie attempted to pick each other up over their heads. Uncle Mateo and Pancho were at the grill, bickering over how to light it. Hijo was barking at something that had scurried up a tree. The next minute, everything went silent around me.

When Manny came around the side of the house, I could hear the roar of the crowd. Here, there was no need for smoke machines and flashing lights because the early-evening sky was its own dramatic backdrop. New Mexican sunsets were overachievers. Tonight, the sky shone like a new penny, red and orange copper lit by the last rays of the sun and dotted with big, fluffy clouds lined in gold. Manny looked like a superhero. Like a Greek god come down from Mount Olympus. Something inside me swelled up, like when the Grinch's heart grew three sizes.

Suddenly, Hijo tore across the yard with a bag of hamburger buns in his mouth. Rosie came out of the house, the door slamming behind her, and just like that, someone had pressed PLAY and the movie of our lives continued.

"¡Perro comelón!" Rosie yelled as the twins took off after the dog. She looked like she wanted to laugh, though, so I knew she wasn't mad at Hijo.

Manny stopped when he saw me, and stared. I stared back. We were like a couple of duelers at high noon, waiting to see who'd make the first move. The twins, who had retrieved the bag of bread from Hijo, had come back to the ring. My grandmother and uncle got to work forming hamburger patties, pretending not to watch us.

"Go," Eva said, pushing me with her toe. I climbed down.

As Manny came toward me, I compared him to the photo in my closet. He was built like Pancho. He looked strong but also a little out of shape. He had stubble on his face, and his dark hair was buzzed close to the scalp. And he was tall. I could see why his nickname was The Mountain and where I got my height.

When Alex moved in with us, he brought with him a set of old encyclopedias he'd had since he was a boy. My favorite thing about them was the section of anatomy transparencies. You could turn each page and see the human body broken down into layers of skin and organs and bone. The Manny in front of me wasn't the skinny teenage boy in the photo anymore, but I could still see that younger version of him. I imagined my father in layers—beneath the person standing in front of me was a layer of Manny the wrestler in trunks and boots. Then the scrawny guy in the goofy Christmas sweater, a kid holding a kid. And underneath it all, layers of bruised and battered muscles.

I clasped my hands, picking at a little piece of skin near a fingernail. We faced each other uncomfortably for a few seconds. Finally, I stuck out a hand at the same time that Manny grabbed me by the arms, and I unintentionally poked him in the gut.

"Oof," Manny laughed and rubbed his stomach. "Nice sucker punch."

"I'm sorry," I said and grimaced. "Are you okay?"

"I'm a little soft around the middle these days, but it takes a lot more than that to hurt me," Manny said, squeezing his sides.

Before I knew what was happening, Manny had pulled me into a bear hug. It caught me by surprise, having his arms around me. The hug felt unsure and a little stiff. He smelled like smoke. Not a comforting outdoor-fire smoke where you warm your hands and toast marshmallows, but a pack-of-cigarettes smoke that makes you want to cough and cover your nose. The smell tickled my nostrils, and I sneezed into Manny's shoulder.

"I'm sorry," I said again, pulling away so I wouldn't get snot all over his shirt.

"No worries." Manny smiled his crooked, dimpled smile.

"Come on and sit down with me," he said.

I followed him to one of the picnic tables. He ran his hands along his knees. Up close, he didn't look like a god or a giant. He looked like just a guy in jeans and cowboy boots and a plaid flannel shirt.

"Wow," he said. "I thought about this moment a lot, you know, what it would be like. Meeting you again. What we would talk about. I didn't think I would be so nervous." He laughed.

"You did?" I said. "You are? Nervous?"

"Heck, yeah," he said. "Aren't you?"

"Maybe a little," I said. But that wasn't the truth. Now that I was sitting next to him and I could see that he wasn't a supernatural being, I wasn't nervous.

"How have you been?" he asked.

It was such a simple question, and at the same time, the hardest question.

Maggie and Eva were in the ring, taking turns climbing to a top turnbuckle and jumping. Every so often, one would run across and throw herself against the ropes, which would propel her back toward the middle. It looked painful. Part of me wished I could be there with them instead.

"Good," I said. I tugged at my braid and let it rest over my shoulder, twisting the end around my index finger.

"That's good," Manny said. "I'm glad."

"Oh," I said, not looking at him. "Do you mean, like, how has my life been?"

"Yeah, I guess," he said. "How has the life of Adela . . . ?"

"Ramírez."

"Right," Manny said. "How could I forget that your mom was so mad she wouldn't let Bravo go on the birth certificate."

"Really?" I was surprised at this new information.

Manny nodded. "It's been a long time, eh?"

"It has." I moved the toes of my shoes like windshield wipers against the dirt, scattering tiny rocks left and right.

"Sorry about the mix-up this morning," he said. "I hope everything was okay."

"It's fine," I said. "I got to spend time with Rosie and the twins and Pancho and Uncle Mateo."

"Cool, cool," Manny said. He scratched his chin absent-mindedly, as if unsure of what to say next. "Hey, so, we don't have to catch up on everything tonight. It'd be impossible anyway, right?" He laughed. "But I want you to know that I'm settling down here. Probably for good."

"Probably?"

"For good," he said, pounding his fist on the table as if to prove he was serious. "I don't know how much your mom has told you about—"

"My mom doesn't talk about you," I said. "At all."

Manny winced.

"I still can't believe she actually let you come," he said. "She doesn't exactly like this place." He looked around, and I couldn't tell if he meant the town or the Bravos' home.

"She doesn't talk about Esperanza either."

"Jeez, lay it all out for me, kid." Manny laughed. "Don't hold back."

"Just being honest," I said. Something the adults around me could stand to be, I thought.

"I appreciate honesty," Manny said. "Your mom was always too good for this place."

I didn't know what that meant, but I didn't like him talking about Mom. Whatever happened between them didn't matter. At least not to me. What mattered was me and him. I had to make sure Manny knew that the decision to be in Esperanza was mine, not Mom's. That I was here because I wanted to be. And that meant that he had to be here too.

"She let me come because I wanted to meet you," I said, placing my hand on my chest. "*Me.*"

"If you're anything like your mom, I bet you two locked horns, eh?" Manny chuckled. "Lulu would've made a good luchadora."

I giggled at the image.

"I'm glad you're here, kid," he said. He patted my cheek. His hand was calloused and sandpapery. "You've missed out on a lot."

"So have you," I said without thinking.

Manny sat up a little straighter, his eyes widened.

"Yeah, I have," he said. "But we'll make up for it, right?"

"Right," I said. Even though I wasn't sure how you made up for so much time.

A human skeleton lasts ten years before old bone breaks down and new bone forms, so Manny wasn't even meeting the same me that I was when he last saw me. That me was already gone.

"You know, I haven't been checked out these past eleven years," he said.

"Twelve," I corrected him. "I'm twelve."

"Yeah," Manny said. "But I was around that first year. I mean, I was always *around*, just not where you and your mom were. I sent your mom money, you know. I tried."

I chewed on the skin inside my lip and watched Maggie roll Eva up like a pill bug. She counted loudly to two before Eva kicked out of the hold.

"Anyway," he said. "That's all in the past. We're here now. I've got some work with the Cactus Wrestling League, so I'm not going anywhere."

"You do?"

"Oh yeah," he replied. "Keep an eye out for me."

"Maybe I can come to a match sometime."

"I'd like that," he said. "That'd be great."

I didn't know when I would see Manny again. *If* I would see him again. Mom had agreed to this meeting, but I knew she would prefer I not spend time with him. I had to know how much he wanted to be with me.

"Maybe you can teach me," I said, motioning to the ring. "Like Eva and Maggie."

He considered it for a moment before responding.

"You need a wrestling alter ego first," he said seriously. "You're a Bravo, so that's nonnegotiable around these parts."

He studied my face for a minute before laughing.

I laughed too. Having a wrestling alter ego didn't sound like such a terrible thing. It was better than being plain old Adela Ramírez.

Manny explained what the twins were doing in the ring and how they kept from getting hurt.

"It's all about timing and trust," he said.

I tried to listen, but I kept thinking about all the questions I had. Easy questions like what did he like to do when he wasn't wrestling? And did he have a favorite city out of all the places he'd been to in the world? And hard questions like why did he leave? And why did he let us go? And how did he feel about legally giving up being my father? Did he, like me, think it was weird that something as important as being someone's father could change because of a piece of paper?

But I had just met him, and I knew this was a lot to cover at once. So when he said it was all about timing and trust, I knew he was talking about wrestling, but it was like he was reading my mind too.

"¡Vengan a comer!" Rosie called from the kitchen door, where she stood with a platter of hamburgers.

"Shall we?" Manny asked, standing. He held out his hand to me.

An old Cyndi Lauper song came on the boom box the twins had in the ring, and Maggie and Eva shrieked. Instead of flinging each other away, they were now dancing in the ring and singing at the tops of their voices.

"Get over here, Adela Candela!" Eva hollered.

"Adela Candela." Manny nodded. "I like it. Maybe that's your alter ego right there."

I smiled and looked toward the ring, then back at Manny.

"Go on," Manny said. "I'll just be inside filling up the tank." He patted his stomach.

"I'll come get food too," I said quickly.

"Have fun with your primas," he insisted. "We'll talk more later. I'm here to stay, remember? Home in Esperanza, with all my family, with you. We've got lots of time to catch up."

Manny squeezed my shoulder, reassuring me. I watched his back as he retreated to the house. I was afraid that if I let him out of my sight, he might disappear again.

Through the window, I could see Manny inside the kitchen. He pecked Rosie on the cheek. Then he leaned in to talk to Pancho. It was like watching a TV show of someone else's family.

Alex says that pulling off a wrestler's mask is a serious deal. It's like a death. Not a real death, of course. But, like, the death of an illusion. It's the end of what you thought you knew. My father had always been an unknown, a masked character in my life. And now I knew who he was. It felt like a mask had been pulled off.

"Come on, prima," Maggie called, snapping me out of my thoughts.

I turned away from the window and walked toward the ring. I had cousins waiting for me.

★ ★ ★

When Manny pulled up in front of my house, the lights were on inside. From the truck, I noticed a curtain on a living room window fall back into place, as if someone had been looking out.

"All right, kid," Manny said. "I'll see you next weekend if your mom says yes."

"Right," I said.

I waited, even though I wasn't sure what I was waiting for.

"Tell your mom I say hi," Manny said. He made no move to get out and see me to the door. Finally, I climbed out of the truck. No way was I passing along Manny's greeting to Mom.

When I walked in, Mom and Alex were sitting on the couch with the TV on. Alex was rubbing Mom's feet.

"How was it?" Alex asked, a little too eagerly for Mom's taste, because she pinched his arm and he flinched.

"It was . . . good," I said, dropping my backpack and glancing at Mom. I wasn't sure how much she wanted to know.

"I'm glad," Mom replied.

"And?" Alex said. He scooted over to make room for me. "Good and what else? Tell us about them. Did you have a nice time?"

I liked how Alex was careful not to say "him," and how Mom was pretending not to listen.

"Don't you want to know, too, Mom?" I asked, sitting.

"Sure," Mom said unconvincingly. She didn't sound like she wanted to hear anything about Manny or the Bravos.

"I like Rosie. And Eva and Maggie," I said. "You know who they are, right?"

"I do," Mom said.

"I don't," Alex said. "Who are they?"

"Eva and Maggie are my cousins," I explained. "My uncle Speedy's kids. He died in an accident when they were really young." I glanced at Mom, thinking she would react. She didn't, but it felt good to talk about the Bravos. They were nice and welcoming and quirky and funny, and I wanted to share this with Alex and with Mom. "Maggie's missing a tooth. Eva knocked it out. And, get this, they *wrestle*. Can you believe it? Rosie makes the tumbleweed snowman. Did you know that? And my grandfather Pancho forgets stuff."

"That's what you can expect from years of concussions," Mom said.

"The twins said that too," I said. "That it's from wrestling."

"And they still want to do it?" Mom asked, frowning. "Interesting."

"Things have changed a bit since your grandfather wrestled," Alex offered. "Brainbusters aren't—"

"Oh yes," Mom said sarcastically. "It's very safe now."

"Lourdes . . ." Alex squeezed Mom's foot gently. Mom pulled away.

Sometimes, when Mom was mad, she acted like a kid. She was practically pouting.

"And my uncle Mateo sews masks and lives in a silver trailer," I said, ignoring her. "And Hijo, the dog, stole a bag of hamburger buns. It was pretty funny."

"Wow," Alex said. "Sounds like a story straight out of . . . professional wrestling."

No one laughed.

"Manny invited me to spend the weekend," I announced. "Can I? Next week?"

"I don't know," Mom said. She massaged her temples. "We agreed to one meeting. *And* he forgot to pick you up."

"But it all worked out, and it was good," I said. "Please? Please, Mom."

"We'll talk about it," Alex said.

"We'll?" I repeated. "You mean you and Mom?"

"Yes, *we'll*," Mom said. "*We* are still your parents."

"I can go, and I won't tell you anything about Manny or any of them again if you don't want to hear," I said, standing up. "He doesn't have to be in *your* life."

"That's fine with me," Mom said, struggling to get up from the couch. "We've been okay without him for a long time."

"You mean *you've* been okay," I shot back. "Not *we*. You never even asked me if I wanted to know him."

"Whoa," Alex said. "Let's all count to ten and take a deep breath." He put his palms together and demonstrated.

"You're a child, Adela," Mom said.

We were both standing behind the couch now, facing each other. Alex joined us, edging between the two of us as if he thought Mom and I were going to wrestle it out in the living room. Manny had said she would've made a good wrestler. If I hadn't been so mad, I might've laughed again at the mental image of my pregnant mom in a singlet.

"Addie—" Alex started, but I cut him off.

"This isn't about you," I said, turning to Alex.

He opened his mouth as if he was going to say something, and then closed it.

"Adela!" Mom yelled in surprise.

But I stomped off to my room before she could say anything else, or before I could say what I was thinking: *And you're not my father!* I slammed my bedroom door. It felt good to stomp and slam. If Mom could act like a baby, I could too.

I threw my backpack in a corner. I knew I'd crossed a line. Mom and I didn't agree on everything, but I had never talked to her or to Alex like that. And even though

I was still angry, I also felt terrible. I waited for them to come after me. I put my ear to the door and heard Alex say *Let her be*, followed by mumbled conversation I couldn't make out.

I opened my closet and turned on the Christmas sweater. In the front pocket of my sweatshirt, I could feel the folded square of paper Maggie and Eva had given me at dinner. I pulled it out and unfolded it. I smoothed it against the floor, then tore a piece of tape off one of the yearbook photos and stuck it to the wall.

Maggie, Eva, and I had eaten our dinner in the ring while the grown-ups sat at a picnic table. Maggie tore a sheet of paper out of her notebook.

"What's your mom's name?" she asked me.

"Lourdes Ramírez," I replied.

"Lourdes," Maggie said.

I chewed on my burger and watched as she wrote names. She still hadn't found her tooth and stuck her tongue in the gap while she worked. When she was finished, she turned the paper around for me to see.

"It looks like a taxonomy chart," I said.

"Sure, okay," Maggie said, pushing her grilled peppers to the edge of her plate like they were contaminated.

"You know, King Phillip Came Over From Greedy Spain," I said.

Eva gave me a blank stare. Her big brown eyes looked otherworldly, framed by blue and gold makeup.

"Kingdom, phylum, class, order, family, genus, species."
I ticked off on my fingers. "It's actually supposed to be King
Phillip Came Over From *Great* Spain, but Mom changed it
because she says Spain was a colonizer and all that."

"You're such a nerd," Eva said and laughed.

But I knew she wasn't laughing *at* me. And even if she
was, I didn't care. Science and mnemonics were cool, and
I didn't really need anyone else to get it.

"What do you think will happen?" Maggie said. "With
Manny?"

"What do you *hope* will happen?" Eva asked.

"I don't know," I said. "I just wanted to meet him. See
what he's like."

"Find out if you're anything like him," Eva added.

"Yeah," I said. "I guess."

"Did you ever think about what would happen if you
didn't like him?" Maggie continued. "What if you end up
wishing you'd never met?"

Maggie wasn't afraid to ask the *what-if*s that hid inside
my brain, the ones I was scared to ask myself.

★★★

I studied the paper on my closet wall. The list of names
reminded me of something Mom once said about her
work. "When there's a species that paleontologists think
has gone extinct because there's no fossil record, but
then it reappears, they have to try to fill in the ghost

lineage. Those are the gaps, the parts of the story that are missing."

It felt like Manny and the Bravos were the species that had suddenly reappeared. Now I was trying to fill in my ghost lineage, the story that had been missing my whole life.

★ CHAPTER 16 ★

"Well?" Cy said. "Are you going to tell me all about them? What's the famous Manny Bravo really like?"

I had given Cy a short text message summary of my visit to Esperanza. But the truth was, there wasn't a lot I could share with her about Manny. Aside from our conversation before dinner on Saturday night, I hadn't spent much time with just him. He seemed busy, rushed. He was there but not there. Was that what he was always like, or was he intentionally avoiding being alone with me for longer than he absolutely had to be?

"I don't know," I said, scanning the selection of seats in the auditorium. "He's tall. He eats a lot. He's . . . He seems like just a regular guy."

"Who happens to be a wrestler," Cy said. "Yeah, totally normal."

I didn't tell Cy that part of me had hoped Manny wasn't just a normal person. That I'd hoped there was something extraordinary, good or bad, that would help me know how to feel about him. Instead, I told her about the twins and about Uncle Mateo.

"Will you see them again?" Cy asked. "I want to meet them all."

We walked past a group of girls who stood against the wall with their arms crossed as if bracing themselves for something awful. I knew the feeling.

"I might spend the weekend," I said. "Manny invited me, but my mom is being cranky about it."

Mom hadn't snapped out of her funk yet. At breakfast that morning, Alex had said that I needed to give Mom time. That this was a lot. As if she hadn't already had twelve years. Mom was acting like this was about her when it wasn't.

"It's just like a soap opera," Cy said. "You meet your long-lost father, and he's a superhero. Isn't it great?"

I laughed.

"It's nothing like that," I said. "He's not a superhero."

We found seats, and I settled in, imagining myself a snail slipping into its shell. I had grown five inches since the last school year. Why was it that the more I wanted to hide, the harder it was to do?

"I'm really nervous," Cy said, looking toward the door at the back of the auditorium. "If I don't get to direct this thing, I don't know what I'll do."

I wished the seventh-grade show were the biggest thing I had to worry about.

"I want to do something fun and lively and totally original," Cy went on. "What do you think?"

She looked at me expectantly, and I smiled back because I knew what it felt like to really want something.

"She'll pick you," I assured her. "You're a natural leader and the most creative person I know. No one else in our class would do a better job."

"You're right," Cy agreed. "Obviously."

"You're also very modest," I joked.

The curtains on the stage were drawn shut, but a bright light shone on the center, reflecting on the polished wood floor. I remembered how exciting it had been to see the seventh-grade performance of *The Nutcracker* for the first time. Every year, I looked forward to the flyers that went up all over town, including at the diner—an open invitation to the community. When I was younger, I wanted to be the Mouse King because even though he had the shortest part, his battle with the Nutcracker was the most exciting thing about the show. But things were different now. The thought of standing in front of a bunch of people, pretending to be someone else, was terrifying. It was hard enough to be just me. Fortunately, I wasn't one of Mrs. González's drama favorites, so I knew I'd be a partygoer or a mouse, maybe even a snowflake, a role where I could just blend in like a chameleon. At least I had that.

"She's here," Cy whispered. She squeezed my hand, crushing my fingers.

"Ow," I said, pulling my hand away. "Relax, will you?"

Mrs. González climbed up to the stage, clip-clopping in her shiny red clogs that always made me think of the ending of the story *Little Snow-White*. Not the sweet cartoon Snow White everyone is familiar with, but the original Grimm tale, where the evil queen has to wear a pair of red-hot iron shoes and dance until she drops dead. The original fairy tales were scarier than the cartoon versions. Mom said they don't call them the Brothers Grimm for nothing. She has what you would call a dark sense of humor.

Cy squirmed restlessly all during class while Mrs. González showed videos from some of the previous years' performances, prolonging the revelation of role assignments. Finally, the drama teacher picked up the stack of papers she'd walked in with and tapped them against the podium.

"Before I distribute the list, I want you to remember that no matter what part you get, you are all stars," Mrs. González said, her voice booming from the microphone. "There are no small roles in this production."

Cy moved to the edge of her seat. I was thankful that her fingers now gripped the armrests. I looked around the auditorium. I noticed Gus sitting alone toward the back, shrouded inside the hood of his sweatshirt as usual.

All around me, the glow of phone screens seeped out from between the covers of loose-leaf binders and from underneath backpacks held on laps. No one seemed to care about big parts or small parts. Maybe no one believed what Mrs. González had said. Maybe they realized that unless you had one of the starring roles, you were just part of a crowd. Just like in middle school. Who cared that no two snowflakes were alike when there were so many of them, all together, all at once, that you couldn't even tell them apart? Maybe they were okay with that too. Maybe it made them feel safe too.

"And as is tradition," Mrs. González continued as she came down from the stage and began handing out copies of the cast list, row by row, "our leads will work with the director to plan this year's surprise twist."

The papers made their way toward us.

"Could they be any slower?" Cy said, loud enough for everyone to hear. She stood, waiting, and sat back down when Mrs. González motioned with her hand for her to sit. When the copies finally made it to our row, Cy snatched them. She grabbed one sheet and passed the others to me. I took my own copy before passing the rest.

"Yeah!" Cy jumped from her seat, hugging the sheet of paper to her chest, and did a little dance.

Mrs. González looked over at Cy. "I'm glad at least one of you is excited."

"I won't let you down," Cy announced. She looked around the auditorium as if addressing all of us. "This is going to be the best *Nutcracker* ever."

"*Addie?!*"

Before I could find myself in the long list of supporting characters, the voice of Letty Anaya shrieked my name from a few rows ahead of us.

She whipped around, her long blond hair swinging like she was in a shampoo commercial. The expression on her face was at once angry and crushed.

"Whoa," Cy said, looking at the cast list. "You're—"

"Marie?" I stared at my sheet. "That has to be a mistake." I looked at Letty and shook my head to let her know I was as surprised as she was.

A few rows behind us, Brandon let out a whoop. "Nutcracker! Yes!"

Mrs. González returned to the podium onstage, seemingly unaware of the chaos she'd created.

"Mrs. González," Letty called to the teacher, waving her cast list. "I think you made a mistake."

"Hey, Mrs. González," Brandon called out. "Is there a yeti in *The Nutcracker*?"

"No mistakes," Mrs. González said. "And don't be silly, Brandon. You know very well there isn't a yeti in the show."

"Maybe it's just me, but I think of Marie as, like, small and delicate," Brandon said, loud enough for me to hear. He turned to look at me and shot me an evil smile. "You could be Addie the Abominable Snowman, since you're so tall and hairy."

"And you're an awful little troll," Cy said, looking past

me and giving Brandon her glare of doom. "Go back to your bridge."

I felt my face burn red like a Chimayó chile. I pulled at the sleeves of my shirt and crossed my arms to make them disappear.

The bell rang, and Brandon jumped out of his seat. He stuck out his tongue at us before taking off toward the exit.

"Prepare to get your nuts cracked, Mouse King," he yelled as he passed Gus.

I felt frozen in place.

"You're Marie," Cy said, a huge smile on her face. "We're going to be a great team. I mean, we already are, but we get to work on this together. I'm so excited. Are you excited?"

"No, Cy," I groaned. "I'm not excited. I don't want to be Marie."

I looked toward the stage, where a few kids had lined up to complain to Mrs. González. Letty was at the front of the line, speaking animatedly while the teacher listened.

"Come on," Cy said, pulling me out of my seat and shaking me. "You'll be a great Marie. Just as good as Letty. *Better* than Letty. We're going to leave our mark on the Thorne Middle School *Nutcracker*."

Letty stormed down the aisle toward the exit. I tried to give her an apologetic look when she passed us, but she didn't meet my eyes.

"Let's go celebrate," Cy said, folding her cast list carefully. "Maybe Alex will make us some fancy milkshakes."

"I have to talk to Mrs. González," I said, grabbing my bag and shaking my sheet of paper at her.

"Really?" Cy pouted.

"Really," I said. "Sorry. Wait for me outside? We can go get those milkshakes and still celebrate you."

"Fine," Cy said. "I'll meet you at the bike racks."

I waited for everyone to leave before making my way to the stage, where Mrs. González gathered her belongings. The empty auditorium gave me the creeps. A few years ago, there had been a bat infestation and almost a thousand bats had been removed. I imagined some of them still hanging from the rafters, preparing to swoop down on us. But it was now or never. I climbed the steps to the stage and walked up to the podium.

"What is it, Adela?" Mrs. González asked. "Or should I say *Marie*?" She looked up from her copy of *The Nutcracker* script. It was highlighted and underlined, dog-eared and food stained. Mrs. González took the show very seriously.

"I wanted to talk to you about my role," I said.

"The most important one," she said. "Everyone thinks it's about the Nutcracker, but it isn't."

"It's not?" I asked. Knowing that according to Mrs. González, Marie had the most important part made it worse. "I always thought it was a story about Christmas and the Nutcracker that comes to life in Marie's strange dream."

"Oh yes," Mrs. González said. "But the Nutcracker doesn't exist without Marie's imagination. None of it does. It's about her growing up and making choices."

"Well, about Marie," I said, hesitating. "Would it be possible for me to switch roles?"

"But *you* are Marie," Mrs. González insisted.

"But I don't want to be," I pushed back. "Please give the role to someone else. Anyone else. Letty really wants it, and she'd be a great Marie."

"Letty has already made her case," Mrs. González said, stuffing her script into her bag. "I picked you."

"Can't I be a mouse?" I asked. "A soldier?" Mrs. González continued smiling. "Is that a yes?" I asked, hopeful.

"Oh, no," she said. "You're my Marie."

"I can't do it," I insisted. "I can't get up onstage in front of people and have everyone staring at me."

"You're scared," she said as if it was a revelation. "That's natural. I can't tell you how many times I've performed scared out of my wits. It's okay to be scared. It's just a sign that you care."

I couldn't imagine anyone who wore lipstick in public as brightly colored as Mrs. González's being scared or embarrassed to be looked at.

"I'm not scared," I said, suddenly not wanting the teacher to think I was afraid. "I just don't want to. I'm not very Marie-like, in case you haven't noticed."

"And what is 'Marie-like'?" Mrs. González asked.

It was obvious that she wasn't going to be easily convinced. It wasn't enough that I didn't want the part and someone else did. Mrs. González needed a debate-level argument. So I thought about Letty and all the Maries I'd seen in the past. What about them made me think that I wasn't Marie-like?

"Well," I said. I held out my arms so that she could take me in. Maybe she would see what Brandon saw—a hulking yeti.

Mrs. González seemed unmoved. She waited for me to go on.

"She seems, I don't know, helpless," I said. "And weak, like she's waiting for someone to save her."

"And you aren't that kind of person," Mrs. González said. "You can take care of yourself."

I wanted to tell her that not only did I come from a family of wrestlers, but I was raised by a single mom.

"Go on," Mrs. González said. "What else?" I took this as a sign that she was considering it. I had a chance.

"In the Thorne shows, Marie is usually a light-skinned girl," I said. "You should know because you always do the casting. Just like the Marie in books and movies. And I've only seen two different ballet companies perform *The Nutcracker* live, but I've never seen a Marie that isn't white."

"You make some very good points," Mrs. González said. "But . . ."

I huffed, feeling on the brink of defeat. "Why *me*?" I groaned.

"Adela, I've been doing this a long time," Mrs. González said. "As a matter of fact, I haven't said anything because it isn't final yet, but this might be my last year of *The Nutcracker*."

"You're dying?" I gasped.

"Oh goodness, no," she laughed. "Just planning my retirement. But you are right."

"I am?"

"Yes," she said. "I always pick the same kind of person for Marie. I've always thought of her the same way, year after year. Just my own subconscious bias, I suppose." She stared past me toward the empty auditorium seats. "But," she went on, snapping out of it, "not this year. This year, I said I would push myself to think differently about the show. You're never too old to change the way you think, you know? And that meant envisioning Marie differently."

"I don't want to be your guinea pig," I said, thinking back to the library books on animal testing. I didn't want to be part of Mrs. González's inspired moment. "Can't you find another way to envision this whole thing that doesn't involve me?"

"When I woke up the day I wrote the cast list, you came to mind for the role," Mrs. González said. "And if there's one thing I trust, it's my instinct."

"What if my mom comes to talk to you about it?" I asked. "Can I change roles then?"

"I'd welcome seeing your mother," she said. "Now, I have to go, and so do you."

I sighed and adjusted my backpack as I started to leave. I knew Mom would never talk to Mrs. González about the role. She had a million other things going on, and she'd say I was old enough to handle this on my own.

"Adela," Mrs. González called.

I turned around, hopeful that she had had a sudden change of heart.

"Have fun with it. Make it your own," she said through her traffic-stopping smile. "I trust you will."

★ CHAPTER 17 ★

Mom and Alex didn't think I could hear them in the kitchen from where I sat at the counter at the diner, waiting. I held the bag I'd packed for the weekend on my lap, hugging it tightly and listening intently.

"You have to stop trying to tell her how to feel about him," Alex insisted. "She isn't you. You're going to end up pushing her away. Is that what you want?"

"Obviously, she isn't me," Mom said. "I didn't have anyone to warn me that he would disappoint me. Just like he's going to disappoint her."

"You don't know that," Alex said. "Maybe he's matured and realizes that this is his chance to make amends, to know his daughter."

I didn't understand it, but I appreciated that Alex was on Manny's side. And that he thought Manny might have changed. It gave me hope.

"He can't just waltz in twelve years later," Mom continued.

"Well, he didn't exactly waltz in," Alex said. "We knew what the adoption would mean, Lourdes. He has to be part of this process."

"I know," Mom said, resigned. "This all just makes me ... nervous."

Dishes clattered nearby, and I glared at Alma, the waitress who seemed to be carrying more than she could handle and making too much noise for me to hear the conversation.

"I know you're trying to protect her," Alex said. "But she wants to know him. She needs to know him. Let her learn who he is on her own."

"She's a kid," Mom said.

"She's growing up," Alex replied. "You can't keep her away from him forever."

There was silence. A few minutes later, Mom came out of the kitchen. Her eyes were red, like she'd been crying.

"Damn onions," she muttered when she saw me looking at her. "You sure you have everything you need?" She jerked her head toward my backpack.

"Toothbrush, toothpaste, underwear, clothes, phone charger," I said, scanning my mental checklist of things to pack. "Got it."

"Hey, before I forget," Mom said, pointing at me accusingly. "Mario at the museum mentioned that Lucy is going to be a soldier in *The Nutcracker*. And that *you're* Marie. Why do I have to find this out from someone else?"

"Ugh," I groaned. "Don't remind me."

"Marie!" Alex held up a hand for a high five. "Congratulations, Adelita. Aren't you excited?"

"Do I look excited?" I asked. "I don't want to be Marie. Why doesn't Mrs. González bother to ask kids before forcing them into roles?"

"You'll be a great Marie," Alex said. He was packing up an apple pie in a white bakery box.

"And if she picked you, there must be a good reason," Mom added.

"Yeah, like maybe she wants to humiliate me in front of all of Thorne," I said.

"I doubt that." Mom frowned.

"Or maybe she trusts you to do a good job as the show lead," Alex offered.

"Can you please talk to her, Mom?" I asked. "Tell her to cast someone else."

"If you don't want to do it, you'll have to talk to her yourself," Mom said. "You're a big girl."

"I already did," I complained.

Mom threw her hands up as if there was nothing she could do. She looked at her watch, then out the window. Manny was a few minutes late already, just as she had expected him to be. She was about to say something when I heard the sound of tires crunching on gravel. I looked toward the window and saw the brown truck pull up outside.

"He's here." I climbed off the stool, relieved that Manny had made it.

"Give this to Rosie, please," Alex said, placing the pie in my hands. "Be careful with it."

"Call me if you need anything," Mom said. She looked like she wanted to say something else, but instead said, "I'll see you on Sunday."

She squeezed my shoulder, glancing out the window one more time before letting me go and heading back into the kitchen. She didn't have to worry about seeing Manny, because he didn't get out of the truck. I grabbed my backpack and walked carefully toward him with the pie.

"What'd you bring me?" he asked, rubbing his hands in anticipation as I set the pie at my feet.

"Eve with a lid on."

"Who with a what?" Manny asked, glancing over at me like I'd lost my marbles.

I laughed. "That's diner lingo for apple pie," I explained. "Alex made it."

"Sounds good," he said. "Ready to hit the road?"

I nodded. He honked the horn and pulled out of the parking lot.

"You must eat pretty well, huh?"

"I guess," I said. "I mean yeah, I do. Alex is a good cook."

"I never really learned how to cook," he said. "But I'm on the road so much, it's not like I have the place or the time for it anyway."

"You do now, right?" I asked. "Since you're staying."

"Yeah, I guess I do," he said.

"When are you wrestling next?" I asked. "I haven't seen you on Cactus."

"It's not too exciting, what I'm doing right now," he replied. "Not sure if it's worth coming to see."

"I don't care," I said. "Can I come? Maybe I can go with Maggie and Eva."

"Sure, soon," he said. He glanced over at me. "Hey, can you keep a secret?"

"Uh, I don't know," I said, hesitating. "Mom says adults shouldn't ask kids to keep secrets."

"It's not that kind of secret," he said. "It's nothing bad. It's about my work. Just not something I can really tell people."

"Okay, then." I was intrigued and happy that Manny was confiding in me. "What is it?"

"I'm wrestling as un enmascarado," he whispered as if there was someone else in the truck who might hear. "That's why you haven't seen me."

"*Really?*"

I tried to think of who he might be. There were a lot of masked wrestlers in the Cactus Wrestling League. Enmascarados were popular in Mexico, so it was natural that they were embraced by Cactus.

"Yeah," he said. "But just for a little while longer, while I get some things straightened out. I'm not supposed to be wrestling here as Manny Bravo right now."

"Why not?" I asked.

"Manny the Mountain was banished from Cactus a few years ago," he said. "I got this great opportunity to wrestle in Japan, but it meant I had to break my contract. Cactus let me go on the condition that I lost a loser-leaves-town match. Your abuelo wasn't too happy about that."

"But, Japan," I said in awe. "Wasn't it great?"

"It was a fun experience," he said. "But now Pa is getting older, and, you know, he's sick. Plus, I'm getting older too. My priorities are a little different."

He looked over at me and smiled. Did he mean that I was a priority now?

"Anyway, Cactus wants me to wrestle as un enmascarado for a little while," he went on. "Eventually, we'll expose my true identity. It'll be the return of Manny the Mountain."

"Who are you?" I asked. He looked over at me, confused. "Your secret identity?"

"Oh." Manny laughed. "Okay, so you know this is top secret. Sometimes masked wrestlers don't reveal their identity to anyone, not even family. That's wild, no?"

"Seems like it would be really hard to do," I said. "To keep a secret that big."

But then I remembered that Mom had kept a big secret from me all my life. Maybe it wasn't so hard after all.

"Believe me, it's not easy," he said.

I pictured Manny in a mask, pushing a shopping cart

around a supermarket or ordering food at a drive-through or checking out books at the library, the whole world unaware of who walked among them.

"Well?" I said. "Are you going to tell me who you are?"

"Oh yeah," he laughed. "But not a word to anyone."

"What about Cy? She's my best friend."

"Nope." Manny shook his head.

"Mom?" I asked.

"I'm guessing she doesn't want to know," he said.

I nodded. No point in pretending. "Okay, tell me already."

"I'm . . ." he said slowly, drawing out the revelation, "The Eagle."

"The Eagle of Esperanza?"

I thought back to the masked wrestler being pounded on by Apollo, the twisted mask, the crowd throwing things at him. The Eagle who always loses was my father.

"Yeah," he said. "Don't know if you follow Japanese wrestling, but I've been The Eagle for a few years now."

"The Eagle," I repeated. "What's it like to lose all the time?"

"Not fun," he said and laughed. "But it's temporary. Right now, my job is to put over a few guys. Soon, El Águila will soar away and Manny the Mountain will return."

"And someone else will be putting you over, right?" I said.

"Right," Manny confirmed.

173

I couldn't wait to tell Mom that she was wrong about Manny. Manny was back for good.

"Heel or babyface?" I asked. "Which do you prefer?"

"Oh boy," Manny said, thinking. "That's actually a tough choice. I like being a face, but playing a heel can be fun too. I'll say heel. But don't tell anyone."

"I'd pick heel too," I said, grinning conspiratorially. "I like The Pounding Fathers."

"You picked the worst, eh?" he said, but I could tell that he appreciated the choice.

"Chocolate or vanilla?" I asked.

"Chocolate," Manny said. "That's easy."

"Me too," I agreed.

"Winter or summer?" Manny said.

"Winter," I answered. "I like the cold."

"So do I," he said.

"Suplex or dropkick?" I asked.

"Suplex," Manny said. "Way more fun to do."

"UFOs, real or not?" Manny asked, glancing up at the sky as if one might fly overhead.

"Real," we both said at the same time and laughed.

I wanted to ask *Do you want to be my dad, yes or no?* but I didn't. I knew Mom had talked to Manny about the adoption, but he hadn't brought it up yet. I wondered when he would.

When we pulled up to the Bravo gate, I grabbed my bag

and the pie and climbed out of the truck. Manny didn't turn off the engine.

"Aren't you coming in?"

"I've got stuff to do, kid," he said. "Hang out with your grandparents, and I'll see you at dinner."

"Oh," I said, trying not to sound disappointed. "Okay."

"Save some of that Eve with a hat on for me," he called out.

He waved and drove away in a cloud of dust.

"Eve with a lid," I said to no one.

I clutched the pie box, feeling the warmth of its contents on my stomach. I stayed in that spot at the edge of the road until the brown truck was nothing but a tiny speck on the horizon.

CHAPTER 18

The house was quiet when I walked in. Maggie had sent me an unidentifiable selfie earlier, a close-up of the space where her missing tooth should have been, and a text message that they would be at the house later because she had to go to the dentist after school for a new flipper tooth. I poked my head in the kitchen, hoping to find Rosie, but it was empty. I could hear a television and followed the sound toward the family room. There, I found Pancho in his recliner chair with Hijo at his feet.

"Hey, hey," he said when he saw me. He seemed to recognize me today. "Tell your abuela her show is on."

Mundo raro was starting, and I was glad to have something to talk about with him. Something that didn't require him to remember anyone in the family.

"What's happening now?" I asked. I sat down in the recliner next to him. He and Rosie had matching leather upholstered chairs. I sank in and propped up my feet. It felt like I was about to blast off into outer space. "Did Paulina find out the truth about her mother?"

"Not yet," Pancho said. "But it's getting good. They just found Simona dead!"

"She's dead?" I gasped. "How? Where?"

"In the oven they use to fire the pencil leads." Pancho laughed and shook his head.

The thing about telenovelas was that they were always "getting good." All the wacky twists and turns were what kept you hooked. In *Mundo raro*, the protagonist, Paulina, had no idea that her boss, the rich heiress to a pencil-manufacturing fortune, was her mother. The heiress had been forced by her parents to give Paulina away when she was born, all because her father was a poor factory worker. The family threatened to disown Paulina's mother. But now, years later, Paulina was an adult, and another employee, the nosy Simona, had found out the truth. She tried to blackmail the family, which was why she ended up baking with the pencil leads.

Telenovela story lines weren't unlike wrestling story lines—hidden or mistaken identity, double cross, good versus evil, and, of course, family drama. It was all very ridiculous, and yet, it made sense too. Maybe Cy was right about my life being like a telenovela.

Pancho moved a wooden bowl of mixed nuts across the little coffee table between the recliners so that it was closer to me. I picked out a few lime-and-chile-covered peanuts.

While the telenovela was interesting, it was the rest of the room that captured my attention. The space was filled with old photographs and awards. It was like one big trophy case.

There were sports medals and wrestling trophies from Esperanza High School. There was Speedy's satin jacket, framed and hanging on a wall—green, white, and red sequins, like the Mexican flag, the name Bravo in black script across the back. There was Pancho's championship belt, the same one he wore in the photo at the historical society.

There were black-and-white photographs of Pancho as a young man in the ring, shaking hands with some of the greats like Mil Máscaras and Gory Guerrero. There were photos of Manny and my uncles together, individual portraits of them in their wrestling attire and flashy jackets like the one Speedy once wore, photos of them goofing around and putting each other in headlocks and Bravo Back Breakers. In one photo, Speedy and Mateo wore the belts they won for defeating Guapo García and The CEO, the former tag-team champions.

There were old family portraits of Rosie and Abuelo and the brothers when they were kids. The boys looked like sets of nesting dolls, different versions of themselves across the years.

I looked over at Pancho, who had dozed off. From where I sat, I could see that he had scars on his forehead, some faint like rivulets and some deep and pronounced like dry arroyos. Sitting there with his head tilted back against the headrest, his hands on his lap over the crocheted blanket that covered his legs, he looked small. Nothing like the photos all around me.

The family room felt like a museum. Mom came to school for career day one year to talk about working in a museum. I had always thought of them as just places with collections of old things, but Mom said museums told stories too. She gave us all these questions to think about when we looked at exhibits. She said that the objects in a museum tell a version of a story, and that it's important to think about who is telling the story, what the story is about, why it's told one way and not another, and who or what is missing.

As I looked at all the objects and photographs in the den, I thought about the story they told. It was a story about family and strength and glory and winning. I thought about what was missing. The photos were old, so you wouldn't know from looking at them that Speedy was dead or that Mateo didn't wrestle or that Pancho was sick. Or that Manny had a daughter. The twins were missing too. And except for the family portraits, there was no Rosie.

Pancho let out a big, loud snore and woke himself up.

"Did I miss anything?" he asked, focusing on the television again.

"Not really," I said. "Just some ugly crying."

He laughed.

I wanted to ask Pancho about wrestling, about Manny, about what it was like to be a Bravo. I wanted to know everything but wasn't sure where to start. So we watched the telenovela and shared a bowl of nuts.

When a commercial break came on, Pancho grabbed the remote and muted the TV.

"I want to tell you something, mija," he said, turning to me.

"What is it?"

"You have to let him go," he said firmly.

"What do you mean?" I asked, confused. "Let who go?"

"He's going to be great," he continued, as if he didn't hear me. His eyes scanned the room, looking at everything in it as proof. "He wants this. And if you try to stop him, he's just going to be unhappy, and you will be unhappy."

"Stop who?" It felt like he was having a conversation with me but also not with me.

"Pues Manny, claro," Pancho said. He sounded angry.

"But he told me he was here to stay," I said. Hijo let out a little yip from where he slept on the floor.

"No, no," he said, shaking his head. "You can go to school anytime. He'll be back to see the baby. It's not like he's leaving forever."

That's when I realized he wasn't talking to me. He was talking to Mom.

"This is his dream," Pancho continued. "And it's like that comet that only comes around once every hundred years."

"You mean Halley's Comet?"

"Ese mismo," Pancho said, pointing at me. "When it's gone, it's gone. Family will always be there. Rosie understood. Greatness is something you have to chase down. It doesn't just come to you."

I felt uncomfortable listening to a conversation he was having with Mom. Like I was invading her privacy again. I looked at the doorway and wished Rosie would appear. Maybe there was something she could do to bring him back to the present.

Earlier in the week, I had looked for information about head injuries and wrestling. I wanted to know what was wrong with Pancho. I read about something called chronic traumatic encephalopathy, which happened to people who played sports where concussions were common. It was a kind of brain damage, and it affected a person's memory and moods. I wasn't sure that was what Pancho had, but I knew that there was nothing that could be done to reverse it. How much of my grandfather was gone forever?

"Where's Lourdes?" he asked.

"Lourdes isn't here," I said.

"Who are you, then?"

"I'm Adela," I said. "Lourdes's daughter. Manny's daughter."

"Adela," Pancho repeated, absorbing the information.

He turned in his chair and looked at me as if he was

seeing me for the first time. Except he didn't seem confused. He recognized me, finally. He reached over and put his hand on mine.

"Tell her I'm sorry," he said. "Tell her I was wrong."

He squeezed my hand, then turned back to the television like he was alone in the room with just Hijo at his feet.

CHAPTER 19

I wandered outside, thinking about what Pancho had said. Did he really want me to tell Mom he was sorry? Was he the reason Manny wasn't around? Halley's Comet is visible every seventy-five years, not every hundred years, but I got the point. It wouldn't be visible again until 2061. That was a long time from now. I could understand that waiting so long for a chance to do something again was too long. But Pancho had also said that family would always be there. And that wasn't true. The twins and I had all grown up without our fathers. How was Manny so sure that *I'd* always be around, waiting for him?

I walked toward the barn, where bundles of tumbleweeds threatened to take over the whole structure. The Bravo property felt like its own universe, a galaxy of planets. Uncle Mateo in his trailer, the twins in the ring, Rosie in her workshop, and Pancho, despite his failing memory, like the sun they revolved around. Manny was a shooting star, visible for a short period of time. Catch him if you can.

I squeezed past tumbleweeds and peeked into the only window that wasn't covered by them. I could see Rosie inside, her head bent over something she was working on. I knocked on the glass. Rosie looked up.

"This way," she called and motioned behind her.

I walked around the side of the barn to the back, where two massive doors were open, letting cool air in. Rosie stood at a worktable surrounded by tumbleweed statues in different states of assembly. She wore a pair of gray coveralls.

"Manny told you where to find me, ¿sí?" she said, looking up. Her curls were pulled back with a red bandanna.

"Sí," I said. It was easier than saying no, that he drove off and told me he'd see me later. Or that I'd left Pancho in the family room having a conversation with the past.

"Mira," she said. "This is going to be the snowman." She pointed to three of the biggest balls of tumbleweed I'd ever seen. Big, bigger, and biggest. "I need to spray-paint them white and finish the scarf." She held up a long blue scarf still attached to a crochet hook. "And then, next month, we assemble it."

The appearance of the platforms along Route 13 was one of the first signs that the holidays were approaching. Every year right after Thanksgiving, the tumbleweed statues went up, starting with the snowman at the entrance to Thorne. There would be tumbleweed Christmas trees between the two towns and a tumbleweed Virgen de Guadalupe at the WELCOME TO ESPERANZA sign.

"We take a photo with the snowman every year," I said,

touching the soft scarf the snowman would wear. "Me and my mom and my stepdad. And Marlene too. She works at the diner. And sometimes my best friend, if she's in town."

"I remember," Rosie said. "Your mami always loved the tumbleweed statues. She would help me sometimes."

"She would?" I asked. Every new revelation felt like a punch to the gut. There was so much Mom had never told me. "I guess since you make these, it's kind of like you were in the photos too."

"Oh, I like that," Rosie said and smiled.

"Where do you get these giant tumbleweeds?" I asked, looking at the prickly dried-out monsters. They were everywhere—on the floor, on shelves, on the table, all over the barn.

"Wherever I can find them," she said. "I don't know if you've noticed, but there's a lot of tumbleweed in these parts." She laughed. "I drive around, and I get some from flood control too. They're always looking for ways to keep the tumbleweeds from clogging up the waterways."

"What are you making there?" I motioned toward the mass of green yarn that trailed off the table.

"This is la Guadalupe's cloak," Rosie said, holding it up. "I work on it a little until I get tired of it, and then I switch to working on the snowman's scarf. I started both over the summer. Little by little, it all gets done."

"You crochet too?" I looked around the barn at all the parts.

"And weld," she said, pointing to steel frames nearby. "Those are for the bodies."

"Wow," I said. "Do you ever sleep?"

"With one eye open." Rosie laughed and closed one eye. "Mateo helps me sometimes, but he has his own work."

"I can help you," I said eagerly. "If you'll teach me."

"I'll teach you anything you want to learn," Rosie offered. "You can be my assistant for next year's statues."

I smiled at the idea of a next year with Rosie.

"How did you start making statues out of tumbleweed?"

"Pues," Rosie started, "one night, I was home alone with three sick boys. Talk about not sleeping! I was up very late, or very early, depending on how you look at it. It was that time of night when there wasn't much on TV, you know? Well, maybe you don't know, because you have el internet, but it wasn't always like that. I found an episode of an old TV show about a couple that gets lost on their way somewhere, and they are held captive by tumbleweeds."

"Tumbleweeds?" I laughed, shaking my head. "Are you sure you weren't dreaming?"

Now it was Rosie's turn to laugh. "No, no, it's real!" she insisted. "The tumbleweeds would not let them leave the house. That happens sometimes, you know? ¡Uy, qué miedo me dio! Because we're surrounded by them here. And here I was with three sick boys. I felt like I was trapped by my own little tumbleweeds."

"I want to see that show," I said. "Maybe we can find it on the computer later."

Rosie nodded. "Tumbleweeds can be dangerous, ¿sabes? They roll when they break from their roots and end up in places where they should not be, clogging and trapping."

"There's a display at the natural history museum where my mom works," I said. "It says they're stowaways. The seeds came from Europe with immigrants."

"That's right," Rosie said. "They are not native plants. They are invasive."

"So what gave you the idea to make statues?" I asked.

"The next day, I was driving us somewhere, and a huge cabezona—"

"Cabezona?"

"Sí," she said, waving her hands wildly around her head. "A big tumbleweed, una cabezona. That's what I call them because they look like heads of wild hair. Como tus primas." She laughed. "Well, this cabezona rolled across the road in front of our car. So big, I thought it was an animal for a second. I had to swerve to avoid running into it. When I saw what it was, I imagined a tumbleweed jackrabbit, and that's where the idea came to me." She motioned around the room. "The cabezonas were at least one thing I could control."

"I thought adults controlled everything," I said.

Rosie laughed and shook her head.

"Maggie said you were one of the best women wrestlers in Mexico," I said, watching her fingers work the crochet hook and the yarn. "Why did you stop?"

"Ah, sí, I was pretty good," Rosie agreed. "That was a whole lifetime ago. That's how I met your abuelo. We were both on the same card one night in Monterrey."

"What happened?"

"We got married," Rosie said. "And then Sebastián happened. And Mateo and your father."

"Yeah," I said. "I guess that's a lot."

"Let me show you something," Rosie said. She put down the yarn and crochet hook and walked to a metal cabinet. She pulled a cardboard box off a shelf and placed it on her worktable. "Open it."

I unfolded the flaps and lifted out the top item. It was a championship belt, smaller than Pancho's but more beautiful. The dark brown leather was lined with green velvet. A silver plate was set into its center. The words CAMPEÓN FEMENIL DE MÉXICO were engraved across the top, and LUCHA LIBRE across the bottom. Her name was engraved in the middle of the silver plate: ROSA TERRONES, LA ROSA SALVAJE.

"*You* were the Mexican champion?" I asked in awe. I picked up the belt. It was heavier than it looked.

"Pues sí," Rosie said. "Women couldn't wrestle in the capital for a long time, you know? But lucha was happening everywhere in Mexico. I won that in Guadalajara."

"Why couldn't women wrestle in Mexico City?" I asked. "Isn't that the biggest city in the country?"

"It is," Rosie said. She did some hand stretches. "The men thought that it was a bad influence on girls to see women wrestling. It scared them to see mujeres fuertes."

She flexed her arms. While the skin under her upper arms jiggled a little, there was no mistaking she had muscles. When she tightened her fists, her biceps popped.

I held the belt against my waist.

"Looks good," Rosie said approvingly.

I blushed and put down the belt, turning back to the contents of the box. There was a scrapbook filled with photos and newspaper clippings from Rosie's wrestling days. One headline in the sports section of a Mexican newspaper announced La Rosa Salvaje victorious over Cathy "Crybaby" Cruz from San Antonio, Texas. Another headline declared her La Reina de Guadalajara. In the black-and-white photo, she held the world championship belt in the air.

I picked up a photograph of a young Rosie. She was dressed in a red wrestling one-piece, black lace-up boots, and a long red cape that touched the ground. Her dark hair shone, her wild curls springing up around her face.

"I was seventeen there," she said.

"Wow," I said, propping my elbows on the worktable to study the photo. "Do you ever wish you had kept wrestling?"

"Forty, fifty years ago, that was all I wanted," she said,

picking up her work again. "I grew up watching Irma González and Chabela Romero and La Dama Enmascarada, all the great Mexican luchadoras. I wanted to travel the world like they did, like the men did."

"Was La Rosa Salvaje a ruda or a técnica?" I asked.

"Técnica, of course," Rosie said.

Looking at the photos and clippings, it didn't seem like there was anything more exciting or interesting than being a professional wrestler and wearing costumes and traveling around the world, performing a story every night, beating up bad guys or being a bad guy. What could compete with that?

"Couldn't you have kept working?" I asked. "Even with a baby? Wasn't there someone who could babysit or something?"

Rosie laughed. "I wrestled when Sebastián and Mateo were very little, but I didn't like to be away from them for so long. Do you know how hard it is to find a babysitter for months at a time?"

"Months?" I said, imagining Mom being gone for that long. "Couldn't you take turns? You travel and then Pancho?"

"Ay, niña, those were different times. What's the point now in thinking about what we could've done?" she said. "I saw how hard it was for other luchadoras to be two things at once. Some of them were single mothers and didn't have many choices. They had to do what they had to do. It wasn't impossible, but it wasn't the life I wanted. Half here and half there and never fully anywhere? Besides, I took care of this family. I've carried and still carry this family through everything, the good and the bad, and that's its own lucha. There's no weakness in that."

Maybe it wasn't Atlas carrying the world, after all. Maybe it was Rosie and women like her. Women like Mom.

"But Pancho got to wrestle," I said. "Why didn't he have to choose between wrestling and family?"

"He had to choose too," Rosie said. "Sometimes it looks like a person gets everything, but that's not possible. You give up something, even if it's not so obvious to others. Your abuelo was never home for long. He would come back, especially when the boys were very young, and they would not recognize him."

"But don't you ever wonder," I asked, "what your life would be like if you made different choices?"

She stopped and looked up from her work for a moment, as if asking herself that question or thinking about what could've been.

"We're here now," she said and looked around. "Maybe things are not always great, but they are good, no? Do I have regrets? Yes. Am I happy with my life? Also yes. Life is full of contradictions."

"Do you think Manny has regrets?" I asked.

"Claro que sí," she said without hesitation. "He always has."

I wanted to believe Rosie, but if he regretted not being

around, why did I have to be the one to find him? It had been eleven years since he'd seen me. In all that time, why didn't he ever try to make things right with Mom? If Marlene hadn't found out that I knew who he was, and if she hadn't said something to Mom, would I even be in Esperanza? Would anyone have answered my email?

I continued working through the contents of the box. In one poster, Rosie stood victorious, with one boot on her opponent's chest, posing with her championship belt. In another photo, it looked like she was shaving her opponent's head.

"Whoa." I held up the photo. "What's going on here?"

"Ha," she yelped with glee. "That's a hair match. Loser has her head shaved."

"Did you ever have to get your head shaved?"

"Nunca," Rosie said proudly. She ran her fingers through her curls.

At the bottom of the box, beneath the photos and posters, was a pair of black wrestling boots, a neatly folded red cape with a rose embroidered on the back, and a red one-piece, the same outfit she wore in the photo.

"Why isn't this stuff in the family room like the other wrestling things?" I asked. I ran my hand up the side of one of the boots. Their red laces ended in neat bows at the tops. I pictured Rosie tying the bows one last time, putting the boots in the box, and saying goodbye to her dream.

"Ay." Rosie waved her hand at the box. "There's no room, and what does it matter anyway? It's just a bunch of old stuff."

"It should all be in there too," I said, placing the items back into the box carefully. I looked at the photo of the seventeen-year-old Rosa Salvaje again. In her cape, she looked like a superhero. "It does matter."

"You can take that if you want it," Rosie said, glancing at the photo.

"Really? I can?"

"Claro, niña," she said.

"Thank you."

In the photo, Rosie had a look of determination on her face, her brow slightly furrowed. She gazed away from the camera as if staring at something in the distance. I imagined that she was looking toward her future. One where she wasn't trapped by tumbleweeds. One where she was going to places all over the world. One where she was La Rosa Salvaje, the world champion.

★ CHAPTER 20 ★

That night, something landed on my bed with a hard thump and woke me up.

"Come on, dormilona," Eva said from where she sat at the foot of the bed, pulling on my big toes.

"Ow." I yanked my feet back. I looked at the twins' outlines in the dark. "What time is it?"

"Heads up," Maggie whispered. I wasn't awake enough to react quickly. By the time I thought to reach out my arms to catch what she was throwing, the rolled-up sleeping bag had already hit me in the face and landed on my lap.

Eva snorted.

"What are you doing?" I asked, yawning.

"Let's go," Maggie said. "Grab your pillow too."

I looked at the clock on the bedside table. Its glowing hands read 12:19. All the lights in the house were off except for the blue of the television in the family room. Was Pancho still awake?

"Should we let someone know?" I asked, following the twins, who carried their own sleeping bags and pillows.

"They won't care," Maggie said in a low voice. "We're just going outside."

In the kitchen, she opened a cabinet and, after looking inside for a minute, pulled out a box of cereal.

With a flashlight that appeared from her sleeping bag, Eva led the way out the back door and to the ring.

"It's freezing out here," I said. I could see my breath. I looked toward Uncle Mateo's place, but there were no lights on.

We threw the sleeping bags and pillows into the ring and climbed up after them.

"You can go back in if you want," Maggie said, settling on the mat. She pulled apart the top of the bag of cereal and held out the box.

I buried my hand and took a fistful of chocolate and peanut butter puffs. There was no way I was going back inside.

We sat in the dark with only the sound of our crunching. It was the first time I'd seen the twins out of their tzitzimime costumes. Tonight, they wore dark flannel pajamas with a sleeping sheep pattern. Their makeup had been washed off, so I could see their faces. Their *real* faces. They looked like a couple of fourteen-year-old girls, not star goddesses.

Maggie pushed the box of cereal aside and snuggled into her sleeping bag.

"Zip me up, please," she said.

Eva zipped her sister's sleeping bag tight around her, then shimmied into her own. "Can you zip me up, Addie?" Eva asked.

I zipped her bag as tight around her shoulders as I could. Then I got into my own sleeping bag. There was no one to zip me up.

"Did you know that the Aztecs believed the earth was a crocodile floating in the ocean?" Maggie said dreamily. "The best thing about sleeping out here is that it feels like we really are just floating."

"Like being on a blow-up alligator in a pool," I joked.

I felt myself warm up a little at the sound of their laughter. I liked that I could make my cousins laugh. What Maggie said was true. It was so dark out that it felt like we could easily be anywhere, even on the back of a crocodile. Just the three of us alone in the world.

"Tell me about the tzitzimime," I said. I'd gotten better at pronouncing the word after telling Alex and Cy about the twins.

"This is what Rosie told us," Maggie said. "The Aztecs believed the tzitzimime were deities, goddesses that protected crops and people, but especially pregnant women."

I thought about Mom being watched over by a bunch of teenage girls that looked and dressed like my cousins.

There weren't many streetlights out where the Bravos lived, so I could see everything in the sky clearly. The moon was a thin golden sliver like the little hoop earrings I wore. I felt swallowed by the darkness. Were the tzitzimime lurking somewhere in the obsidian sky?

"When the world ends, the tzitzis will eat all the people," Eva said. She broke free from her sleeping bag and grabbed my arm, smacking and grunting as she pretended to devour it.

I yelped and pulled my arm away, but I couldn't help giggling.

"I thought they protected people," I said.

"The Aztecs believed that whenever there was an eclipse, or at the end of a fifty-two-year cycle, or whenever there was some kind of big change happening was a good time for the tzitzimime to come down to earth," Eva explained. "They were powerful, and they could make scary times go well or not."

It suddenly made sense that the twins had come into my life. Between meeting Manny and Mom having a baby soon and the adoption and even the whole ridiculous *Nutcracker* thing, there was a lot of change happening. Maybe the twins, the tzitzis, were here to make it all go smoothly. At least that's what I hoped.

An owl hooted somewhere, and I realized that there were probably all kinds of creatures hiding in the dark. Skunks, deer, wolves, star goddesses, La Llorona. Maybe the hooting was her crying for her children and not an owl.

"They're good and bad," Maggie picked up. "Depends on how you look at them and depends on the situation."

"Kind of like a jobber, huh?" I asked, thinking about

The Eagle of Esperanza. "Not really good, not really bad." Did the twins know Manny's secret?

I shifted in my sleeping bag and snuggled deeper into it, the sound of nylon swishing with each movement.

"Why'd you pick them?" I asked. "For your wrestling alter egos?"

"When Rosie told us about them, we thought they were cool," Maggie said. "Some people think they're female and others describe them as male. I like the idea of them being something you can't identify by gender. Just being."

"And if they are female," Eva said, "I like that they don't fit stereotypes. That people respect them but also fear them."

"Mujeres fuertes," I said, remembering what Rosie had told me in the barn.

"Exactly," Maggie said. "The tzitzis can nurture and protect, but they can also destroy."

"Who taught you all the stuff you do in the ring?" I asked. "Uncle Mateo?"

"Uncle Mat? No way," Maggie said. "He helps us sometimes. But it's Abuela who showed us most of what we know."

"Rosie?" I propped myself up on my elbows. "I thought she quit all that a long time ago."

"She did," Maggie said. "But she's still really strong."

"I *know*," I said, excited. "She flexed her arms for me today. She has some serious muscles."

"She still works out," Eva said. I detected pride in her voice. "She says the body doesn't forget."

I wanted to be a tzitzi. A powerful girl, una mujer fuerte.

"When did you know?" I asked. "That you wanted to wrestle too?"

The twins didn't answer right away. They seemed to be waiting for the other to speak first.

"Always," Maggie finally said. "For as long as I can remember. It's what we do."

I knew that by *we*, she meant the family. Eva and Maggie didn't have their father, either, but in a way, they had more of a relationship with him than I did with Manny. They were connected through wrestling. They knew who they were, and what they wanted.

"I want to wrestle until I can't," Maggie said. She turned to me, and I could see that she wasn't wearing her new flipper tooth. "I'm trying out for the wrestling team this year. I'm going to be the first female wrestler on the Esperanza High team."

"That sounds really tough," I said. "But you're so good. I bet you'll make the team. Manny was on the Esperanza wrestling team."

"They all were," Eva said. "Manny, Speedy, Mateo."

"What about you?" I asked Eva. "Are you trying out too?"

"Nah, not me," Eva said. "That's her thing."

"Eva plays softball," Maggie informed me.

"But what about the tzitzimime?" I asked, afraid the star goddesses were losing their light.

"I'm going to tag-team with Maggie after high school," Eva said. She sniffled and wiped her nose on the sleeve of her pajama top. "For a little while at least. Then maybe go to college. But I don't want to be old and beat-up and forgetful like Abuelo."

"Jeez, Eva," Maggie grumbled. "Just because you wrestle doesn't mean you'll be like Abuelo."

"What else would you want to be?" I asked as if I couldn't imagine any other possibility for a Bravo except being a wrestler.

"I don't know." Eva shifted in her bag. "Mom says the sky is the limit. Maybe an actress or a judge or a dentist so I can fix up Maggie every time she gets a tooth knocked out in the ring."

Maggie gave her sister a playful shove.

The three of us lay on the mat in silence. I thought about Manny and about wrestling. I thought about Rosie and about Mom. Was it strange for Eva and Maggie that one of them didn't want to follow in the Bravo footsteps? I tried to identify the sounds in the dark. Were those coyotes howling? Crickets chirping? I searched for constellations. Orion's belt was always the easiest. Three stars side by side. I imagined the three of us star deities, an asterism on the hunter in the sky. I thought of the

Bdelloidea, microscopic organisms that live in water and have existed and survived without males for millions of years. Mom says they're her kind of rotifer. I turned over to tell the twins about it, but they were curled together, fast asleep.

★ CHAPTER 21 ★

Rosie moved around the kitchen, agile and quick, making Sunday breakfast. Underneath her coveralls and her flowery apron, I could see La Rosa Salvaje.

"Eyyy," Manny said, pulling out the chair next to him for me.

Manny, Pancho, and the twins sat at the table. Hijo joined them at their feet, waiting for food.

"You're such a sleepyhead," Maggie teased.

I looked at the time on the stove.

"It's only nine thirty." I sat in the chair Manny offered. "And it's a Sunday. *And* someone woke me up in the middle of the night." I had made my way back to my bed in the early morning, cold and shivering.

"Early bird catches the worm, kid," Manny said. "That's the Bravo way."

"¿Y quién es esta muchacha?" my grandfather asked, squinting at me from across the table.

"Pa, this is my girl, Adela," Manny said, squeezing my shoulder. "Looks just like her old man, no?"

I felt myself blush.

"Adela," the old man repeated as if searching his

memory. "I remember you. How are the dinosaurs, eh?"

Manny laughed. "No, Pa," he said. "That's Lulu."

"She looks like her," Pancho said.

"Because it's her mom, Abuelo." Maggie got up and began setting the table.

"Lulu has a daughter?" Pancho asked.

I could feel the collective sigh in the room as they went around and around with him.

"She sure does." Manny smiled at me proudly.

Rosie set a plate of bacon on the table.

"If anyone feels like helping, that would be great," Maggie said, looking from person to person.

"You're the best, Mags," Manny said. But he didn't get up.

Maggie shook her head and huffed. "You'd think we lived in, like, the fifties or something," she muttered as she walked to where Rosie handed her a bowl of fruit salad. "How do you stand it, Abuela?"

Maggie placed the bowl at the center of the table hard. Manny didn't seem to notice. He was drinking his coffee and looking at his phone. Pancho was in his own world, having a conversation with Hijo in Spanish.

Rosie went on working like it was no big deal. Eva rolled her eyes but didn't get up.

"I'll help," I offered.

The back door opened, and Uncle Mateo came in.

"Good morning, my people," he said, grabbing a strawberry out of the fruit salad.

"Spoon, please, Mateo," Rosie said. "Are you eating?"

"No breakfast for me, Ma," Uncle Mateo said. "I just came to look through your eye shadows. Do you have anything glittery?"

"I don't think so, mijo," she said and laughed. "Have you ever seen me in glitter?"

"True," Uncle Mateo said, looking around the table. "It's plaid and denim for this crew."

Manny, Rosie, and Pancho were all wearing plaid flannel shirts. I thought about Rosie's shiny red cape and her beautiful belt. She did wear glitter. At least she used to.

"We have glitter eye shadow," Eva offered. "I'll be right back." She got up and ran to the room she and Maggie shared.

"What's the eye shadow for?" I asked Uncle Mateo.

"I do drag story time at the bookstore," he said. "You should come."

But before I could say anything, Pancho slammed his fist down onto the table, making all the plates jump like a terremoto would.

"What kind of man wears glitter?" Pancho frowned.

It felt like had sucked the air out of the room.

"I do, Pa," Uncle Mateo said. "You know that."

"I can't believe you gave it all up," Pancho said, shaking his head. "For what?"

"Abuelo," Maggie interjected. "He does amazing things outside the ring."

"Yeah, Pa," Manny chimed in. "Remember? ¿Las máscaras? And the jackets? I'll take you over to the trailer later so you can see what he's working on."

Uncle Mateo smiled at them appreciatively.

"But *inside* the ring is what matters," Pancho insisted. "What about the world championship, mijo?"

"That just wasn't for me, Pa," Uncle Mateo said gently. He stood behind my grandfather, his hands on his shoulders, and kissed the top of his head like Pancho was the son and he was the father.

"Besides, Abuelo, you have other contenders in the room," Maggie said. "What am I? Chopped liver?"

Everyone laughed, including Pancho. I looked at Manny, and he was smiling. But there was a look in his eyes that wasn't happiness. Maybe he was disappointed that Pancho didn't think of him as a contender.

"Funny girl," Pancho said.

"What's so funny?" Maggie asked.

"A girl can't be world champion," Pancho said. He looked at Maggie as if it was the most obvious thing.

"¿Y por qué no?" Rosie asked, turning from the stove. She looked like she was considering putting him in a headlock.

"Yeah, why not?" I said. "Rosie was."

"Yeah, Pa," Manny added. "Maybe Adela will get in on the action, too, someday." He winked at me.

Eva walked back in with a handful of makeup containers.

"Are you ganging up on Abuelo?" she asked, dropping the makeup into Uncle Mateo's extended hands.

"Finally," Pancho said, grabbing Eva's hand. "Here's mi Evita, come to protect me."

Eva leaned her side into him and put an arm around his shoulders. "I'll protect you," she said, smiling at Pancho. "But you have to admit that women are good wrestlers too. And that the women's championship is as important as the men's."

"Oh boy," Manny whispered under his breath.

"*And* that glitter is for everyone," Maggie added.

Rosie leaned against the sink. Uncle Mateo and Maggie stood with their arms crossed. We were all frozen in place, waiting for Pancho's response. I was afraid this would bring us back to what set him off to begin with.

Pancho looked at all of us.

"Fine," he said. "Women are good wrestlers."

"Go on," Maggie said.

"The women's championship is as important as the men's," he added with a sigh.

"And what else?" Eva prompted.

"Glitter is for . . . everyone," Pancho mumbled.

Eva kissed him on the cheek. Uncle Mateo and Maggie high-fived each other.

"There's hope for you yet, Abuelo," Maggie said.

Pancho waved us off and turned to Hijo.

"Mi único amigo," he said, scratching the dog behind his ear.

"Okay," Uncle Mateo said, grabbing a piece of bacon from the plate on the table. "Thanks for the makeup." He pinched Eva's cheek. "I'll get it back to you. Story time bus leaves in an hour if you three chickens want to come."

"Can we go, Abuela?" Maggie asked.

"Vayan," Rosie said. "Have fun with your uncle."

When the door slammed behind him, we all dug into the breakfast spread.

Jokes, a little tenderness, and some tough love had made it so that Pancho's comments about Uncle Mateo didn't turn into a big fight. There was relief in the air. It looked like a normal family at the table, eating and laughing.

But I couldn't help wondering how much of it was a mask for whatever hurt Pancho's words or lack of them caused each person—his disapproval of Uncle Mateo's choices, his disregard of Manny, his dismissal of Rosie and the twins. And then there was me. Pancho seemed lucid now; he recognized me. He asked questions about me and about Mom. But there was no mention of my absence from his life, as if it were perfectly normal for me to be gone and then reappear so many years later without wanting answers.

★ ★ ★

I didn't go to story time with the twins, because Manny said he had plans for us, but I ended up spending the day hanging around, doing my homework, trying to not get in Rosie's way in her workshop, waiting for Manny to finish running errands. By the time he returned, the twins had already gone back home, and it was time for me to go home too. I said my goodbyes to Rosie and Pancho before Manny drove me back to Thorne.

"I'm sorry, kid," he said. "I had to take Pa's truck to my mechanic friend. Since he can't drive anymore and Ma needs her truck for her work, I'm using it until I can get my own wheels. Only time my pal could look at this old junker."

"It's okay," I said, even though I wished I could've gone to story time with the twins. I stuck my fingers through the opening at the top of the window and felt the cool air.

"I'm still getting my bearings," he said, driving up the path that led out of the property. "My plan isn't to live with my parents and borrow my dad's truck forever like some teenager, you know." He laughed. "Once I'm all set, then things will be different. You'll see."

Manny turned on the radio, and rock music blasted out of the speakers.

"What's wrong with Pancho?" I asked. "Why does he forget stuff?"

"The doctors say it's dementia," Manny explained, not seeming too concerned.

"Oh," I said, thinking. "The twins say it's from wrestling."

We stopped at a red light, and a roadrunner bolted in front of us, reminding me of Rosie.

"I don't know what caused it," Manny said. "Maybe wrestling, maybe genetics, maybe just age."

"Was he really mad at Uncle Mateo?" I asked. "About the makeup?"

I didn't want Pancho to be someone who would disapprove of Uncle Mateo's life. Thinking about it made me angry.

"Pa's always been a little old-fashioned," Manny admitted.

"I think what you mean is closed-minded," I said and rolled my eyes.

Manny laughed, a whole-body-shaking laugh that made me afraid he would drive off Route 13 into a ditch.

"You know who used to put him in his place?" Manny said. "Your mom."

"Really?"

"Oh yeah." Manny laughed. "Those two would get into it."

"About what?"

"About everything," Manny said, peering into the rearview mirror. "Politics, feminism, wrestling, even the weather." He shook his head. "She would never let him get away with saying stuff like that."

"Cool," I said, feeling proud of Mom. "It's good that

Maggie and Eva challenge him on those things too."

"Yeah," Manny agreed. "Anyway, he never got over Mateo leaving wrestling. Pa had big plans."

"A dynasty," I said, remembering the Bravo biography.

"Something like that," Manny said.

I had so many things I wanted to ask Manny. Like how it felt to have so much pressure on him. And how he could be such a supportive brother and such a caring son, but abandon me. Before I could ask anything else, Manny changed the subject.

"Hey, have you seen the statues?" he asked, pointing his thumb out the window to where the WELCOME TO ESPERANZA sign stood. "That's where the Guadalupe will go. Your abuela used to have us help her collect tumbleweeds. She'd pay us something like a quarter for each one she used."

"A quarter?"

"Yes, ma'am," Manny said. "A quarter went a lot further back then. If she offers to pay you for helping her, don't settle for a quarter."

"I won't," I said. "You know, Mom and I take a photo with the snowman every—"

"Year," Manny finished. "Yeah, I know. Who do you think started that?"

Of course, Mom had never told me about that either.

"I have the photo from my first Christmas," I said. "That's how I found you."

Manny chuckled, but I noticed he gripped the wheel more tightly.

"Where have you been?" I asked, feeling couragous.

Manny glanced over. "I thought I told you. I started here at Cactus, then went to Mexico. I moved around there a bit. Then I was in—"

"No," I said. "I mean, why didn't you come to see me?" Manny let out a low whistle as he exhaled. "It's just a question." I tugged on my ear, suddenly unsure if I wanted to hear what he would say next.

He let out a sigh as if he was tired. "It's hard, Addie," he said. "This life I live. I don't ever stop. I've never even had my own place. No point, since I've been moving around for the past decade or so."

"If you and Mom had stayed together, you would've had a home," I said quietly. "You could've come back to us."

"I wish it had been that easy," Manny said, staring at the road ahead.

Why did adults make everything so complicated? It was almost like they tried to be unhappy.

"Wrestling sounds like a carnival," I said. "Aren't you tired of traveling?"

"I go where the work is," Manny said. "Wrestling's roots are in the carnival, you know. Kinda makes sense, eh?"

"So what's your plan now?" I asked. "Once you can wrestle as The Mountain again?"

"Glad you asked," Manny said. "First, the identity of

The Eagle will be revealed. Then I'm going to win the Cactus Wrestling League championship belt. And from there it's going to be world domination. The way it was always meant to be."

"What does that mean?"

"Speedy died and Mateo quit before either of them could wrestle for the Atlantic Wrestling Federation's world championship," he said. "It's up to me."

He nodded as he drove, as if picturing himself wearing the world championship belt.

"Can you dominate the world from Esperanza?" I asked. "You said you weren't leaving."

"Once I win the world championship, then I'll be done," Manny said, shifting in his seat.

"Done wrestling?"

"The AWF world championship is the peak," he said. "That's the big time. That's the belt your abuelo won. But, hey, let's take things one day at a time, okay?"

He looked over at me and gave me the now-familiar Manny grin. But he hadn't answered my questions. I thought about Mount Olympus, the home of the gods, and imagined Manny trying to climb it.

"What if it doesn't happen?" I whispered, mostly to myself, but Manny must have heard.

I could feel his mood change. He wasn't smiling anymore. He stared at the road with that same intense look I saw on all the Bravo faces in photos. I wanted Manny to fulfill his dream, but all I could think about was getting what *I* wanted. And if the past twelve years were any indication, I wasn't so sure that both could happen.

I rested my head against the window. A minute later, I heard Manny whisper, "It *will* happen."

★ CHAPTER 22 ★

"It isn't bad enough that I'm Marie, but we also have to meet during lunch?" I complained.

"At least you get to do something cool with your best friend," Cy said, grabbing my hand and pulling me into the auditorium.

Inside, Mrs. González was sitting on a chair up on the stage. Brandon and Gus were already there with her.

"Excellent," Mrs. González said, clapping. "My stars are all here."

"And your director, reporting for duty." Cy pulled off the baseball cap she wore and tipped it toward Mrs. González.

Normally, Cy would never wear a baseball cap, but when she showed up at school that morning, she said it was de rigueur for a director to wear one.

Cy and I sat down, forming a circle that Mrs. González closed. Cy pulled a clapboard out of her backpack.

"This isn't a movie," Gus said.

"He speaks." Cy snapped the clapboard at him.

"The purpose of our meeting is to discuss the plan for this year's show," Mrs. González said. "I picked each of you because I know you'll bring something special."

"Obviously," Brandon joked.

Gus and I looked at each other as if we were both trying to figure out what Mrs. González believed we could offer. For a moment, I thought he might lean in and say something, but instead he looked away.

"Now, as you know," Mrs. González went on, "*The Nutcracker* is a classic, but what really brings out the crowd is their curiosity about each year's twist."

Cy clapped her hands with giddy excitement.

"Can we do a sock puppet version?" Brandon asked.

Mrs. González rolled with it. "Why not?" she said. "But that's something you four should all discuss and agree on. And, of course, you need to decide by Monday so that we have as much time as possible to prepare."

"The show's not until December," Gus said. "Do we really need that much time?"

"Of course," Mrs. González and Cy snapped in unison.

"Hello, December is *next* month already," Cy said, looking at Gus like he had something strange growing on his face.

"Gustavo, you're new to Thorne, so perhaps you don't know that this is something the town looks forward to every year," Mrs. González explained. "Not some fly-by-night production."

"Amen," Cy agreed.

"Now, Cy, as our director, do you have any words for

us?" Mrs. González smiled expectantly. Today she wore purple lipstick that made her look like she'd just eaten a grape Popsicle.

Brandon, Mrs. González, and I turned to Cy. Gus looked up at the rafters.

"That's where the bats live," Brandon said. "Careful you don't get bat poop in your eyes."

"Shhh." Cy glared at him and stood up.

"It's called guano," Gus said. "Not bat poop."

I tried not to smile at the fact that he knew this.

"The Thorne Middle School production of *The Nutcracker* is an important tradition for the school and for our community," Cy said. She paced outside of our circle. "It's been my dream to direct the show for years, and I'm proud to have been chosen. Thank you, Mrs. González."

The teacher nodded approvingly. "Thank you, Cy, and as I mentioned—"

"I'm not done," Cy said. Mrs. González raised her hand in apology. "I'm going to do everything in my directorial power to make this the most memorable show in the school's history," Cy continued. "But even though I am the director, I recognize that I can't do it alone. That's where you come in. I'm really looking forward to working with you. Together we'll make a great team. Thank you!"

She looked at each of us before sitting. Brandon made a face like he'd smelled something terrible. Marlene called that a *fuchi face*.

"She's right," Mrs. González said. "From here until the end of the show, you *are* a team. And maybe even after that. This is a bonding experience."

"I'd rather not be bonded to a yeti," Brandon said, jerking a thumb at me.

Instead of hiding my arms like I typically did, I thought about what the twins would do if someone called them a yeti. I certainly couldn't pick up Brandon and toss him off the stage, so instead I reached over and pinched him.

"Did you see that, Mrs. González?" he whined, rubbing his arm.

"I'm not here to bond," Gus muttered under his breath.

"I don't care if you're here to bond or not," Cy said, staring him down. "If you want to hang out by yourself under a rock on your own time, go for it. But when we're together, I want one hundred percent from all of you. Got it?"

Gus stared at Cy, flabbergasted. Brandon stood and stretched.

"Can we go now, sarge?" Brandon asked.

Mrs. González ignored him. "Remember, I'm here to support your vision," she said. "Now, as far as your meetings go, you're welcome to gather in here during lunch or after school this week. And, of course, you can meet on your own outside of school if you choose to. But by Monday, I will need your plan so that we can get this show on the road."

★ ★ ★

217

When I got home from school, I found Mom in the baby's room, trying to put together a dinosaur mobile.

"I'm about to send these guys back to the Mesozoic," Mom muttered.

"Let me try," I said, taking the wooden pieces and the tangled strings.

"Thank you," Mom said and began folding tiny shirts.

Ever since I started going to Esperanza, I tried to imagine Mom there. At the high school, in the Bravo house. Once, while I was helping Rosie, she drove me past the house where Mom grew up. I imagined her in the tiny space, dreaming of dinosaurs and college and something beyond that little town. After my first night in Esperanza, it seemed we had come to an unspoken agreement that she wouldn't ask, and I wouldn't tell. Unless I had something to tell, of course. So I had told her about sleeping outside with the twins and about Rosie's workshop. But I didn't tell her about Manny disappearing for a lot of the weekend. Even though he wasn't around much, I liked Esperanza and being with the Bravos. I didn't get why Mom thought it was so awful.

I couldn't stop thinking about Pancho's apology the day we were in the family room alone, though.

"Pancho said to tell you he's sorry," I said, looking at her for a reaction.

Mom stopped folding.

"Huh. Did he say anything else?"

I shook my head. "He gets confused. Sometimes he thinks I'm you."

"Interesting," Mom said.

"What?"

"Nothing." She continued folding.

"What was he apologizing for?"

"Who knows." Mom shrugged. "Like you said, he gets confused. I'm sure he's got plenty to apologize for."

"What do you mean?"

"How's that mobile?" Mom asked, ignoring my question.

I held it out to her, all the strings untangled.

"Perfect," Mom said. She took the mobile and clipped it into the attachment on the crib. "You're going to be a good big sister."

The dinosaurs dangled delicately from the ends of their strings.

"Why don't you ever want to talk about Manny or the Bravos?" Every time I asked I thought might be the time she finally gave in. "Not even now that I know who they are."

Mom put some clothes in a drawer and slid it shut. "There really isn't much to say. That's all in the past."

"If it's all in the past, then what's the big deal?"

Mom sat down on the rocking chair. She looked like she was trying to remember what the big deal was.

"Are you happy?" she asked. "Being with Manny and

his family? Do you feel like you're getting what you went there to find?"

I gave the mobile a spin, making the dinosaurs go around and around. I went to Esperanza looking for my father, to find out if he wanted to be in my life, to find out what things about me came from him. I met a family I never knew I had, but Manny still felt distant.

"I don't know," I said. "Sometimes, I guess."

"You don't have to keep visiting if you ever feel like you don't want to," she said.

"I know," I said. "I want to."

"Okay." Mom nodded. "I just don't want you to feel trapped or obligated. Or like you owe it to anyone."

In a video in science class, I learned that cells in different parts of the body regenerate at different rates. The ones that don't, that are around for all our lives, are the ones that live in the heart, the brain, and the eyes. But maybe it's those that *should* regenerate. Otherwise, how do you forget? How do you start over? All the adults around me seem weighed down by stuff from the past.

As Mom folded laundry for the baby, I pictured the heart halves Mom and Manny each wore in their yearbook photos. I knew it was supposed to be a sign of love, a shared heart. But I couldn't help thinking of it as what it actually was—a broken heart.

CHAPTER 23

Alma stood on a ladder, hanging cardboard turkeys from the ceiling. It looked dangerous.

"I would've just put them on the tables," Marlene said, looking up at her.

"Same," Cy agreed.

Watching the waitress maintain her balance while the turkeys twisted on their strings, their yellow-orange-and-brown honeycomb bodies twirling, was the only thing distracting me while I waited.

The bells on the door of the diner chimed, and Gus walked in.

"Flying turkeys!"

He laughed, pointing to the ceiling. I had never seen Gus even crack a smile at school. He wore braces with green rubber bands that matched his Bob Marley T-shirt.

When he saw me, he seemed to remember that he wasn't supposed to smile. He threw himself onto the padded bench with a frown.

When I told Alex about our school meeting, he offered to feed everyone if we met at the diner. I had no plans to invite Gus or Brandon to the diner, but Cy had been with me when Alex made the suggestion, and she thought it was a great idea.

Cy moved over on her side of the table, and I sat down.

"Some turkeys can fly, you know," I said.

"Really?" Cy asked. "They're so big. I had no idea."

"Your dad owns this place, right?" Gus asked, looking around the diner.

"Alex is my stepfather," I replied.

"Tell him about Manny," Cy urged.

"Who's Manny?" Gus asked.

"Manny Bravo"—she paused for dramatic effect—"is her father."

I glared at Cy.

"What?" she said. "It's not a secret anymore. Right?"

"Like, the wrestler Manny Bravo?" Gus said, a look of disbelief on his face.

"Do you know another Manny Bravo?" Cy asked, raising an eyebrow. "Tell him, Addie."

"Yeah, right," Gus said.

Cy and Gus waited. I looked over at Alex, who was frosting a cake with the concentration of someone solving a difficult math problem.

"He is," I admitted.

"Pretty cool, huh?" Cy propped her chin on her fist.

"Is it true that he's wrestling as The Eagle?" Gus asked. "If you're really his kid, you'd know, right?"

"No!" I shook my head a little too vigorously. "I mean,

he's not. I mean, I don't . . . I don't know anything."

"That's the rumor. I read it on Pro Wrestling Today." Gus looked me in the eye. "But maybe you don't know because he's not really your father."

"Nice try, Gustavo," Cy said. "If that was true, I would know because I'm her best friend. Right, Addie?"

Now they both looked at me for confirmation. Gus was finally talking. But I had promised to keep this secret. I hadn't even told Cy, and she would be furious if I revealed it in front of Gus.

"Does he wear a mask all the time?" Gus asked.

"Of course not." I frowned, sure I was wearing a mask of guilt myself.

"Of course not because he takes it off? Or of course not because he's not The Eagle?" Gus grilled me like a detective trying to wear down a suspect. "Or of course not because you're making up this whole story about him being your father?"

"I liked it better when you didn't talk," I said, glancing at the door.

I never imagined I'd wish for Brandon to be anywhere near me, but I wanted him to show up already so we could move on to talking about the show.

"Did you know El Santo never took off his mask in public in his entire career?" Gus asked. "Well, he did after he retired. And not long after that, he died of a heart attack. Strange, huh? He was buried in it too."

"You're thinking of Bela Lugosi," Cy said, opening a notebook to a blank page. "He was buried in his Dracula cape."

"Look it up," Gus insisted. It was the most animated and engaged I'd seen him since his arrival at Thorne Middle.

The diner door opened, and Brandon came in, startling Alma. The waitress attempted to catch a falling turkey and almost went down with it.

"Idaho tumbleweeds with a yellow blanket and dragged through New Mexico," Marlene announced, placing a basket piled high with cheesy tater tots doused in green chile in the middle of the table. "Compliments of the chef."

"I have no idea what she just said." Brandon grabbed a fork. He was wearing a sock puppet on one hand and forked a tater tot with it. "But looks like I'm right on time."

"What's your deal with the sock puppets?" Cy said, slapping his hand. "Get that thing out of here."

"I thought you were supposed to be open to ideas." Brandon snapped his sock puppet's mouth at Cy. "I didn't realize you were a dictator and not a director."

"What if we do *The Nutcracker* from someone else's point of view?" Cy asked. "Like from the Mouse King's. What do you think, Gus?" She dipped a tot in salsa and gave Brandon a spiteful look. "The Mouse King doesn't get enough stage time."

"*The Mouse King and the Nutcracker* instead of *The Nutcracker and the Mouse King*?" Brandon shook his head. "No way."

"Why not?" Cy asked, kicking him under the table.

Brandon kicked back. The two were about to get into a kicking match when Alex approached with a glass stand holding a three-layer cake with pink frosting sprinkled with crushed candy canes.

"Mmm," Cy said. "What is that beautiful creation?"

"Peppermint mocha cake," Alex said. "Who wants a piece?"

"Me!" Brandon yelled.

"Can we all get some?" I asked. "Please?"

"Of course," Alex said. "Four slices coming right up."

"If we don't figure out something better by Monday, I say we go with the sock puppets," Brandon said. "I'll even volunteer to make them."

"You?" I tried not to laugh.

"Sure," Brandon replied. "My mom's an art teacher, and she was making them with her classes. It's easy."

Cy and I now looked at him, surprised.

"What?" Brandon said. "Can't I like sock puppets?"

"Of course you can," Gus said, coming to his defense.

"But maybe we should discuss a little more," Cy said, looking around the table. "What about you, Gus? Addie? Any ideas?"

"I don't care what we do," Gus said. "The show is goofy.

And anyway, I like art that makes a statement, not this old-fashioned stuff."

"We're in seventh grade," Brandon said. "What do we have to make a statement about?"

"Just 'cause we're in seventh grade doesn't mean we don't have opinions," Gus said, tapping his fingers against the table. "At my old school in Las Cruces, we organized a class walkout because our math teacher said boys were better at math than girls."

"Well, it's true, isn't it?" Brandon said and laughed.

Cy leaned across the table and swatted at him.

"And when I lived in San Antonio," Gus went on, "I was at this private school and boys couldn't wear shorts even on super-hot days, so we protested by wearing skirts. And when I lived in—"

"Exactly how many times have you moved?" Cy asked.

"Never mind," Gus mumbled, as if he'd said too much. "Do whatever."

Gus retreated. I studied him and started to think. Maybe there was more to him than what he let us see. Maybe there was a reason he didn't want to be friends. Maybe it had something to do with his moves.

"I do like the idea of making a statement," Cy said. "What do you think, Addie?"

"Snowflakes don't make statements," I muttered. "Besides, I think Mrs. González is already on top of that."

"What do you mean?" Cy asked.

"Well, for one, me as Marie," I said. "What was she thinking?" I told them about my conversation with Mrs. González.

"This is our *Nutcracker*," Cy said. "And you're the perfect Marie for it. And I think it's cool that Mrs. González wanted to change things this year."

"Yeah, but she shouldn't use Addie as her experiment," Gus said. "Especially if Addie doesn't want to be a part of it."

"Thanks, Gus," I said. "That's exactly what I thought."

I smiled at him. He shrugged and looked away.

Alex walked over and placed four slices of cake on the table.

"Time to get working on the eggnog latte cake," he declared before turning back toward the counter, mumbling something about corporate coffee.

"What's wrong with him?" Cy asked, scraping her fork across her frosting.

"He hates the new big chain coffee place that just opened," I explained. "He's been making cake versions of the seasonal coffee drinks on their menu. He says it's his way of working out his anti-corporation anger."

"Making a statement with flour and sugar," Cy said. "I like it."

"If the eggnog latte is as good as this, I'm here for it," Brandon said through a mouthful of cake.

"Okay, so far we have sock puppets and something that

makes a statement," Cy said. "What about a New Mexican *Nutcracker*? Something that screams Dos Pueblos?"

"I think that's been done," I said. "Remember the year of the native New Mexican animals?"

"Oh yeah." Cy crossed a line through what she'd written in her notebook. She tapped her pencil point against the paper. "What about aliens? Not exactly Dos Pueblos, but still New Mexico."

"Aliens are kind of . . . predictable," I said. "Don't you think?"

"Predictable?" Cy said the word as if I'd called her idea dog poo. She scribbled all over what she'd written down.

"It could be okay, though," I offered. But I knew Cy would never accept okay or predictable for the show.

Gus swiped a tater tot across a smudge of frosting on his hand and popped it into his mouth.

"Ugh." I scrunched my nose.

"Sweet and salty is a good combination," he said defensively.

We all tried it to see if Gus was right.

"Can we sleep on it?" I asked, putting down my frosting-covered tater tot. "And decide next time?"

"Or," Brandon offered, "we can do ALIEN sock puppets!"

Cy threw a tater tot at him, which Brandon picked up and happily ate.

We finished the tater tots and Alex's pink cake. We tried, unsuccessfully, to get more information out of Gus about his many moves. Brandon and Cy provided commentary as Alma put up the Thanksgiving decorations, and we tried to guess if she would manage to get all the turkeys up on the ceiling without falling.

Even though I didn't want to be Marie, and even though I hadn't wanted the group to come to the diner, it felt good to have a moment when I wasn't thinking about the adoption or about Mom's feelings or about what I wanted from Manny. Sitting in the diner felt like an ordinary moment. Or at least as ordinary as flying turkeys, fathers who wrestle, and alien sock puppets.

★ CHAPTER 24 ★

I waited for Manny to drop me off at the Bravo gate and drive away like he always did on Friday afternoons, but he didn't take the usual route.

"Where are we going?" I asked, confused.

"It's a surprise," he said, tapping his fingers on the steering wheel.

When we turned onto Yucca Road, I could see the Esperanza Arena and knew that was where we were headed. The arena held all kinds of events—high school basketball games, trade shows, kiddie camps—but everyone knew that Friday night was lucha night. They recorded matches live, and these aired later on TV.

"Really?" I gasped. "I get to see you wrestle?"

"Think of it as our own take-your-daughter-to-work day," Manny said. "Not exactly alone time, but I think you'll have fun."

"This is so awesome," I said, trying to contain my excitement. I felt like a jack-in-the-box, wound up tight. "But . . ."

"What's wrong?" Manny said, pulling into a parking space.

"I don't want to see you get your butt kicked and lose," I said. "Sorry."

Manny laughed and playfully tugged my braid. He reached over and opened the glove compartment. He grabbed The Eagle's mask and pulled it down over his face.

"Now we're ready," he said. "Let's fly."

I climbed out of the truck and followed him through the parking lot to the back entrance of the arena.

Behind the arena floor were all the things that the audience never got to see. I read names on dressing room doors and saw the green room, where the wrestlers did their interviews and called out their enemies. A few guys were lifting weights in a workout room. We passed a spread of food, where Manny grabbed a handful of almonds.

"Does anyone here know you're The Eagle?"

"A few people do," he said. "Most don't. At least not for sure. The bookers, those are the guys who write the story lines, have tried to keep my identity a secret. Either way, I like to keep the kayfabe going, at least around here."

"What's a kayfabe?"

"Kayfabe," Manny repeated, waving to a wrestler. "It means staying in character even when you're not in the ring. The idea is that no one knows The Eagle is Manny the Mountain."

I remembered El Santo, who never took off his mask in public, and the twins, who almost always dressed in their tzitzimime outfits. Manny nodded at another wrestler.

Of all the things I saw, the most interesting was seeing wrestlers dressed like regular people. No makeup, no outrageous outfits, no kayfabe. We walked past a man sitting on a folding chair, absorbed in a book.

"Was that Apollo?" I asked turning my head to look at the blond wrestler in shorts, a T-shirt, and sneakers. He didn't look anything like the god of the sun who flies off the top turnbuckle to pin his opponents.

"Sure was," Manny said and opened a curtain that led to the arena floor.

"Head on down there," he said. "If you want to get some food, let them know you're with me."

"The Eagle or Manny Bravo?"

"The Eagle," he said. "Gets a little confusing, eh? I'll see you soon."

The curtain swung shut behind me, and I found myself swept into the crowd. There were families with young kids, groups of teenagers, couples on dates, old men who looked like they'd seen some real-life battles themselves. A few people in wheelchairs and motorized chairs rolled up to the front, where there was more room. Some people carried poster boards with messages for their favorites or least favorites, hoping they'd catch the cameraperson's attention and end up on TV. A few kids wore lucha libre masks like the ones Uncle Mateo made. I saw a woman about as old as Rosie wearing a black T-shirt with the faces of the Bravos on it, which was totally bizarre. Some people came dressed like their favorite wrestlers. One guy wore a long green homemade robe like the one Guapo García wore.

The smell of food from the concessions stand and the electric excitement of the crowd filled the air. The arena floor was covered in rows of metal folding chairs and seemed to get warmer as people filled the seats. I got a box of popcorn and a root beer and made my way to the front, right behind the table where the two TV commentators sat.

There were four matches on the card that night. The bell for the first match rang just as I got to my seat. Two young wrestlers I'd never heard of circled each other for a few seconds before locking arms. I was glad Manny wasn't in the opening match, since those were usually at the bottom of the card because they were the least popular.

The two wrestlers in the ring headlocked and arm-barred and flipped each other, an occasional slap or punch or kick to the midsection, until one managed to pin the other long enough for the referee to count to three. People cheered, probably as much for the winner as for the match being over.

The next match on the card was between Marvelous May Mendoza and La Lechuza, the current women's Cactus Wrestling League champion. La Lechuza wore a hooded cape covered in feathers so that she appeared to be part woman, part owl. I was surprised at how scary she looked close up, just like the owls that turned into witches in stories. She removed her cape to reveal the championship belt around her waist. It made me think of Rosie, and I wished she was there with me.

The owl woman let out a bone-chilling "Whooooooo" before grabbing May by the hair and driving her headfirst into a corner of the ring. Anyone who thought women didn't wrestle as hard as the men had probably never seen a women's match. La Lechuza and Marvelous May were two of the best wrestlers in Cactus. They were strong and quick and put on as exciting a match as any I'd ever seen.

It ended with La Lechuza taking down Marvelous May in flying head scissors before rolling her up for the count in what she called the Owl Pellet. I'd seen a real owl pellet before. It's all the stuff an owl can't digest from the prey it swallows whole—bones and fur and talons and feathers—regurgitated into a mass. An owl pellet, a real one and the one in the ring, definitely made a statement. I cheered for La Lechuza as she made her way out of the arena, her championship belt over her shoulder.

Manny's match was next. I was so nervous for him that I had to run to the bathroom before it started. The woman with the Bravos T-shirt was in the bathroom line. She caught me staring and smiled.

"I like your shirt," I said.

Even though she was a stranger, it felt like we had something in common.

I hurried back to my seat just in time to see The Eagle

coming down the aisle toward the ring. He flung his arms in the air, trying to get the audience riled up. A kid behind me threw a handful of popcorn at him as he passed us.

I turned and yelled, "Hey, don't do that!"

"Or what?" The kid laughed and flicked a palomita at me.

I looked down at the popped kernel that ricocheted off my chest. Then I locked eyes with the kid.

"Or I'm going to put *you* in a Bravo Back Breaker," I threatened. I was taller and glared down at him to let him know I meant business.

He laughed again but sat down and stuffed a handful of popcorn in his mouth.

Manny leaped over the top rope into the ring, where he waited while The Scorpion made his way in. The Scorpion was a heel, so people didn't really cheer for him, either, though a few stuck their hands out for the wrestler to slap as he passed.

I knew the match between La Lechuza and Marvelous May should've been higher on the card. It was a championship match, and it had been a better match than I anticipated this one would be.

The Scorpion slid under the bottom rope, and the two wrestlers squared off. The Scorpion was also an enmascarado, so in addition to trading blows, the two attempted to pull off each other's mask. You'd think it'd be as easy as yanking off someone's hat, but masks were made to fit tight. They were secured with laces and sweat and the determination to not have your identity revealed.

The Eagle clung to his mask with one hand and gave his opponent a chop to the throat with the other, causing The Scorpion to fall into the ropes, grabbing at his neck. The Eagle turned to face the audience. He flapped his arms and cupped his hand to his ear as if asking the crowd if The Eagle should fly.

I got on my feet to cheer. The kid behind me yelled something rude, but I ignored him. I was too busy flapping my arms, hoping Manny could see me from where he stood.

As The Eagle climbed the turnbuckles, The Scorpion came up behind him and ran him into the corner, knocking him off. He flipped The Eagle over the top rope, sending him down onto the floor outside the ring. The referee began to count.

The Eagle got up and paced for a few counts before climbing back into the ring. But The Scorpion was there to greet him with a stomp to the back. He grabbed The Eagle by the ankles and tried to drag him like a wheelbarrow to the center of the ring, but The Eagle held on to the bottom rope. The Scorpion dropped The Eagle's legs and kicked him in the side until The Eagle let go.

It was hard to watch Manny getting beaten on, preparing to lose another match. I found myself thinking *Get up get up get up*, like I had a few months earlier, when The Eagle was on the little diner TV. When I had no idea who The Eagle really was.

The Scorpion pulled The Eagle by the leg, and the crowd, including the kid behind me, chanted for a figure-four leglock. I sat down knowing the match would be over soon. The Scorpion gripped The Eagle's ankle, preparing to twist his foot. But while his back was turned, The Eagle managed to use his free leg to knock The Scorpion away.

I whooped and jumped out of my seat again. Even if The Eagle didn't win the match, I wanted to see him put up a good fight.

The Scorpion stumbled, giving The Eagle time to stand. Once back up on his feet, The Eagle ran across the ring and pushed off the ropes, catching The Scorpion in a clothesline as he straightened back up. Just like that, the dynamics of the match had changed. The Eagle made it up to the top of a corner of the ring. This time, he didn't waste a second flapping his arms. As soon as The Scorpion stood again, The Eagle flew, flattening his opponent under a cross-body press. The Eagle lifted The Scorpion's leg, holding his weight on the wrestler so that he couldn't lift his shoulders from the mat.

The referee dropped down and counted. I waited for The Scorpion to kick out, but he never did. The referee slapped his hands against the mat three times, and the bell rang. The Eagle had won the match!

The Eagle rolled off the mat and out of the ring, quickly making his exit. I managed to touch Manny's sweaty arm as he passed. He looked at me and I could see him grinning underneath the mask. The Scorpion stood in the ring for a minute as if confused before jumping down.

The main event was next, but all I wanted was to run after Manny.

"I can't believe that guy actually won," the kid behind me said. "He's such a loser."

I didn't think twice before turning around again to face the boy.

"That guy is my father," I said.

"Really?" The boy looked at once confused and impressed. "That's cool."

"Yeah," I said. "It is."

I turned back around and waited for the main event. It was a championship match between Apollo, the current champion, and Guapo García. Apollo made his way to the ring to the cheers of his fans. He removed his belt and handed it to the referee, then waited for his challenger.

When Guapo García finally appeared, he strutted toward the ring like a rooster. He wore sunglasses and the beautiful green sequined robe that Uncle Mateo had made. He tossed his long dark hair, posed, and blew kisses to the booing crowd. I got caught up in the booing and joined in. Someone pelted him with a handful of popcorn, but I stuck to yelling. I wouldn't be responsible for butter stains on Uncle Mateo's work.

Once inside the ring, Guapo removed his robe and made a show of taking his time, folding it carefully. When the bell rang to start the match, the two wrestlers met in the middle. Guapo extended his hand, as if offering to shake. But when Apollo leaned in to take it, Guapo grabbed his arm and twisted it behind his back. Apollo grimaced in pain. I couldn't believe he'd fallen for that trick.

The advantage went back and forth. Apollo had Guapo in an arm bar, and then Guapo had Apollo in a toe hold. Guapo tossed Apollo through the ropes, and Apollo came back with a slingshot jab to the midsection.

Guapo wrestled dirty, putting Apollo in an illegal choke hold and using the ropes for leverage. At one point, Apollo fell onto the floor. Guapo picked him up and threw him onto the commentator's table right in front of me. I could see Apollo gasping for air. He slowly rolled off the table and back onto his feet as the referee counted. He had to get back inside the ring or risk losing the match. When he finally did, Guapo greeted him with an overhand punch.

Things weren't looking good for Apollo, and I was convinced he would lose the belt. But just as quickly as he'd gone down, he was back up. He bounced off the ropes and flew into Guapo with a dropkick. The crowd roared.

Guapo lay on the mat, writhing in pain. Apollo threw an elbow onto his opponent's chest, then stood and quickly moved toward a corner. The crowd went wild in anticipation of the Sunset.

Guapo was still on the mat when Apollo reached the top turnbuckle. If he could flatten Guapo and pin him, the match would be over. The arena shook with the noise of the audience. But the cheers were suddenly interrupted by screams as someone came running down the aisle. It was The Scorpion!

The Scorpion ran up to the edge of the ring and grabbed Apollo's ankles, knocking him from where he'd climbed. Apollo went crashing down to the mat, giving Guapo time to recover. The crowd yelled for Apollo to get up. Guapo taunted the crowd, doing a little dance around the fallen wrestler before throwing himself on top of Apollo.

The referee, who hadn't noticed The Scorpion's interference, started the count. It looked like it was going to be lights-out for Apollo this time. Meanwhile, on the floor outside the ring, The Scorpion taunted the crowd, pleased with himself for helping take down the champion. But he stopped suddenly when he saw something that startled him.

A flash of black and gold ran past me.

"Manny!" I gasped and then quickly slapped a hand over my mouth, afraid someone had heard. But you probably couldn't hear a marching band playing in the arena, the audience was so loud.

The Eagle climbed onto the ring apron and pulled Guapo by the leg, breaking the pin and allowing Apollo to raise his shoulder before the count of three. The Scorpion attacked The Eagle, and now there were two wrestling matches going on—one inside the ring and one on the floor. The Scorpion slammed The Eagle's head against the edge of the ring. The Eagle shook it off. The Scorpion grabbed him by the arms, but The Eagle broke out of his grasp, twisted behind him, and ran him into a corner pole.

The audience was going wild. The commentators leaped out of their chairs. The referee, who had gotten knocked out when Apollo swung Guapo into him, lay on the mat. Meanwhile, Apollo was beating on Guapo, and The Scorpion was still on the floor, getting pummeled by The Eagle. The Scorpion managed to escape The Eagle and slide into the ring. He stumbled toward where Guapo was slowly getting to his feet, still dazed. As if it had all been part of a plan, The Eagle climbed into the ring. He and Apollo tore across the squared circle and pushed off the ropes. They used the force of the impact to fly into the air, and when Guapo and The Scorpion turned around, confused, they were met with twin dropkicks.

Apollo rolled Guapo for the pin just as the referee raised himself from where he lay. He crawled over to the two wrestlers and slammed the palm of his hand against the mat. One! Two! Three! The bell rang. The referee raised Apollo's arm in victory.

I realized I'd been holding my breath and let out a big sigh of relief.

The match was over, but the action wasn't, because inside the ring, The Eagle was holding The Scorpion faceup across his shoulders like he had him in a stretching rack. I knew what he was going to do because I'd seen him do it in all the videos I'd watched online.

"What in the world is happening now?" one of the commentators yelled from his table. "The Eagle has The Scorpion in a Bravo Back Breaker!"

The commentators looked at each other, shocked.

"No one does the 3B except the Bravos," the second commentator said. "What is going on here tonight?"

The Scorpion's face twisted in pain, and he waved his arm for someone to help or for the referee to stop the match, but the real match was over, so there was nothing to stop. When The Eagle finally released him, The Scorpion plummeted to the mat.

Suddenly, Guapo García came up behind The Eagle and grabbed him in a sleeper. The Eagle struggled to get out of it but got no help from Apollo, who was now fighting with The Scorpion at the other end of the ring. The Eagle slumped over, and Guapo took hold of the bottom of The Eagle's mask and pulled. He tugged and struggled, and then, as if in slow motion, the mask rolled up to reveal the person underneath.

It felt like the entire arena gasped collectively. And even though I knew who The Eagle was, I gasped too.

Guapo stumbled backward. Manny stood and roared, pulling Guapo out of the ropes where he cowered and tossing him over the top. Then he turned to look at the crowd,

and the place erupted. I looked around me and saw people jumping and high-fiving. They were wide-eyed and
open-mouthed in astonishment. They were screaming
and cheering and whistling. Someone was even ringing a
cowbell. The kid behind me had climbed up onto his chair
and was jumping up and down. I spotted the woman with
the Bravos T-shirt a few rows over. She had tears stream-
ing down her face. All of it was for Manny.

The Scorpion and Guapo slithered out of the ring like
a couple of snakes, their eyes wide in disbelief, and hurried out of the arena before Manny and Apollo could start
pounding on them again.

In the ring, Manny picked up The Eagle's mask and
shook it in the air. The fans screamed. He threw the
mask into the crowd, where people jumped to catch
it. Manny's face was covered in sweat, and he looked
exhausted but happy. He looked like he was where he
belonged. He looked like he was home. We had all just
witnessed the return of Manny "The Mountain" Bravo.
Manny and Apollo raised their arms and turned to each
side of the ring to acknowledge the crowd. Like they
were performers on a stage, taking a bow. And that's
when I got an idea.

CHAPTER 25

The four of us had agreed to meet on Monday morning before school to vote on a plan to give to Mrs. González. Cy pushed open the door to the auditorium and ran down the aisle toward where Gus and Brandon waited in the front row.

"Addie has come up with the best idea," Cy declared. "Hurry up!" She motioned for me to join her.

"Better than sock puppets?" Brandon asked. "I doubt it."

"Tell them, Addie," Cy urged.

"Okay," I said. "Instead of the battle scene between the Nutcracker and the Mouse King, we should—"

"Have a wrestling match," Cy finished for me. She hugged herself. "Ughhh, it's so good, I can't stand it. It's special to Dos Pueblos, and it definitely hasn't been done before. You're a genius, Addie." She grabbed me and shook me.

I blushed. It *was* a good idea.

"I'm in!" Brandon jumped out of his seat and swiped at Gus. "I can't wait to put the Mouse King in a sleeper hold."

"Gus?" Cy asked. "What do you think?"

We all turned to Gus. He pulled back his hood and pushed his dark bangs out of his face.

"Is your *dad* going to teach us how to wrestle?" he asked, as if he still didn't believe me.

Cy looked at me expectantly.

"Manny will help us," I offered proudly.

"Don't you mean The Eagle?" Gus asked.

"Him too," I said with a grin. "We start tomorrow after school. He'll pick us up and drop us here after. Get permission from your parents. And my mom wants their phone numbers too."

Mom had reluctantly agreed to the plan even though she called it "concerning."

The bell for first period rang, and Gus stood up. "Good luck putting me in a sleeper hold." He gave Brandon a push. Brandon chased after him out into the hallway.

"I'm going to find Mrs. González right now," Cy said. "See you at lunch." She rushed off, leaving me to walk to first period alone.

I hurried out of the empty auditorium, thinking back to Manny's final match as The Eagle. After the show at the arena, I had waited for Manny while he showered. When he came out of the locker room, he looked like he was floating on a cloud. I felt like I was floating on a cloud, too, as we walked through the parking lot and he waved goodbye to other wrestlers, who congratulated him on his triumphant return. He introduced me to everyone with *This is my daughter, Adela.*

On the drive to the Bravo house, we had gone over the

details of the match. I had asked him all kinds of questions like how long he'd known about the unmasking and what was it like to be up in the ring again as Manny Bravo. Then I told him about *The Nutcracker* and how we couldn't decide on what to do and needed to tell Mrs. González what our plan was on Monday. I described Brandon's puppet Nutcracker, a sad-looking tube sock with a face drawn on with marker. And I admitted that while I just wanted to get it over with, I also had what might be a really good idea.

"Eyyyy!" Manny nodded after I finished telling him about it. "That's a great idea."

"You think so?" I asked. "Wrestling is a big part of Thorne and Esperanza. The battle scene between the Mouse King and the Nutcracker as a wrestling match would be perfect. There's only one problem."

"What's that?" Manny had asked.

"How do you do it?" I said. "How do you wrestle?"

"Don't worry," he said. "I'll show you."

As I approached my first-period classroom, it felt like everything was finally falling into place. I'd met my father. Mom was letting me spend the weekends in Esperanza with him. I was getting to know the Bravos. Manny had taken me to see him wrestle not just any match, but his return as Manny the Mountain. And he was going to help with the *The Nutcracker*. Things felt right.

I wanted to skip down the hall, I was so happy. I realized I had walked past my classroom and I turned back just in time to see Gus coming out of the custodian's closet down at the end of the hall. I watched him look around as if checking that the coast was clear. The late bell rang, and I rushed into my social studies class no longer thinking about Manny, but instead wondering what Gus had been up to.

★ CHAPTER 26 ★

"All aboard the pain train," Uncle Mateo called to us. He had pulled up outside the school in his black truck.

Brandon looked at him, bug-eyed.

"Just kidding," Uncle Mateo laughed.

"Who is that?" Brandon whispered, grabbing his backpack from the ground.

"Not my father," I muttered, stomping over to the driver's side.

"I thought Manny was picking us up," I said. "He's supposed to help us. He said he would."

"He got a call from work." Uncle Mateo gave me an apologetic look. "He told me he would text you to let you know."

"Who's going to help us now?"

"What?" Uncle Mateo looked around, as if insulted. "He's not the only wrestler in the family, you know?"

I sighed and walked to the passenger side.

"All your adults know where you are, yes?" Uncle Mateo asked after we had all piled in. He looked over at me. "That includes you."

A chorus of affirmations called from the back seat.

"Mom knows where I'm going and why," I said.

Once we were on the road, Brandon, Cy, and even Gus bombarded my uncle with questions the entire way to Esperanza while I wondered why Manny had backed out of our plan without even bothering to let me know. All day, I'd replayed his words in my head. *I'll show you.* And now he wasn't here.

In Esperanza, we spilled out of the truck and walked around the house to the backyard.

"No! Way!" Gus yelled. He rubbed his eyes in disbelief and ran toward the ring.

Brandon took off after him. They climbed into the ring and immediately began play fighting.

"Are your cousins here?" Cy asked, looking at the house. I'd been telling her all about Eva and Maggie, and she had been looking forward to meeting them.

"No," I said. "They're usually only here on weekends."

"So it's just us and all of these boys?" Cy asked, making a face.

"Gather round, children," Uncle Mateo called to us. He kicked off his sneakers and climbed up onto the apron of the ring, but instead of entering between the ropes, he leaped over the top rope in one swift move.

"I can do that," Brandon said as if it was no big deal.

We all laughed as he attempted to imitate Uncle Mateo's move.

"Sit before you break something," Uncle Mateo said, pacing the ring.

We fanned out at his feet, and I imagined this was what it was like when he did drag story time at the bookstore. Except today he wore jeans and a T-shirt and didn't have glittery makeup on.

"Adela tells me you want to wrestle," he said.

"Well, at least these two," Cy said, pointing to Gus and Brandon. "I have no interest in getting hurt."

"Show us how to jump over the top rope like you just did," Brandon said.

"No, show us how to suplex someone," Gus interjected, giving Brandon an evil glare.

"Are you two done?" I asked. I glanced at Uncle Mateo, who waited patiently.

"Okay," Uncle Mateo said, taking command of the group. "First things first. No one is getting hurt on my watch. That means you need to listen. You can't just start yanking each other around. Wrestlers train a long time to be able to do what they do. The goal is to avoid getting hurt and to avoid hurting someone else. Understood?" He leaned in close to Brandon and Gus, who both nodded quickly. "Wrestling is an art," Uncle Mateo went on. "There's technique. But it's also story. It's the body and the imagination combined."

"And also lots of punching and pounding and kicking, too, right?" Brandon said, looking around at us, hopeful.

Everyone ignored him.

"It's like science," I said while my uncle moved around the ring. "And mythology."

"That's right," Uncle Mateo said. "I like that, Adela. Science and myth. That's exactly what it is. It's about all these things working together—the laws of gravity, the power of the human body, people's imaginations. You're putting on a show. So that's the idea behind what I'm going to teach you. You don't have to be able to pick up someone like this."

He grabbed Brandon and lifted him over his head.

Brandon screamed, and we all laughed. Uncle Mateo put him down carefully.

"That was awesome," Brandon said, laughing nervously. "I wasn't scared."

"It's kind of like we're dancing," Cy said.

"Right," Uncle Mateo said. He held his hands out to me, and I let him pull me up. "Instead of choreographing a dance, you're choreographing a fight."

"Adela, I want you to swing me against the ropes, and when I come back toward you, get me with an elbow to the chest, okay?"

I knew I couldn't physically move my uncle, but he leaned in the direction I was pulling and with his cooperation, I flung him across the ring. He hit the ropes and bounced back toward me.

"Elbow *now*," he said.

I crooked my arm and directed an elbow at my uncle's

chest, just like I'd seen the twins do. I didn't want to hurt him and hardly made contact, but he went down hard on his back, the mat under us trembling.

"Daaaaaang," Cy said, eyes wide.

"Are you okay?" I knelt where my uncle lay. "I didn't think I hit you that hard."

He winked and turned on his side to look at the group. "Remember, it's all about timing and being aware of each other. Like a dance. It took me a while to learn how to use my body to make sound, how to move so it looked like I was being hit hard when I wasn't."

"If it's acting, does that mean none of it is real?" Gus asked. He sounded concerned.

"No way," Uncle Mateo said, standing up. "People get hurt in all kinds of ways. It's very real." He turned his head quickly in the direction of the house. I wondered if he was thinking of Pancho.

Rosie came out from behind the barn in her work coveralls.

"Rosie," I called and waved to her. She made her way to the ring, and I introduced her to everyone. "Rosie was the women's champion in Mexico," I said proudly.

"We are in the presence of greatness," Cy declared. She bowed down to Rosie, and Rosie laughed.

"Oh, stop," Rosie said, shooing at Cy.

"It's true," Uncle Mateo said. "She *is* great. When we were little, she would teach us her moves."

Rosie laughed and shook her head.

"And she still teaches my cousins," I said. "Right?"

"Those two have gotten so good, they don't really need me," Rosie replied.

"You're the coolest," Cy said, admiring my grandmother. "Will you teach *us* something?"

"Please," I said. "Come on, Rosie."

"Do you want an old woman to break a hip?" Rosie asked.

But she climbed onto the apron and rolled into the ring as if she did it all the time. Like her body *did* remember. She stood up and paced the ring.

"Who wants a piece of La Rosa Salvaje?" she growled. "You?"

She pointed at Gus, who shook his head, wide-eyed. I had never seen this Rosie. Her stare was intense. She moved like an animal preying on her next meal. Her footsteps made the mat rumble beneath us.

"Or maybe you?" She turned on Uncle Mateo.

Uncle Mateo swiped at Rosie, and suddenly Rosie was on him. She kicked into his midsection, sending him onto his butt. When he was back on his feet, she grabbed him and tossed him with an arm throw.

"What do you think?" she asked Brandon. I could tell Brandon was hoping she wouldn't drag him into her fight with Uncle Mateo.

"He's getting up," Brandon warned, pointing to my uncle.

"No, he's not," Rosie said. She went behind Uncle Mateo and wrapped her arms around his head. Uncle Mateo appeared to struggle in her hold but couldn't get out of it.

"Dudes, Granny has gone mad," Brandon whispered urgently. "Who's gonna stop her?"

"Not me," Gus and Cy said at the same time.

Rosie caught my eye, and I knew Uncle Mateo would be okay. When she finally let him go, he slumped onto his back, and Rosie hooked one leg with her arm and covered him with her body. I looked at the group and crawled over to them. I slammed my fist against the mat.

"One!" Cy yelled.

"Two!" Now the whole group was in on it.

But before we could get to three, Uncle Mateo's body convulsed off the mat, sending Rosie flying.

He sat up, laughing, and leaned over to check on her. Rosie sat up laughing too.

"It's been a little while since I've done that," she said, wiping away tears. "I'm going to be sore tomorrow."

"Will you be my abuela?" Cy asked, sidling up next to Rosie.

"That was so cool," Gus said appreciatively. "Show us how to do it."

"Yeah," I said, forgetting for a moment that Manny had stood me up. "Show us everything you know."

CHAPTER 27

Thanksgiving always meant waking up early and help-ing Alex at the diner. Every year, there was a food drive, and then on Thanksgiving Day, the diner would give away boxes of food and Alex's Thanksgiving-in-a-Pie, which was exactly what it sounded like—turkey, stuffing, sweet potatoes, cranberry sauce, greens, and gravy in a double pie crust. We'd turn on the TV to a football game or wres-tling or whatever holiday movie was on.

At two o' clock, we'd close up the diner and have din-ner with any staff who had no place to be. Thanksgiving dinner was a spread of everything from calabacitas and menudo and empanadas to whipped sweet potatoes with marshmallows and Marlene's natilla for dessert. Then we would take all the leftovers and a pumpkin pie back home, and Mom and Alex would let me pick a movie. But all of that would happen without me this year, because I was spending Thanksgiving with the Bravos.

I learned that the Bravos didn't celebrate the holiday. Not since the year when Speedy died. He was headed home for Thanksgiving when the small plane he was flying in crashed in the mountains. Manny said they kept it very "low-key." Maggie explained that "low-key" meant no big dinner and a trip to the cemetery to visit Speedy.

"You sure you want to spend Thanksgiving there?" Mom asked when I told her, a concerned look on her face.

I wasn't, but I decided to go anyway.

Mom dropped me off on Thursday morning with a Thanksgiving-in-a-Pie. I felt a little like Peppermint Patty inviting herself to Charlie Brown's house, like maybe I was intruding on a day that was reserved for family who knew Speedy. At least I brought food.

"The Bravos have always been good about hiding their pain," Mom said with a sigh. "It's part of the job."

"Part of the job of wrestling," I asked, "or part of the job of being a Bravo?"

"Both, I guess," Mom answered.

She climbed out of the car and pushed the gate open for me, but she didn't cross the entrance. "Tell Rosie . . . Tell them I wish them a happy Thanksgiving."

"I will," I said, holding the box of pie carefully. It was the first time Mom said anything even the tiniest bit kind about the Bravos.

When I walked into the house, it seemed especially quiet. There were no smells of delicious food being prepared, nor the bustling energy of family getting ready for guests to arrive.

"Hola, Adela," Rosie said when I got to the kitchen.

I set the box on the counter. "This is from my mom."

"It looks wonderful," Rosie said, opening the top. "Please thank your mamá for me."

"You can thank her too," I said, tired of being in the middle. "If you want."

Rosie nodded but didn't say anything about contacting Mom. "We'll see your cousins at el cementerio tomorrow. They celebrate Thanksgiving with their mamá's family."

"Okay," I said. "Is Manny here?"

"He'll be back soon."

Back soon. Always back soon. Ever since the return of Manny the Mountain, he was around even less than when he was wrestling as The Eagle. He had been apologetic about not picking us up that first day he was supposed to help us with the show, but every time the group met, it had been Uncle Mateo or Rosie who picked us up and helped. Even the twins had pitched in. But never him. He was always busy. And it seemed like there was never a good time to talk about Mom and Alex and the adoption.

I left Rosie in the kitchen and went out into the yard with Hijo. We walked toward Uncle Mateo's trailer.

Even though the door was open, I knocked and ran my fingers through the wind chimes to let him know I was there. I didn't feel right just walking in. On the other hand, Hijo, who had followed me, didn't wait to be invited. That dog had no manners.

"Come in," Uncle Mateo's voice called.

My uncle wasn't alone. He was taking in the sides of the velvet jacket that was no longer on the dress form. Instead, it was on a tall, muscular man whose skin matched the soft brown of the fabric. The man held his arms stiffly, just slightly out to his sides, while my uncle stuck pins into the fabric.

The man wiggled his fingers in greeting. "Hey," he said. He had a short dark beard and kind eyes.

"Hi," I said back, sitting down across from Uncle Mateo. "I know you. You're Carter 'The Crusher' Jones."

The man tipped his head.

Uncle Mateo took a pin from between his teeth and stuck it into the jacket. "Carter, this is my niece Adela," he said to the man.

"I'd shake your hand, but he might stick a pin in me instead of this thing," Carter said, raising his eyebrows in exaggerated fear.

"I'll do it too," Uncle Mateo threatened, and he pointed a pin at his friend.

Carter squeezed his eyes shut as if dreading the pinch.

"Is that yours?" I said, motioning to the jacket. "I thought it belonged to one of The Pounding Fathers."

"It is," Carter said, turning only his head in my direction. "And it does."

"Quit moving," Uncle Mateo warned. "I'm serious."

"I'm *not* moving," Carter insisted.

"Anyway," Uncle Mateo said, turning to me. "Carter The Crusher has a new identity."

"Promise not to tell anyone?" Carter asked.

"I promise," I assured him.

"There's a new Pounding Father in town." He grinned.

"*You?*" I asked, surprised.

Uncle Mateo looked up at Carter from where he sat and beamed with pride.

"I'm making my debut at the Thanksgiving Throwdown in Atlanta tomorrow night."

"Really? Wow," I said. "How do you even get to be a Pounding Father?"

"It wasn't easy, that's for sure," Carter said. "Are you almost done?"

Uncle Mateo put one more pin in the jacket and then threw his hands in the air like a contestant in a cooking show competition when time's up.

"Take it off," my uncle said.

Carter carefully removed the jacket and handed it to Uncle Mateo, who placed it under the needle on the machine.

I made room for him at the table, and Carter squeezed in, his tall frame barely fitting.

"I heard they were auditioning a new member. I've been wrestling with Cactus for a few years and felt ready to move on to a bigger promotion," Carter said. "And hey, they're The Pounding Fathers, so I figured I'd give it a shot."

Manny had explained that a lot of wrestlers spent their careers working mostly in obscurity, moving from territory to territory. They were the guys in the opening matches, the ones who wrestled before the main event. Or the guys whose job it was to lose. Not everyone got to be a main-event wrestler, top billing on a card.

"And they picked you," I said. "That's so cool."

"Very," Uncle Mateo agreed from the other side of his machine. "Especially since it almost didn't happen."

"Why not?"

"I walked in, and they looked me up and down," Carter said.

"They?" I asked. "Like *The* Pounding Fathers?"

"Yep," Carter said. "All of them were there. Alexander, John, Thomas, George."

"Were you nervous?"

"Was I nervous?" Carter laughed. "You've never been in a room full of giant zombies, have you? They looked at me and before I could say a word, John Addams says to me, 'Thanks for coming, but no.'"

"Why?" I asked.

"They said it wouldn't make sense because there were no Black Founding Fathers," he explained. "And I said if we're talking about making sense, there were no zombie Founding Fathers either."

"The American Revolution might've ended sooner if there had been," Uncle Mateo joked, and we all laughed.

"But they picked you anyway," I said. "How did you convince them?"

"I told them, look, give me a chance, see what I can do compared to the rest of these guys," Carter said. "And after that, I'll give you a history lesson."

"Yes," Uncle Mateo said, shaking his index finger in the air. "School's in session."

"They laughed, but they said sure," Carter continued. "So I did my thing."

"And then what happened?" I asked, imagining Carter making his case in front of the other wrestlers.

"And then it was undeniable that I was the best wrestler in the ring that day," Carter said, slapping his hands on the table. "That's what happened."

"They hired you?" I asked. "Just like that?"

"Well, no," Carter said. "They told me they wanted to, but I didn't fit the gimmick. They were hung up on the idea that there were no Black Founding Fathers. Said it wasn't believable."

"This from a business that is all about illusion." Uncle Mateo rolled his eyes.

"I told them about James Armistead Lafayette and Salem Poor," Carter said. "Ever heard of them?"

I shook my head.

"Well, Black Founding Fathers exist whether you've heard of them or not," Uncle Mateo added.

"Anyway, I made my case, and I convinced them to give

me a shot," Carter said. "I even had my name picked out. Say hello to Crispus *Attacks*." He stood and did a little turn for us.

"Like Crispus Attucks!" I shouted. "I know him. He was the first person to be killed in the Boston Massacre. We learned about him in history last year. My teacher said there's not a lot of information about him. Historians know that he was a sailor, and he was probably Black and Indigenous, and that he was protesting because British soldiers made it hard for sailors to work and make a living."

"Dang," Carter said, looking at me. "You know more than I do."

"Told you she was a smart kid," Uncle Mateo said. "Addie's got a new role too."

"Yeah?" Carter said like he was genuinely interested. "Tell me about it."

"Oh, it's nothing as exciting as The Pounding Fathers." I folded a piece of fabric into little squares. "Just our school's *Nutcracker*."

"With wrestling," Uncle Mateo added, looking up from the sewing machine.

"That sounds like fun," Carter said. "How's it going?"

"It's fine." I shrugged.

"Fine? She's so modest," Uncle Mateo said. "They look great. Your friends are good."

"Yeah, I guess Gus and Brandon are getting all the

moves down," I said. "You and Rosie have been really helpful. Unlike someone else."

"I know you're disappointed," Uncle Mateo said. "I remember that feeling."

The three of us were quiet for a minute. It felt like there was nothing else to say about Manny.

"Anyway," I said, breaking the silence. "I'm just glad *I* don't have to wrestle."

"A Bravo . . . who doesn't want to wrestle," Carter said, looking confused. "Does not compute." He and Uncle Mateo laughed.

"I'm not a Bravo," I said, glancing at my uncle.

"But Addie has been training with us too," Uncle Mateo said. "And she's not bad."

"Not bad?" I wrinkled my nose. "Thanks a lot."

My uncle laughed. "Thought you didn't care."

"Maybe you can do a shoot," Carter suggested.

"What's that?" I asked.

"A shoot is when something unscripted happens in a wrestling match," he said. "You should just jump into the action."

"No thanks." I shuddered. "Besides, that's not how the story goes. Marie *watches* the battle happen."

"You don't have to follow the script, you know?" Carter said. He hadn't met Cy, so he couldn't possibly know that Cy would wring my neck if I ruined the show.

"Yeah," Uncle Mateo added. "Some people choose to improvise and write their own story."

I got the feeling he wasn't just talking about me and *The Nutcracker*.

"Is that what you did?" I asked, looking around his trailer. "Did you go off script?"

"I make masks," Uncle Mateo said, lifting one from the table. "But I don't believe in wearing them." He tossed it dramatically back onto a pile.

Carter snapped his fingers, as if applauding what my uncle had said.

"Besides, performing is in your blood," Uncle Mateo said. "You just have to believe." He removed the jacket from the sewing machine and handed it to Carter. Carter put it on and faced us. "Perfect," Uncle Mateo declared.

Carter did a turn to model. Sunlight shone through the windows, reflecting on the deep-brown velvet fabric. Carter looked like a superhero. Like a zombie Founding Father. And in that moment, I believed.

★ CHAPTER 28 ★

I had never been to a cemetery before. Mom had made me pack something nice to wear, but Rosie said not to worry about it, since we'd be doing some cleaning. Rosie, Pancho, and I piled into Manny's truck, and Uncle Mateo drove on his own. The twins met us there with their mom, a big woman with a sweet face like a kind fairy godmother. She didn't look like someone who had star goddesses for daughters. She greeted everyone with hugs and kisses, and when Rosie introduced us, she hugged me tight, like she'd known me forever.

There were angels carved out of stone on either side of the entrance. Rosie said it was a Catholic cemetery, and since I had never been to church, I watched everyone to see if they did anything special, like make the sign of the cross or bow before entering. But everyone just walked through the gates.

I followed the twins down a paved road past a mausoleum with little built-in vases along its front wall. Some of the containers were filled with real flowers and some with plastic flowers, while others were empty. Next to the vases were tiny plaques with people's names and dates of birth and death. Sometimes there was a little photo of the person, too, or a line that said something like BELOVED MOTHER or ALWAYS IN OUR HEARTS. It looked like a wall of drawers, like a file cabinet of lives.

Beyond the mausoleum was a small chapel with stained-glass windows, an office, and a groundskeeper's shed. And all around these were graves; some had headstones that stood upright, others were marked with crosses, and some had stones set into the ground. The most interesting ones looked like grottos that held statues of la Virgen de Guadalupe and other saints and the flowers and gifts people left.

We found Speedy's gravesite past the chapel. It was marked with a marble headstone that had an oval-shaped opening with a photo of him wearing the jacket that hung framed in the Bravos' family room. The inscription on the headstone read SON, BROTHER, HUSBAND, FATHER, BRAVO. I thought about how someone's life could be summarized with a list of words that described how they related to other people, as if our connections to others were what mattered most in life. What would my list say? *Daughter, stepdaughter, long-lost daughter, best friend, cousin, niece, granddaughter.* Something like that.

The twins, their mom, and Rosie bowed their heads and held hands for a minute. Then they got to work. Everyone seemed to know what to do. The twins' mom pulled weeds and cleaned the area around the grave. Rosie wiped off the stone with a rag and a spray bottle of some kind of special cleaning solution.

I knelt by the twins, who were collecting items left on the grave and putting them into a box.

"What's all this stuff?" I asked, picking up a wrestling action figure.

"People leave gifts," Maggie explained. "They're just little tokens of respect, to let him know they were here."

"Gross," Eva said, holding up a ratty-looking luchador mask.

There were photos and prayer cards and notes. Could the dead enjoy the things left for them? Did Speedy's ghost wake up at night to see what gifts people brought him? Did he put on the mask and have the little action figures wrestle it out?

"You come every year?" I asked in a whisper.

"Yeah," Eva whispered back. She glanced toward Maggie. "I know he's our dad, but it feels like we're visiting a stranger."

"Maybe to you." Maggie raised her voice and frowned at her sister.

Rosie shushed them from where she worked.

"Do you remember him?" I asked, picking up a crumpled dollar bill and dropping it in the box.

"He died when we were almost three," Eva said. "Maggie says she does, but—"

"I do," Maggie insisted. She glanced up at Rosie and her

mom to make sure she wasn't too loud. "I remember laughing while he chased us around the yard. And I remember him training in the ring at the house."

Eva gave me a look that said she didn't believe her sister. "I don't know why we have to keep coming," she muttered. "He's been dead for so long. Eleven years."

"That's as long as Manny has been gone," I said.

"At least your dad is alive, though." Maggie tossed something into the box.

"Yeah," I said. "I'm sorry."

Even if I hadn't seen Manny for most of my life, at least I could still talk to him, and maybe someday he would teach me the Bravo Back Breaker. And that was more than the twins would ever have. I felt guilty for wishing Manny wouldn't disappear so often.

Maggie pulled a slip of paper out of the pocket of her jacket and set it on the ground in front of Speedy's tombstone. She found a small rock nearby and placed it on top so that the paper wouldn't fly away.

"What's that?" I asked.

"I made the wrestling team," Maggie said. She seemed to be talking to Speedy's grave. "It's the team roster."

"Wow," I said, smiling at her. "You made history. First female wrestler on the team. I bet Speedy would be proud."

Maggie was silent.

I thought she might want to be alone, so I stood up and brushed off my knees. Rosie had finished polishing the stone and carried her cleaning supplies back to one of the trucks. Eva picked up the box of tokens and followed.

I walked over to where Manny crouched nearby, opening white paper bags.

"Can I help?"

"Sure can," Manny said. "Scoop sand into each bag, just enough that they can't blow away."

"Got it," I said. I knelt next to the bucket and opened a bag.

"This is our family plot," Manny said. He passed his hand across our line of vision. "You're my only kid, so when I die, you know where I want to be buried, eh?"

"Is that your way of saying you're glad I'm around?" I asked, scooping sand into a bag.

"Yeah," Manny said. "I'm glad."

The wind was blowing, and my face was starting to feel numb.

"Come here," Manny said. "I want to show you something."

I dropped the little shovel into the sand bucket and followed Manny, stepping lightly between graves but feeling like I wasn't being careful enough. Manny stopped at a grave a few feet away from Speedy's.

"Who is that?" I asked, reading the headstone of Armando "El Jaguar" Jiménez. I calculated his age when he died: fifty-seven. Pretty old, I thought, but not too old.

"Jaguar Jiménez and my dad pretty much started the

Cactus Wrestling League," he said. "They were tag-team partners for a long time. And he was one of my mentors. He was like an uncle to me."

"What happened to him?"

"His body wore out," Manny said. "He had a heart attack. No family, so we had him buried here with our people."

Manny stared at the grave as if waiting for Jaguar Jiménez to suddenly leap out of his plot.

"Every time I'm here, I think about having to do this someday for my parents," Manny said. "I bet you're wishing you hadn't come now, huh? Get stuck with this job?" He laughed.

"I don't mind," I said. "I would do it. That's what family does, right?"

"Yeah." Manny nodded.

Back at Speedy's grave, Rosie arranged fresh flowers and the twins' mom collected the bags of sand we'd filled, lining them on either side of the grave.

"You know, my dad was never around," Manny said out of the blue. "I'm not telling you that to make excuses for myself," he added quickly.

I knew Manny was trying to answer one of my questions: Why? Why wasn't he around?

"In my head, my dad and that guy in the ring that I saw on TV were one and the same," he said. "Even though he was always gone, I knew it was because he was fighting the bad guys, always doing the right thing. I wanted to be just like him."

Manny looked over at Pancho, who was standing on the paved path with Uncle Mateo. It seemed like Manny was still trying to please his dad. Like Maggie, even though her father wasn't around either.

"Why did you want to be like him?" I asked. "Couldn't you just be yourself?"

"I am myself," Manny said. He seemed surprised by the question. Maybe he'd never thought about it. "But he's my dad. Isn't that enough of a reason? People all over the world loved him. He was a giant. Isn't that what everyone wants? To be like their old man?"

Not really, I thought. I liked that Manny pursued his dreams so hard. In the same way Mom did hers. But I didn't understand why he had to do it while sacrificing other important things . . . like me.

"I guess he was the best dad he knew how to be," he said. "At least he came home. Can't say the same for myself, eh?"

"You can still be a good dad," I said. "But you might need some practice."

"Right." Manny patted my head. "Hey, looks like they're about done. Let's head over." He motioned toward Speedy's grave.

"Da—" I started to say as he walked away, but I lost my nerve. "Manny?"

He turned back to me.

"Do you think you can show me that 3B sometime?" I asked.

"Really? You want to learn the 3B?"

I nodded.

"What would your mom say?"

"She probably wouldn't like it," I said. "But it's my decision."

"All right, then," he said. "You got it."

Uncle Mateo and Pancho joined the rest of us at Speedy's grave. I helped the twins turn on the battery-operated tealights and placed one in each of the paper bags framing the tombstone.

"¿Dónde están mis hijos?" Pancho suddenly asked no one in particular. He sounded just like the Sleepy Reading Lady impersonating La Llorona. "Who are all these girls?"

"These are your nietas," Rosie explained.

"Bah," Pancho grumbled.

Maggie sidled up next to him and took his hand. He didn't look happy, but he let her.

I walked over to his other side. My heart pounded as I took his other hand. Pancho stared at Speedy's headstone as if remembering something.

Pancho turned to Maggie and then to me. "Maybe one of you can win the championship, since my sons can't seem to do it."

I glanced at Manny, whose eyes wouldn't leave the

ground. I didn't know if he'd heard Pancho. If he had, he pretended not to. I hoped he hadn't.

There were a few other families that seemed to be doing the same thing as us—cleaning, lighting candles, and praying, visiting loved ones during Thanksgiving. Maggie and Eva and their mom held hands. Rosie knelt on the ground, whispering. I couldn't tell if she was praying or talking to Speedy. Pancho pulled away and moved to her side. Manny stood next to Uncle Mateo, each in their own thoughts.

I looked out at the graves. What would Manny have done if I'd never reached out? Who would have made sure he was buried with all the Bravos and that his headstone listed the ways he was important to others?

We left the cemetery as the sun set. From the back seat of Manny's truck, I could see farolitos flickering throughout, little phantom lights, will-o'-the-wisps, out of reach. Each tiny flame was a memory someone somewhere was trying to keep from extinguishing.

★ CHAPTER 29 ★

I emptied out my locker in search of a library book. Meanwhile, kids hurried past me, walking over my stuff as they rushed toward the school exit to freedom. Ms. Baig had sent a student to distribute overdue notices earlier in the day. When the kid visited my class and placed the notice on my desk, everyone had oohed. I sighed with relief when I found the book crammed between the pages of a notebook at the very back of my locker. I had already lost one library book. Mom was not going to be happy if I lost another. I shoved everything into my locker and hurried to the library. Ms. Baig was at the counter, but I didn't go inside. Instead, I dropped the book in the return slot.

The school had cleared out as I made my way toward the exit. At the end of the hall, near the stairwell, I could see Gus in his brown hoodie. The four of us had been training in Esperanza a few times a week, plus regular rehearsals for the show during drama class. Sometimes he would let his guard down. But just when it seemed that he might be getting comfortable with us, he would go back to acting like his usual grumpy and aloof self. It was like he really just didn't want to be friends. Even Brandon was a little less annoying each day we spent together.

I waved to Gus, but he seemed distracted. He did a full 360-degree inspection of the space around him before disappearing into the custodian's closet. It was the second time I'd seen him go in or out of there.

I hurried down the hall and stopped outside the closet door. Mrs. Murry approached, and I realized that I was the one looking suspicious now. I unzipped my backpack and dug around, pretending to search for something.

"See you tomorrow, Addie," the teacher said as she passed.

I looked up and waved.

It felt like an hour went by before the door of the closet opened slightly.

"The coast is clear," I whispered into the crack.

The door slammed shut. A few seconds later, it opened again. Gus poked his head out.

"What are you doing here?" he asked, frowning.

"I think the better question is what are *you* doing in *there*?" I replied. I held the door open for him, keeping watch.

"None of your business," Gus said. He slipped out toward the school exit.

I hurried to catch up. "I saw you come out of there the other day." I followed him out of the building. "What are you up to, Gus Gutiérrez?"

"Leave me alone," he barked.

"Are you moonlighting as a cleaning person?" I asked, trailing him as he quickened his pace.

"What if I was?" he said. We'd reached the bike racks, and he unlocked his bike.

"I don't care what you're doing," I said, shrugging. But the less he told me, the more I wanted to know. "Just tell me."

"You really are nosy," Gus said, climbing onto his bike. "Thorne, New Mexico—home of the nosiest people!" He made a face at me that said he didn't approve.

"Not nosy," I offered. "Curious. What are you doing? Do you need help?"

"No," he growled. "I don't need your help. I don't need anyone's help."

Before I could say anything else, he sped off, pedaling so hard, he and his bike wobbled left and right and left and right until he rounded the corner and disappeared. He had some nerve saying Thorne was a weird place when he was the one acting weird. I was about to unlock my bike, but instead I turned and headed back into the school. I passed Mr. Pace, the music teacher, on his way out.

"Forgot something in my locker," I said and hurried inside before he could ask any questions.

★ ★ ★

Mom sat down across from me. I was putting off doing my

math homework by flipping through an issue of *National Geographic*. She had flecks of dried plaster on her arms and hair.

"Any good dinosaur news in there?" she asked, motioning toward the magazine.

"No," I replied. "But do you have any pockets of skin where you might store things?"

The look Mom gave me—part puzzled, part horrified, part grossed out—made me laugh. "That might be the strangest question I've ever been asked." She looked down at her stomach. "But there's a chance I do."

"Otters have loose skin under their forearms, where they store stuff," I said. "Isn't that cool?"

I went back to looking at my magazine, hoping Mom would leave. Mom was always moving, working, doing stuff. When she stopped moving, she started thinking. But not just thinking, *ruminating*. And that would lead to talking and talking would lead to Manny and the adoption. And I didn't want to talk about either. Mostly because it felt like there was nothing to say.

"Very cool," Alex agreed, serving us two pieces of cake and saving the day. "Look, I've got loose skin too. Think I can use it to hide things?" He extended his left arm and tapped at the skin under his bicep. It shook. His biceps looked nothing like Manny's. Alex didn't work out, unless you counted sweating at the flat top working out.

"What's this?" Mom asked, picking up her fork.

"I said I was making eggnog latte cake, and I meant it." He pounded his fist on the table.

I took a bite. It was yellow cake with eggnog buttercream sprinkled with nutmeg.

"Well?" Alex said.

I nodded my approval.

"I don't know why I'm losing so much sleep over that new coffee place," he said, shaking his head. "I guess it just makes me nervous that people, even people who've been coming here forever, get excited over the shiny new thing."

"This is delicious," Mom said. "And don't worry. The newness will wear off."

"In the meantime, I'll work on the gingerbread latte cake," Alex said. "Who in the world would drink a gingerbread latte?" He made a face and threw his hands up before walking away.

I stuffed another bite in my mouth, wishing Alex would take Mom with him. Mom nibbled at her cake and put her fork down.

"I've been trying not to pry too much about your father, you know," Mom started. "But are things going okay?"

"Yeah," I said, looking up from my plate. "Why wouldn't they?"

"Because I know Manny," Mom said, running the tips of her fingers across the tabletop.

"You *knew* him," I said. "Maybe you don't know him anymore. Maybe he isn't the Manny you knew in high school."

Mom looked surprised.

"Maybe," she said. "I hope you're right."

"People can change," I said. "It's called *evolution*." That made Mom laugh. Sometimes I had to talk to her in a language she understood.

I thought about all the adults I knew—Mom and Alex and Marlene, and now Rosie and Manny and Pancho and Uncle Mateo. How much had any of them evolved in their lives? Would I always be the me I was at that moment?

"He said he's staying," I said, feeling like I had something to prove to her. "He's wrestling as Manny the Mountain again. He's home, Mom."

"I don't want you to get too attached," she said.

"Why not?" I asked. "He's my father."

"Because I don't want you to get hurt, Adela."

"He can't hurt me," I said. "I'm not you." I wasn't sure why I said it. I wasn't even sure it was true. I just wanted Mom not to worry about me being with Manny.

I knew that Manny was frozen in time in Mom's memory. He was like a prehistoric bug caught and preserved in a drop of amber, never changing. But somewhere inside, I was afraid of Mom being right. Manny said he would help train us for the show, and he hadn't. He said he wanted me to visit and spend weekends, but he was gone a lot.

"You're right," Mom said. "You and Manny have a different relationship."

"I like going to Esperanza," I said.

"What do you like about it?" she asked. She leaned in, moving her plate out of the way as if to listen better. I could tell that she really wanted to know. She wasn't just looking for something to criticize.

"It's really different than being in Thorne," I said. "I feel like there's another side of me that comes out when I'm there. Like with *The Nutcracker*. Gus and Brandon are going to do a wrestling scene, but Cy and I have been learning the moves too."

"This plan still makes me so nervous," Mom said, frowning.

"Don't worry," I said. "Uncle Mateo and Rosie are showing us how to move so it looks like we're fighting but no one gets hurt. The point is, that's something that I never would have done if I hadn't met them. It's something I never knew I could do. And it's so much fun. I like being with Rosie and Uncle Mateo and the twins."

"I can see how that would all seem fun," Mom agreed. She turned the plate in front of her, thinking. "You know, I don't have very many memories of my parents."

Mom's parents died in a car accident when she was really young. She was like Aphrodite, the goddess whose parents were unknown. Did Aphrodite obsess about who her parents were? Maybe that was the kind of thing only mortals thought about.

"I understand what it's like to want to know more about something that's been missing from your life," Mom went on. She had a faraway look, like she was trying to remember them. "To wonder in what ways these missing factors make you who you are."

"Exactly," I said. "It's like that."

"Yeah," she said, poking at her cake but looking at me. "I was going to ask you about the adoption, but I won't. I know you have a lot going on right now."

"You say you aren't going to ask," I said. "But just mentioning it is your way of asking."

"You're too smart," Mom said. "And that brain, for your information, definitely comes from *me*."

We both laughed, and the conversation about Manny and the adoption faded, tucked away for later like something a sea otter hides in its skin.

★ CHAPTER 30 ★

"Final costume fittings are happening on Monday." Cy stood onstage, waving her arms to get everyone's attention, but all the seventh graders were busy collecting their things. She grabbed the microphone from the podium.

"Hello," she called out. The microphone squealed, and everyone stopped. "You need to sign up." She held up the sign-up sheet. "I see a lot of names still missing here. Don't make me have to come find you." She stared lasers down at us and shook the mic.

"Okay," Mrs. González said, gently taking the microphone out of Cy's grip. "Thank you, Cyaandi."

Cy jumped down from the stage and hurried over to me. My cool best friend had turned into a tightly wound spring now that the night of the show was getting closer.

"Hey, you should come shopping with me and Manny on Saturday," I said hopefully. "Maybe you can spend the weekend with me in Esperanza."

Cy took a deep breath through her nostrils and slowly exhaled through her mouth. "Thanks, Addie," she said. "But I can't. I have too much to do." She looked around the auditorium as if controlling the end-of-day chaos was something she needed to tackle.

"You should really relax," I said. "You look like my mom."

Cy stared at me like I'd called her an awful name.

"I'm sorry," she said, yanking her sweater over her head. "Did you just tell me to relax?"

"Yes," I said. "What are you so stressed about? Everything is running smoothly under the leadership of General Fernández." I saluted her.

"You're funny." Cy smirked. "Have you seen the snowflakes? I think they're plotting a rebellion."

"What are you talking about?" I laughed.

"They're a complete mess," Cy insisted. She picked up her bag. "And I think Letty is intentionally trying to sabotage the show."

"Why would she do that?" I asked, following her out of the auditorium.

"Because she's a snowflake, that's why," Cy said. She started walking backward down the hall.

"Home is this way." I motioned with my head toward the exit.

"I have to go check in with props," she said. "A director's work is never done."

"Well, if you change your mind about the weekend, let me know." I gave her my most supportive look. "It'll be fun."

But as I watched Cy charge down the hall, her orange Wallabees like two headlights, I knew she wouldn't be changing her mind.

With Cy busy, I turned to the other business I had to take care of. I poked my head into the auditorium to see if Gus had come out yet. There was no sign of him, so I hurried toward the exit and out the door.

He was at the bike racks.

"Hey!" I yelled. "Wait!"

He looked up from his lock and rolled his eyes.

"Wait," I said again as he got on his bike and began to wheel away from the racks. "I have a question for you."

Gus stopped.

"Actually, it's a joke," I said when I caught up to him.

"Oh brother." Gus sighed. "You stopped me for a joke?"

"Why do earthworms love Beethoven?" I asked.

A look of surprise crossed his face, just as I'd expected. He shook it off.

"I don't know," he said, gripping his handlebars. "Why?"

"Because he was . . ."

I started laughing before I could deliver the punch line. When I came up with the joke, it hadn't seemed that funny, but now I couldn't stop laughing. I needed a way to break the ice with Gus. To let him know that I knew his secret and that I was on his side.

"Because he was *what*?" Gus asked. "Stop laughing and finish the joke."

"Because—" I took a deep breath and tried to speak, but I doubled over again.

"I gotta go," Gus said, but he didn't leave. He might not have cared about the punch line, but there was something else he did care about.

"Okay, okay," I said, making a straight face. "Why do earthworms love Beethoven?"

Gus gave me a blank stare.

"Because he's de-composer!" I grinned and looked at Gus through teary eyes. He seemed confused.

"Get it?" I said. "De-composer? *Decomposer*? Because earthworms—"

"Okay," Gus said. "I get it." I detected a hint of a smile.

"I made it up myself," I said proudly. "And I *know*."

"You know what?" Gus asked, playing off his curiosity.

"You know what I know," I said, narrowing my eyes at him. "Custodian's closet? Anything you want to share?"

"Were you snooping?" he asked, acting all affronted.

After going back into the school, I had snuck into the custodian's closet. It was a small space crammed full of cleaning supplies and other junk. It smelled weird, like disinfectant and moldy rags and who knows what else. I searched around, the flashlight on my phone providing extra visibility. What would Gus be doing in there? That's when I found the box shoved into a dark corner. It was marked with the science lab room number, and it smelled terrible. Inside the box were little plastic bags of preserved earthworms and dissection trays.

"What?" I said. "You're not even supposed to go in there. Not to mention . . ."

"Is this blackmail?" he asked, frowning.

"That's dark," I said, shaking my head. "It's not blackmail."

"Then what do you want?"

"Well," I said, thinking. "I want to know why you took the earthworms from the science lab. And I want to know what you're going to do with them."

"Why do you care?"

"It's not every day that someone steals the worms we were supposed to dissect," I answered. "I heard there was a manifesto, too, which means you must care about the whole thing. So tell me."

"If I tell you, will you leave me alone?"

"Maybe," I said. "Depends."

"I took them in protest," he said. "I don't think we should dissect anything that was once alive."

"Why not?"

"Because it's gross, and it's not right," he insisted. "How would you like it if you died, or worse, were killed, just so a bunch of kids could cut into you and look at your insides and then throw you away? It's undignified."

"You know, people donate their bodies to science."

"Yeah," Gus said. "And that's a choice. These poor earthworms can't choose. They barely even have a brain."

"So . . . what are you going to do with them?" I asked. "Just leave them in the custodian's closet?"

"For your information, I have a plan," Gus said.

"Which is?"

"I'm not telling you." He frowned. "I don't even know you."

"What do you mean you don't know me?" I asked. "We see each other every day."

"I mean, you're not my friend."

"I'm not?" I was a little surprised.

We'd been spending a lot of time together at school because of the play. And he'd been going to Esperanza, to the Bravo house, to learn to wrestle. Mrs. González said working on the show together would be a bonding experience, and if learning to wrestle from a grandmother even *I* had just met wasn't a bonding experience, I didn't know what was. But maybe he was right. He didn't want to be friends no matter how much I tried. Maybe I should just give up.

"No, you aren't," he said. "And that's fine with me. I prefer it that way."

"You prefer what?" I pressed. "Not having friends?"

"Yeah," he said. "I do."

"I think that's really strange," I said. "And if you don't want friends, that's fine. Tell me anyway. What's up with the worms?"

"You're really annoying," Gus said. "Fine, I'll tell you.

I'm going to dump them on Brandon during the show."

"You're what?!" I yelled. "You can't do that."

"Why not?"

"Because it'll ruin the show and this means a lot to Cy and she's my best friend and I won't let you," I said, not stopping to breathe.

"The worms are going to be my illegal weapon," Gus said. "The Rain of Worms! Or maybe the Worm Wallop. I haven't decided."

"How is that any more dignified for the worms?" I asked. "Just dumping them? Since you care so much."

Gus looked at me like he regretted telling me anything.

"And that doesn't make a statement," I added. "I thought you were all about making statements. How is anyone going to know why you took the worms?"

"Good point," Gus said, thinking. "Okay, I'm going to do a monologue. Mid-match. I'll stop the action and go into my speech about the worms."

"You can't do that either," I said. I imagined how disappointed Cy would be if Gus derailed the show. "*The Nutcracker* isn't the place for your worm agenda."

"I have to go," he said.

"Wait." I stood in front of his bike to stop him from leaving. "Let me help you. I'll come up with a plan. Something that makes a statement and that won't affect the show."

Gus looked away, but he didn't ride off.

"If you come up with a better idea before the show, I might consider it," he said. "But if you don't . . ." Gus moved his bike around me and rode away.

"Don't worry," I called out to him. "I'll think of something!"

★ CHAPTER 31 ★

Downtown Esperanza was decked out for the holidays.
The plaza was decorated with farolitos and bright red
ristras and green-ribbon-wrapped columns. Large papier-
mâché stars hung overhead. The branches of a pine were
adorned with recycled tin ornaments. In the center of the
square, one of Rosie's tumbleweed statues, an angel, had
been assembled. It was painted gold, and a halo made from
a metal hanger rested on its head. A mom took a photo of
her two little kids in front of it, and I couldn't help feeling
proud. Rosie had shown me a scrapbook of articles about
her work. Her tumbleweed statues must be in hundreds,
maybe thousands, of photos.

The smell of piñon smoke and hot chocolate and fried
dough wove through the tables that lined the square,
where vendors sold everything from handmade jewelry to
beeswax candles to homemade salsas, both red and green.
I'd brought the money I'd saved up from doing chores and
diner work and was ready to shop.

"Your mom ever bring you here?" Manny asked. We
stopped in front of a puppet theater on a bike where two

patchwork coyotes were howling along to "Mi burrito sabanero."

"No," I said, smiling at the puppets. "We never came to Esperanza together."

"This is pretty neat, right?" Manny asked, looking around. "I used to love coming here with my brothers when I was a kid. We'd come with your abuela. Pa would sometimes make it home in time for Christmas and join us."

"It must've been hard," I said. "Not having him around for the holidays."

Manny held out a dollar and motioned for me to place it in the tip can. I moved closer and shoved the bill into the slot cut in the plastic lid. The coyotes shook their tails at me in thanks.

"Yeah," he said, stuffing his hands in the pockets of his jacket. "But it was almost easier when he was gone too."

We stopped at a stand selling spices, and I scanned the little jars for something to get Alex.

"Why's that?" I asked, picking up a star anise and sniffing it. I held it out for Manny to smell.

"When he wasn't home, we knew the deal," Manny said, leaning in to smell the spice. "Rosie was la jefa. And it was confusing having him there and then not. Sometimes he'd be home for a few days, sometimes for a few weeks. We never really knew. Mateo would cry his head off every time Pa left."

"Do you think you would've been better off if you didn't have a dad around at all?" I asked, not looking at Manny.

"I didn't say that," he replied. He stared at me as if he were trying to see inside my brain.

I paid for a jar of a spice combination called La Llama. The little homemade label was decorated with orange flames. The woman behind the stand wrapped the jar in white tissue paper and placed it inside a small paper bag before handing it to me. I busied myself placing the package inside my canvas shopping bag.

"I don't know if there's anything I can say that's going to make you think differently about me and us," Manny said. "I can't change anything that happened, you know? I'm here now. And I'm not trying to pretend it was okay that I wasn't around for you more."

"At all," I corrected. "That you weren't around at all."

"Fair," Manny said. "I know your mom would probably love this."

"Please don't talk about Mom," I said, moving toward another vendor.

Manny held up his hands. "Sorry."

"Can we just shop?"

"Yeah," Manny said. "We can do that."

Manny had opened the door for me to tell him exactly what I thought about him leaving us, and I closed it. He had been gone a lot while I was in Esperanza, but I had been avoiding talking about Alex and the adoption too. Maybe I didn't want to know. Maybe I was afraid of what I would learn.

We walked around the square, pointing out interesting things we noticed, like how the eyes on the wooden saints at one stand seemed to follow us and when the puppeteer climbed out of the back of his bike theater and hurried to the porta potty. We stopped for tamales and ponche. At another stand, we ate warm sopaipillas with honey. I bought gold star-shaped face glitter for the twins, a jar of homemade chamomile bath salts for Mom, a lotería tarot deck for Cy, and a black onesie with a wrestler's masked face printed in silver for the baby. He wasn't around yet, but I thought Mom would appreciate that I thought to get him a gift too.

"Let's see what this guy is up to." Manny motioned to a young long-haired man sitting on a folding chair just past a row of vendors. The man had an old-fashioned blue typewriter set up on a card table. Next to the table was a chalkboard sign that read POEMS $10.

"It's a poet!"

"You really selling poems?" Manny asked, looking from the sign to the man.

"Sure am," the man replied. "Would you like one? Maybe for the young lady?" He shot me a smile.

"How do you do it?" I asked. "You just write?"

"That's how poetry works," the man said. "You give me

a little information and about ten minutes, and I write a poem."

I was impressed. When we wrote poetry in school, it always seemed to take a lot longer than ten minutes.

"How 'bout that?" Manny said. "All right, I'd like a poem for the kid. My daughter."

"You got it," the man said. He took a fresh sheet of paper from a wooden tray and rolled it into the typewriter's carriage. Then he picked up a pad and a pencil. "So this young lady is your daughter," he said, looking at Manny. "What's her name?"

"Adela," Manny said.

"That's a nice name," the poet said. "Tell me about Adela."

"We, well, her mom, really, named her for the Adelitas," Manny said. "Mexican lady soldiers."

I knew the story. The Adelitas weren't just "Mexican lady soldiers," like Manny said. They were women who fought alongside male soldiers during the Mexican Revolution. But they were also girls and women who were kidnapped, like Persephone, taken from their families, and forced to join the men. Mom said they were women who persevered despite the difficult situations they found themselves in, whether voluntary or not. She said she wanted me to be a fighter, too, for me to determine my own fate.

"Mexican lady soldiers, all right," the poet said. "What else?"

"Well," Manny said, "she's twelve." He looked at me as if to confirm.

"Uh-huh," the poet said, writing.

"And she's tall like her old man," Manny went on.

"Okay," the poet said. "And what is she like?"

I suddenly had a feeling in my gut that the poem was a bad idea.

"What do you mean, what's she like?" Manny asked and laughed. "She's like a twelve-year-old kid."

"I like science," I offered the poet.

"Cool," the poet said, jotting it down. He looked up at Manny again. "What's special about Adela?"

The tamales and ponche and sopaipillas churned in my stomach. I felt like I wanted to run—away from the square and the poet and the awkward way Manny was standing there, looking down at the guy holding his pencil to his notepad. I worried Manny might put the poor skinny poet in a Bravo Back Breaker if he didn't stop asking him questions.

"I don't need a poem," I whispered to Manny. "Let's just go."

"Aw, don't be embarrassed of all the great stuff your dad has to say about you." The poet looked at Manny, waiting. "What are some things you love about Adela, Dad?"

I held my breath and couldn't bring myself to look at Manny.

"Hey, man, I thought *you* were the poet," Manny said,

his voice loud enough to catch the attention of a couple walking by. His face was red. "What am I paying you for if you want me to write the poem for you?"

The poet laughed nervously. "Sure, but I don't know Adela like you do."

"Just write the damn thing," Manny said.

He threw a ten-dollar bill on the ground near the poet's shoes and walked off. I could feel my face burning with embarrassment. I picked up the money and put it on the table.

"Don't worry about the poem," I said. "Thanks for trying."

I walked away, leaving behind the poet and any notion that I'd get to hear all the things Manny knew and loved about me.

★ ★ ★

That night after dinner, I found Manny sitting outside in the ring. He was smoking a cigarette that he quickly threw on the ground and stubbed out with the toe of his boot when he saw me.

"Sorry about that."

"You shouldn't smoke."

"Yeah, I know," he said, patting the mat. His legs dangled over the edge of the ring. I pulled myself up next to him and scooted closer.

"What are you doing out here?" he asked. "Aren't they watching a movie or something?"

"Yeah," I said. "I wanted to look at the stars. The lights are too bright in Thorne. It's hard to see them." Seeing the stars was only a fraction of the truth.

"Hey," Manny said, not looking at me. "I'm sorry about today. The thing with the poet. I shouldn't have lost my cool like that."

"It's not like the poet knew we'd just met." I let out a half-hearted laugh.

From where we sat, I could see the red-and-white holiday lights Uncle Mateo had strung up outside of his trailer. They blinked in the darkness like a fairyland in the distance. For a moment, I wished I could be there instead, drinking a cup of flowery tea, listening to classical music, helping him with a sewing project.

"When I was a little kid, I thought my dad was a god," Manny said, leaning back on the ropes. "Like Zeus or something."

"Zeus was a jerk," I said, thinking about all the Greek myths I'd read. "He had a bunch of wives, and he was always doing crummy things like turning people into animals."

"He kinda was, right?" Manny laughed. "Anyway, your abuelo was the strongest person I ever met. He was tough. There was no one and nothing that could beat him."

I thought about how weak and confused Pancho seemed sometimes. How he got headaches and had to sit in the dark in the family room. How sad it was that he couldn't remember things. Was Manny thinking of that too?

"But like I said before, he was never around," Manny continued.

"Yeah, Greek gods are too busy messing up mortals' lives to show up for Christmas," I joked.

"Or graduations," Manny added.

"Or to know anything about their kids." I looked at him and smirked.

"I deserved that," he said. "I don't think my dad really knew much about me."

"What was it like when he was around?"

"When he was here, it was all about us training," Manny said. "We didn't want to let him down. For a long time, that was cool with us because we wanted what he wanted."

"What happened?" I asked, scooching back to sit even with Manny. "Did something change?"

"Yeah," he said. "My brother died."

"Speedy." I nodded.

"My dad always said to us when we got hurt, 'Mijo, there's no crying in wrestling.' When Speedy died, it was the first time I saw *him* cry. It was like everything we thought we were as a family began falling apart. It changed everything. It changed me, I guess."

When Manny talked about Pancho, it seemed like it was as close to an apology as he could get. But I was tired of adults being so busy thinking about themselves and how they were hurt that they couldn't see when they were hurting someone else.

The sound of the twins' laughter rang out from inside the house.

"You should go back in there," Manny said, hopping off the mat. "I need to go see your uncle for a bit anyway."

"Okay," I said. I hated that the spell had been broken. I didn't want our time together to end yet.

"Oh, hey." Manny turned back to me. "I'm sorry I haven't been around to help you with your play."

"*The Nutcracker*," I said.

"That's a good name for a wrestling move." Manny laughed. "When is it again?"

"On Thursday," I said, cringing at Manny's joke.

"Okay." He tapped his temple. "Thursday. I'll be there."

"Promise?"

"I'll be there," he said, tugging my braid. "I promise."

★ CHAPTER 32 ★

The twins and I sat at the kitchen table, working on school assignments. They were reading a book titled *Bless Me, Ultima*, and I was working on my mythology project. Mrs. Murry had told us to think about mythology in our lives, so I was creating a pantheon with my own family. I was taking photos of everyone with my little blue instant camera. So far, I had Mom at the museum with some of her tools. In the photo, she's wearing her respirator that makes her look like someone out of a sci-fi movie and the T-shirt Alex and I gave her a few birthdays ago that reads I'VE GOT A BONE TO PICK.

I was carefully writing out my heading, bubble letters in purple gel pen, when the door flew open and Uncle Mateo appeared with a gust of chilly air.

I gasped. The twins squealed.

"You look—" I started.

"Amazing," Maggie finished.

"Perfect," Eva added.

He wore a dark green velvet gown that swept the floor, its full skirt decorated with tin birds and hearts and flowers. A gold boa wrapped around his neck like a garland of tinsel. On his head was the pink beehive wig I'd seen in his trailer. His face was made up in golds and pinks, two bright red spots on his cheeks.

"You're a real-life Christmas tree," I said, admiring my uncle.

Uncle Mateo curtsied, then twirled. The hooped skirt spun hypnotically. "All right, Santa's helpers, ready to roll?" he asked. "Who's coming?"

"We are," Maggie said, dropping her paperback.

"I don't know," I said. I snapped and unsnapped the cap of my gel pen. "I'm waiting for Manny."

The twins looked at each other. I could see Eva roll her eyes.

"Come on," Maggie urged. "It'll be fun."

"Besides," Eva added, "who knows when Uncle Manny will show up?"

My cousin's comment felt like a metal chair across the back, knocking the wind out of me. I imagined myself on the floor of the arena, writhing in pain. I knew she was right, but it still hurt.

"Eva, Mags, can you grab that bag and take it out to the truck?" Uncle Mateo asked, pointing to a duffel bag by the door and shooing them before they could protest. "Thank you."

When Eva and Maggie were gone, Uncle Mateo turned to me.

"I understand why you don't want to come," he said,

smoothing his skirt before carefully sitting down at the table.

"But I do want to come," I said. "I just don't—"

"Want to miss seeing Manny," he said. "I get it."

"I thought things would be different now that he's staying at Cactus and wrestling as The Mountain again."

"When I was a kid, I was like that, too, with my dad." Uncle Mateo patted his beehive. "I would wait and wait and wait, afraid I would miss him if I went out to play with friends or did anything outside the house."

"Manny told me," I said. "He said you would cry."

"I did," Uncle Mateo said. "But that's before I knew there was no crying in wrestling." He winked.

"Can't forget that," I mumbled.

"Even when he was home, he didn't really spend much time with us unless we were training," Uncle Mateo said. "He had a one-track mind that way. Wrestling was his work, but it was also an obsession, and anything that got in the way was just a distraction."

This was all sounding familiar to me. My stomach ached. "Like Manny."

"I know the truth isn't easy to hear, sweetie, but you're twelve and you're here because you want to know the truth," Uncle Mateo said. "I told you that I don't believe in wearing masks, so I'm pulling this mask off the Bravos."

He took my hand in his, something I imagined Manny might do. But Manny still seemed to mostly keep me at arm's length. Telling me about growing up with Pancho, as if that explained everything. It was like he was still the teenage boy in the photo, afraid and unsure.

"Is that why Manny wasn't around?" I asked. "Why he still isn't? Because it's an obsession?" This was starting to feel like a Greek tragedy.

"You like science, right?"

I nodded.

"Then you know that sometimes stuff gets in your genetic makeup. Do you know what that means?"

"Yeah," I said. "Like things you get from your environment."

"Right," Uncle Mateo confirmed. "Environmental factors. Not having a dad around was one of the environmental factors that affected us. That affects *you*." He twisted and untwisted his gold boa around his hand. "I'm not making excuses for Manny. All I'm saying is that I know it wasn't easy for Manny or Speedy to be fathers so young when they were still just kids hungry for our dad's approval. It does things to how you think about yourself."

"So what you're saying is that Manny is doomed to follow Pancho's example," I said, looking my uncle in the eye.

"No, I'm not saying that," Uncle Mateo replied. "But I'm trying to give you some idea of why he is the way he is."

Outside the window, I could see Hijo sniffing the ground.

"We all have to figure out our own paths," he went on.

"We make choices. It's possible to break the cycles, those environmental factors, but it's not always simple. It's easier for some people than for others, of course."

"I can't tell if you're defending him or not," I said.

"Neither," Uncle Mateo said, getting up. "I'm just trying to be honest with you. I know adults aren't always good about that."

"Not at all," I agreed.

"I believe people can change," Uncle Mateo said. "But you can't force it. And I don't think anyone should sit around waiting for that change to happen."

"Are you saying I should stop waiting for Manny?" I asked. "Did you stop waiting? For Pancho?"

Uncle Mateo looked up as if remembering. His fake eyelashes fluttered like spider legs against his gold-dusted face. I waited for him to answer. He seemed to have everything figured out. He was the one adult I knew wouldn't lie to me. His shoulders rose and fell as he slowly let out a deep breath, like years of waiting being released. He opened his mouth and then closed it. Then he tried again.

"Eventually, I realized that everything was passing me by while I sat around waiting for my dad to come home," he said. "I wrestled for a while because it was the only way to be close to him. But it wasn't what I loved. I knew that if I lived my life to please him, I wouldn't be happy. So, yes, I guess I did stop waiting." He looked me in the face and leaned in. "But I'm not saying you should stop waiting. You make your own choices, okay?" He squeezed my hands and let them go.

"Why can't everything in life just have a right or wrong answer instead of all these possible choices?"

"I know what you mean," Uncle Mateo said. He looked inside his canvas tote bag and pulled out some books. "Why don't you start with an easy decision?" He held up two holiday picture books. "What should I read today?"

I studied the colorful covers. "That one," I said, pointing to *A Piñata in a Pine Tree.*

"Good choice," my uncle said. "I do have a pretty great singing voice."

He held out his elbow to me, and I hooked my arm through his.

Outside, Maggie was chasing Hijo around the backyard while Eva laughed uncontrollably.

"What in the world is going on?" Uncle Mateo said.

"Gimme that!" Maggie yelled, lunging for the dog.

"Hij—" Eva tried to talk and laugh and gasp for air at the same time. "Hijo."

"What about Hijo?" I asked. Maggie was now struggling to pull something out of the dog's mouth.

"He was digging near your trailer." Eva sniffled and wiped tears from her eyes. "We went over to see what he was doing, and he had dug up Maggie's—" She started laughing again. Streaks of mascara ran down her face.

"Maggie's what?" Uncle Mateo and I asked at the same time.

"He had Maggie's flipper tooth," Eva shrieked and laughed. "He must've swiped it the day it went missing and buried it."

Maggie stomped over to us, her black wrestling boots kicking up clouds of dirt behind her.

"Got it," she declared victoriously, holding out a disgusting dirt-covered tooth, its pink retainer mangled by Hijo's bite marks. She stuck it in the pocket of her jacket and climbed into Uncle Mateo's truck.

"What's she going to do with that?" I asked Eva.

"I don't know," Eva said as she got into the truck. "But she better keep it away from me or it's going out the window."

On the drive to the library, through the sounds of Uncle Mateo's classical music and the twins arguing, I thought about what Uncle Mateo had said. I had to make my own decisions about Manny. It felt hard and scary. Making choices seemed so final. And I realized that all this time, I had been missing having my father around, but I had also been missing something no one had given me—a choice.

★ CHAPTER 33 ★

When Brandon limped into the diner, his weight held off his right leg by a pair of crutches, Cy screamed. Everyone in the diner looked over at our table, afraid something terrible had happened. And it had.

"Brandon Rivera, this is the worst prank you've ever pulled." She gritted her teeth and grabbed for one of his crutches.

But I could tell by the pained look on his face that it wasn't a prank. Brandon had missed school. He'd missed dress rehearsal. Cy had already been fretting, and with good reason.

"Everything okay?" Marlene called over from the counter.

"Not really," Brandon said. "I have a sprained ankle and zero sympathy from the deranged director."

Marlene looked at our group as if she had no interest in getting involved with our drama. She went back to organizing her tickets.

"What happened?" Gus asked, making room for Brandon, who sat down carefully and leaned his crutches on the table.

"Thank you for asking," he mumbled in Cy's direction. "Glad someone cares. I tried to put my brother in a figure-four leglock, and he twisted out of it. The doctor said it could've been a lot worse."

"So even though Mateo and Mrs. Bravo told you repeatedly not to try new moves on your own, you did it anyway," Cy said, shooting flames with her eyes. "And now you've ruined everything!"

She reached across the table as if trying to wring Brandon's neck. Brandon scooted out of her reach. He looked down at his hands guiltily.

"If it makes you feel any better," he said, "it hurt a lot." He smiled apologetically

Cy shook her head. "I'm sorry you got hurt," she said, coming down from her rage. "Really. I hope your leg is okay."

"Thanks," Brandon said. "I'm sorry I ruined the show."

"If you can't be in the show," I said. "Who's going to be the Nutcracker?"

Before Cy could say anything, Marlene set a tray of shakes on the table. "Four Posadas shakes," she announced. "Bon appétit."

"Guess I'll drown my sorrows," Cy said, sliding a glass toward herself.

We drank our shakes in silence, everyone somber as if we were at a funeral. I'd been trying to think of a way to dispose of the earthworms and keep Gus from ruining the show. I hadn't come up with an idea, and when I snuck back into the custodian's closet, the box was gone. Gus said he didn't trust me to keep them there. But now the show had been ruined anyway.

"You kids want anything else?" Marlene asked, looking from face to face. "Y'all look like someone died."

"Oh, I'd like to kill someone," Cy muttered under her breath.

"Is that a no on food?" Marlene asked, tapping her pen on the table.

"No, thanks," I said.

Marlene turned on her orthopedic shoes and walked away.

"You need to chill out," Gus said. "It's just a show. Someone else can play the Nutcracker. And we can just do a fake fighting scene. No one will know the difference."

Cy stood up.

"First of all, don't tell me to chill out," she said. "Second of all, *we'll* know the difference. There's already a regular fight in the original. This is supposed to be a wrestling match. That's the twist. And the only ones who know the moves are us. We can't just train someone else in a few days."

"Okay, then why don't *you* play the Nutcracker?" Gus said. "Like you said, you know the part."

"Because I'm the director," Cy said, gripping the edge of the table. "I need to keep all the plates spinning."

"Something is definitely spinning out of control," Brandon said, "and it's not the plates." He slurped his shake loudly.

Cy got up in a huff and carried her empty glass to the plastic tub of dirty dishes near the counter before heading for the door.

"Where are you going?" I called to her.

"I need to go to my thinking place," she said.

"Where's that?" Brandon asked.

Cy didn't answer, but I knew she was just going for a walk. Her thinking place wasn't an actual physical place.

"Guess I'll see you tomorrow," Brandon said, struggling to get out of his seat. He knocked one of his crutches over, and I picked it up for him.

"Sorry about your leg," I said. "Cy didn't mean any of it. She's just stressed."

Brandon shrugged and waved. Gus held the door open for him.

"He lucked out," Gus said when he returned to our table.

"Why?" I asked. "Doesn't seem very lucky."

"Now he won't get worms dumped on him," Gus said with a sour face. "But someone else might."

"You said you wouldn't do it," I argued.

"I'm kidding," he said. "I'm not dumping the worms. But something else is going to happen unless you come up with a good plan."

"You know what? You're mean," I accused. "Maybe

that's why you don't have any friends. Because you're mean, and you know that no one will want to be friends with you for long."

"Whatever," Gus said. But for a moment, I thought he might have looked hurt. "Did you come up with something?"

"Yes," I said with as much certainty as I could, even though I hadn't. "Are the worms still at school?"

"In my locker," Gus informed me. "Safe and sound."

"Okay," I said. "Have them with you on Friday."

"But that's after the show," he said. "Are you going to tell me the plan?"

"Not yet, but I will after the show. Okay?"

Gus looked at me as if he was trying to decide whether to believe me.

"I know we aren't friends, but trust me."

Maybe he didn't know what it was like to trust someone, but finally, he nodded. And I knew that I had no choice but to trust him too.

CHAPTER 34

The backstage area thrummed with the noise and energy of seventh graders dressed as soldiers and mice and snowflakes and partygoers. The high school drama club kids were putting last-minute touches on costumes and makeup, attaching safety pins and Velcro strips to keep everything in place, putting lipstick on the snowflakes and making sure mouse whiskers had enough glue to stay on under the heat of the stage lights. Cy, Mrs. González, and Mr. Pace rushed around calling out orders.

The stage had been transformed into Marie's living room. A couch from the teachers' lounge covered in an afghan sat on one side. Next to it was a small cardboard Christmas tree surrounded by empty boxes wrapped to look like gifts. Sleeping bags were rolled in a corner, waiting for Marie and Fritz. I peered out from behind the curtains. *The Nutcracker* overture played on the sound system and snowflake lights reflected on the walls of the auditorium. Sixth-grade ushers greeted people with candy canes and programs.

I scanned the crowd, hoping to catch a glimpse of Manny and the twins and Rosie and Pancho and Uncle

Mateo. I had asked Mrs. González for eight tickets. Now I was almost hopeful no one would come. When Cy had called an emergency meeting and announced her idea, I would've thought she was kidding. Except I knew Cy would never kid about the show.

"You look fantastic!"

I closed the curtains and turned to face Cy. She was dressed in black bell bottoms, a black-and-white-striped button-down, a black bow tie, and white platform sneakers. She wore a headset with a microphone and carried a clipboard. Tonight, she was doing double duty as the director and the referee.

"I look like a fluffy kitten," I said, flicking the bow at my neck. "No, I look like one of those creepy old-fashioned dolls. The ones that wake up in the middle of the night and stand over you to watch you sleep."

"You have some serious feelings about this costume," Cy said and shuddered. The dress I wore was white with little pink flowers. My hair was loose and pulled off my face with a pink headband. Cy laughed. "The shoes are fabulous."

I looked down at my ballet shoes—Mom bought white ones, but Uncle Mateo helped me dye them red. They were the only thing about the whole silly outfit I liked.

"Are you ready?" Cy asked.

"Do I have a choice?" I tugged on my white tights, which were beginning to roll down at the waist.

"Have I told you that this is going to be the best *Nutcracker* in the history of Thorne Middle School?" she asked, shaking me by the arms.

"Yep," I said.

"And have I also told you that you are the best friend in the whole world?" She smiled. "And that this wouldn't be possible without you?"

"Trust me," I said. "If you weren't my best friend, I would not be doing this."

"It's going to be a-ma-zing." She spun in a circle, arms stretched out wide.

"Sure," I said, unconvinced.

The lights dimmed and came back on.

"It's time," Cy squealed.

"Already?" I asked. "I think people are still coming in. Shouldn't we wait?"

"I have to find Brandon." She grabbed me in a quick hug before skipping away. "Break a leg! But not literally because, well, you know."

★ ★ ★

The audience clapped as the guests departed and the stage darkened to just the eerie blue lights that made it appear as if night had descended on Marie's house. I slipped into my sleeping bag while Cy directed the mice to the dark living room. The audience laughed as the mice scurried around frantically, bumping into one another.

The tree music played, at first quietly and then rising to a crescendo, as a couple of soldiers rolled the large wooden Christmas tree out onto the stage, replacing the small cardboard one. A stage light turned on to reveal the tree. It sparkled with green glitter and silver tinsel. The audience clapped with delight.

A soldier pushed the cardboard cannon out, and the boom of a bass drum sounded twice to represent an explosion at the start of the battle. I sat up in my sleeping bag as mice and soldiers came running from opposite sides of the stage, swinging cardboard swords. I hurried out of the way and huddled near the tree, a fearful Marie. Godpapa Drosselmeier stood next to me, looking on in his eyepatch, top hat, and cloak.

Gus ran onstage dressed in gray sweatpants with a belt that held a cardboard scabbard, a gray sweater under a gray felt cape with ragged edges, gray sneakers, and, of course, the mask of the seven-headed Mouse King. He swished his tale and clawed at the audience as they cheered. And then, from the other side of the stage, Brandon appeared as the Nutcracker. He was supposed to lockstep to the middle and pull his foil-wrapped sword, but instead, he hopped out on his crutches, an air cast on his ankle.

Four pairs of mice marched out carrying planks of plywood. They turned the boards to reveal the turnbuckles and ropes painted on their sides. The mice connected the ends to create a square. When the audience realized what was happening, they went wild.

Two mice opened one corner of the squared circle, and Gus stepped into the middle. Then the other two mice opened another corner for Brandon.

"Good evening, everyone." Cy's voice boomed from backstage. "Tonight's main event is a championship match. At stake? The heart of the fair Marie."

The light shone on me, and I clasped my hands and held them to my cheek, pretending to be flattered. I picked up the belt the wardrobe kids had made. I had shown them a photo of Rosie's, and they modeled it after hers. It was cardboard covered in red velvet and sequins, with a tin foil heart glued to the center. I held it up for everyone to see. The audience cheered.

"First, from the sewers of Thorne, New Mexico, weighing in at one hundred and nineteen pounds, the Mouse King!"

Gus flexed his arms and pumped his fists in the air. The audience booed and laughed. He waved his hands, dismissing them.

"And from the workshop of Godpapa Drosselmeier, weighing one hundred pounds, the Nutcracker!"

Brandon waved one crutch in the air, and the audience hooted and whistled.

A bell rang, and the two began to circle each other. The mice holding the boards moved to the perimeter of the stage to give Gus and Brandon room.

"Friends, the Nutcracker appears to be injured," Cy said in her announcer voice. "Unbelievable. Just can't imagine what he was thinking. Hope you don't mind an early dinner, because this match should be over soon."

The Mouse King cornered the Nutcracker, backing him into the couch. He took both crutches and tossed them aside. They locked hands until the Mouse King had pushed the Nutcracker down to the couch. The Nutcracker shook his head and held up his hands as if begging for mercy. The Mouse King strutted around.

"Looks like Marie is going to have to make herself comfortable with the sewer life," Cy said. "Hope she doesn't *waste* away down there."

The audience laughed at Cy's joke.

While the Mouse King goaded the booing audience, I slipped behind the Christmas tree and tied on the red cape from Rosie's old wrestling outfit. I yanked off the headband and pulled on the red mask I'd borrowed from Uncle Mateo.

While the Mouse King strutted, the Nutcracker slid off the couch and crawled behind him. He slowly got on his one good foot, but the Mouse King turned, surprising him with a headbutt. The audience gasped as the Nutcracker fell onto the couch.

Rosie had taught us that the secret to making it look like a real headbutt was to make a loud stomp with the movement. The sound and the big motion created the illusion that you were slamming into someone when you weren't.

Gus busted out some dance moves that hadn't been part of our rehearsals, and the audience cheered him on.

"The Mouse King is pulling out all his moves," Cy announced. "I believe that one is called the Running Man. Which, by the way, would also be the Nutcracker's nickname if not for the injured ankle."

The Mouse King pulled the Nutcracker up off the couch. The Nutcracker tried to hop away, but the Mouse King crossed the ring with an exaggerated bounce off the side of a board and ran back, whipping the Nutcracker across the chest with his tail in his return. The Nutcracker staggered in a funny, slow-motion fall to the floor.

"The Nutcracker is getting a royal lashing from the rodent ruler," Cy bellowed.

With the Nutcracker down, the Mouse King lifted his uninjured leg to pin him. Cy ran out from backstage, dropping down next to them.

"One," Cy called out.

When I heard the first slap, my insides quivered like gelatin. The audience yelled along, just like we knew they would.

"Two," Cy and the crowd counted. That was my cue. I came out from behind the tree. The mice holding the side of the ring closest to me raised it, and I ran under it into the ring, Rosie's red cape billowing behind me.

From behind my mask, I could see the audience on their feet. They were whooping and whistling and cheering, just like the crowd at the arena had. I looked to the side of the stage, where Mrs. González and Mr. Pace stood with puzzled looks on their faces. They had seen Brandon and Gus rehearse, but my appearance was a surprise. Then Mrs. González's face slowly transformed to a delighted Santa-suit-red smile.

"What is going on?" Cy yelled as she stood and moved back into the darkness. "Who is that mysterious masked maiden?"

I dropped an elbow to the Mouse King's back. He rolled off the Nutcracker, and I gave him a fake stomp to the leg. The Mouse King grabbed his leg and squirmed in pain. While he writhed on the floor, I dropped another elbow on the Nutcracker's midsection.

"Wait a minute," Cy hollered. "She's fighting them both! This is chaos!"

While the Nutcracker and the Mouse King slowly got up, I faced the audience, and for the first time, I knew why Manny and Pancho and Maggie loved the squared circle. My insides buzzed with the electricity of the crowd's excitement. They were cheering for *me*. Or at least for the person in the mask and the cape. So I gave them a Rosie pose, hands on hips, then flexed my arms. The audience roared with appreciation.

"Those arms are puny, but they're powerful," Cy said.

"The question is, can she finish this match?"

The Mouse King and the Nutcracker looked around in confusion. I grabbed the Mouse King by one arm and flung him toward one end of the ring. As he moved in slow motion, I grabbed the Nutcracker and did the same, sending him hopping in the opposite direction. The two pretended to bounce off the ropes and moved toward each other, with Brandon struggling to hop while Gus moved like molasses so that they got to the center of the ring at the same time. I looked at the invisible watch on my wrist and yawned. The audience laughed. When they reached me, I grabbed their heads and pretended to knock them together. They dropped exaggeratedly next to each other and onto their backs.

I looked behind me and saw that four mice had turned one plywood board so that the flat side faced up. I climbed up onto it as if I were on the top turnbuckle. I cupped my ear toward the audience like I'd seen Manny do in some of his matches, letting the crowd know I wanted to hear them. Kids, parents, teachers—everyone was on their feet. Somewhere in the crowd I could hear the chant starting: *Ma-rie! Ma-rie! Ma-rie!* It felt like I was back at the arena watching Manny help Apollo, revealing the true identity of The Eagle. I could see why this meant so much to him. *This* felt more exciting than Christmas morning.

I looked down at Gus and Brandon on their backs. This was the scariest part. The board was less than two feet off the floor of the stage. I needed to land next to Brandon without stepping on him. In the couple of days we had between Brandon's injury and the show, we had practiced with me jumping off a chair. It was no big deal. But at that moment, I wasn't sure I could trust my legs not to fail me.

"Jump," Gus urged from where he lay.

"Please don't land on my leg," Brandon pleaded, his eyes squeezed shut tightly.

I took a deep breath and jumped. My slippered feet hit the floor, and in a not-so-swift and not-so-graceful move, I threw myself across Gus and Brandon.

"Oof," Brandon groaned when I elbowed his stomach.

"Sorry," I whispered.

Cy came running out again. She dropped to the floor and counted, the audience counting with her.

"One! Two! Three!"

I pushed myself up, trying my best to not smash anyone. Cy grabbed the belt and handed it to me.

"The winner of the match, with a *double* pin," Cy said, holding up my arm, "Marie!"

I waved the belt in the air, victorious. If there had been any bats left in the rafters above, they would've surely been shaken out by the noise in the auditorium.

★ CHAPTER 35 ★

I was just Marie again, in my flowered dress, when I found Mom and Alex waiting for me in the hall.

"Okay," Mom said, "I can admit it was pretty cool. Even if it involved wrestling. You kids were great."

"That was the best thing ever," Alex said, grabbing me in a hug. "I'm glad you didn't go with the sock puppet idea I overheard."

"Rosie and Uncle Mateo were good teachers," I said. I was grinning so hard, my face hurt.

Mom nodded, willing to acknowledge this too. "Your little brother seemed excited," she said. "He was kicking a lot. I think he thought you might need a tag-team partner, but you seemed okay up there on your own."

"It was a team effort," I said proudly.

Alex waved to someone behind me. I turned to see Rosie and Pancho, the twins and Uncle Mateo, but no Manny. They stood a few feet away from us, as if unsure if they should approach.

"Why don't you go say hello," Mom said, motioning to them. "We'll wait for you."

Uncle Mateo and Rosie waved back. Pancho stared at

us, and Rosie whispered something in his ear. Finally, he smiled and waved too. I hurried over, and the twins pounced on me.

"That was the coolest!" Eva yelped.

"The best *Nutcracker* I've seen!" Maggie agreed.

"The only *Nutcracker* you've seen," Eva said.

"You looked just like a wrestler I once knew," Pancho chimed in. "Her name was La Rosa Salvaje."

I couldn't tell if Pancho was joking or if he was forgetting that the woman next to him was La Rosa Salvaje.

"I hope Brandon didn't hurt himself," Uncle Mateo said, looking concerned. "He really should've just sat out."

"He's fine," I said. "Tired from hopping on one foot, but no seventh graders were hurt in the making of this show."

I looked past the group.

"Where's Manny?"

No one said anything for a few seconds. The twins stared at the floor, avoiding my face.

"I'm sorry, niña," Rosie said. "Your father wanted to be here, but he had to go out of town."

"Out of town?" I asked, frowning. "But he knew the show was tonight. He said he'd be here. He *promised*."

Uncle Mateo squeezed my shoulder. "Come on, Pa," he said, leading Pancho out. "You too." He motioned for the twins to follow.

"We'll see you this weekend," Maggie said, giving me a hug.

Rosie stood next to me as Uncle Mateo led Pancho and the twins outside.

"Where is he?" I asked when they were gone.

"There was a meeting with someone about an important job," Rosie said. "Lo siento."

"I thought he already had a job," I said. "Here. At Cactus."

"He wanted to come, Adela," Rosie said. She looked sad. I wondered if it was for me.

"Right." I fought back tears. I wouldn't cry in front of Rosie. "He couldn't even call or text and tell me he wasn't coming?" I looked at my phone in case I had missed a message.

"He's returning late tonight," she said. "He wants to have breakfast with you tomorrow morning at the diner before school."

"Does my mom know?" I said. "That he's coming tomorrow?"

"I think so." Rosie nodded. "You can tell him all about the show, ¿sí?"

"If he cared about the show, he would've been here tonight," I muttered. "What kind of person doesn't follow through on a promise?"

Rosie held my hand. How many times had she apologized for fathers who couldn't make it to first days of school and high school wrestling matches and birthdays and other important days? I was mad at Manny, but I was also mad at myself for believing that he would be at the show. How many chances had Mom given him before she finally stopped believing?

"Did you ever wish Pancho and your sons didn't wrestle?" I asked. "Or Maggie? She wants to wrestle. Don't you get tired of apologizing for them?"

"I cannot control what people do," Rosie said. "If I could, I never would have lost you." Her eyes glistened like smoky quartz.

"Manny and Mom?" I said. "You wanted them to stay together?"

"No, mija," she said. "They didn't have to stay together for us to be in each other's lives."

"Did you know anything about me?" I asked. "All these years?"

"A little bit. Not much. I loved your mamá," she said. "And one of the things I loved about her was that she's a woman of her word. When she told Manny she was done, she meant it. I can admire that."

"Even if it meant I didn't get to see any of you," I said. "That's not right."

"No, it's not," Rosie said. "What they did was selfish. And confusing, yes?"

"Very," I said. "Maybe it would be easier if life really was like wrestling and you knew who the good guy was and who the bad guy was."

"But even in wrestling it is never certain," Rosie said. "We're all a little of both sometimes, no?"

I thought about Rosie's words. Families trickled past us out of the building.

"You were wonderful tonight." Rosie squeezed my hand. "I'm very proud of you, Adela."

"Thank you, Rosie," I said. "And thank you for your help."

"Will I see you on Saturday?"

I nodded. She kissed my cheek and began walking toward the exit to find Pancho and the rest of the family.

"Rosie, wait," I called to her. She turned. "I need to get your cape. I left it backstage."

"Ay, don't worry about it," Rosie said, smiling. "You can keep it. It looks better on you."

CHAPTER 36

Every few minutes, Mom waddled out of the kitchen. She looked like my baby brother would arrive at any minute even though she wasn't due for another two months. She pretended to do tasks that had to be done at that exact moment. She wiped down the counter. Again. Checked if the sugar containers needed to be refilled. They didn't. Made sure all the empty tables had napkins and silverware. Part of me wanted her to leave. Her nervous energy filled the air. But part of me was glad she was hovering. She'd taken the morning off from the museum so that she could be at the diner when Manny came.

Marlene appeared from the kitchen and walked over. She set a smoothie down in front of me.

"Monkey and cow in a twister," she announced, placing the glass on the table with authority.

"I'm not hungry," I said, looking at the peanut butter, banana, and chocolate milk smoothie.

"Should I bring you a bowl of hope instead?" Marlene threatened.

"Uh, no." I shook my head. If hope was something you

could order off a menu and eat from a bowl, I might've accepted it.

"Then drink it," Marlene said.

I took a sip of the smoothie and felt it move down my throat like cold cement. I was nervous, but it was a different kind of nervous than last night. *The Nutcracker* was an if-I-mess-this-up-I-hope-the-Earth-swallows-me nervousness. What I felt as I waited for Manny was an everything-depends-on-this nervousness. It was almost too much.

I didn't want to look at the face of the clock on the wall. I could hear each move of the minute hand pounding, just like the telltale heart in the creepy story we'd read in Mrs. Murry's class for Halloween. There was a jumble of feelings in the pitter-patter of my own heart—anticipation, disappointment, sadness, anger. And, somewhere in all that, there was still a dash of hope.

Two-thirds of a smoothie gone and seven minutes late, Manny walked in. He wore a black ski cap over his shaved head, a beat-up leather jacket over a black T-shirt, jeans, and work boots. His face was freshly shaven.

I instinctively turned to look at the kitchen window in relief, forgetting for a moment that I was mad at him for missing the show. I knew Mom would be there, watching. She was, along with Alex and Marlene. They all quickly turned away.

"Sorry I'm late," Manny said, sitting down across from

me. He mumbled something about traffic. Or maybe it was something about alarm clocks.

I was about to say *It's okay*, but it wasn't. I'd said those words so many times, they didn't seem to mean anything anymore, just like Manny's apologies.

"First, tell me what's good," he said, opening the menu as if nothing was wrong. "Then tell me all about the show, eh?"

"Everything's good," I said, looking at the menu that was so familiar to me.

"Mmm," Manny said. "I think I'm going with the blue corn pancakes. And the scrambled egg breakfast."

"That's a lot of food," I warned.

"Have you seen me?" Manny asked, patting his belly.

Marlene brought Manny coffee and took his order.

"I'm sorry I missed the show," Manny said when she walked away. "I really am. Ma said it was something else."

"It's . . ." I almost said it again but stopped myself. "You *should* be sorry. Where were you?"

Manny smoothed the paper place mat with his fingers.

"Something came up. Well, not just *something*. This is a really big something."

"What is it?" I asked.

"An old friend at the Atlantic Wrestling Federation has a story for me," he said. "It'll lead to a shot at the belt."

"The belt? That's great," I said. "What does it mean?"

"It means . . ." Manny hesitated. He took a sip of his coffee and placed the mug carefully on top of the coffee ring that had soaked through the place mat. "Well, it means I'm going to Delaware."

"Delaware?" I tried to picture Delaware on a map in a cluster of other tiny states. "For how long?"

The *ba-rum-pa-pum-pum* of "The Little Drummer Boy" filled the diner. Alex turned the volume up a little bit. The deep, heavy baritone gave me a strange feeling, scary and uncomfortable, like when you ride a roller coaster and it feels like your stomach drops out of you. I wanted to run out of the diner.

"The thing is, I have to reestablish myself for a bit," he said. "Before I can get that title shot."

"But you said you were going to stay," I reminded him. "Are you leaving . . . for good?"

"Staying *was* the plan," he said. "But when a chance like this comes along . . . I have to do this, Addie. I won't be leaving for good, but I do have to go."

"I thought you loved Cactus." I frowned. "I thought Cactus was home."

"It is," Manny said. "But it's also small potatoes. You understand, don't you?"

"Small potatoes can be good too," I insisted, thinking about the baby yellow potatoes Alex would sauté in butter in a cast-iron Dutch oven. "What about Pancho?"

"What about him?"

"He's sick," I said. "Don't you want to be here? What if something happens?"

"He gave me his blessing," Manny said. "He wants this for me."

Marlene brought out Manny's food. She looked at me as if she could see something in my face that I didn't know was there.

"You okay, hon?" she asked. She looked at Manny and glared.

I nodded. Marlene hesitated before walking away.

"What about me?" I asked. "Don't you want my blessing? Is that why you came here?"

"This doesn't change anything, Addie," Manny said, cutting into his corn cakes. "You can come visit."

"In *Delaware*?"

"You make it sound like I'm inviting you to outer space or something," he said, laughing nervously. "Delaware's a nice place."

"I don't want to go to Delaware."

"Okay, well, then I'll see you when I come through Esperanza," he said. "No big deal, right?"

Manny poured syrup onto his pancakes. I wanted to tell him that you never pour directly on them. Otherwise, the syrup gets absorbed and disappears. You pour on the side, for dipping. It was my syrup secret. I wanted to share this with Manny, but I didn't.

"What about the adoption?" I could feel the anger

growing in me. "Are we ever going to talk about it? Or were you just going to leave again and not mention it? That's why I looked for you, you know? What do you think about that? Do you even care?"

"Of course I care," Manny said. He sat back in his seat and ran his hands over his face.

"You don't act like it." I stared at him.

"What do you want me to do, Adela?" he asked. "Your mom kept you away from me because I couldn't be who she wanted me to be. This is who I am."

I looked at what he had to offer. Was it enough?

"I want you to act like you want to be my father," I practically yelled. "Or is that not who you are?"

"I want to be your father," he said, looking around the diner to see if anyone was paying attention to us. "Jeez, I *am* your father." He exhaled.

"Then why are you leaving?"

"I don't have a choice," Manny said, leaning into the table toward me.

"Like you didn't have a choice before."

I remembered my conversations with Rosie and Uncle Mateo about choices. I knew it wasn't that he didn't have one. It was just that he wasn't choosing me.

"Don't be this way, Addie," he said.

"When will you be back?"

"Soon," he offered. "Really soon."

"Will you be here for Christmas?"

"I . . . I don't think so," he said. "I don't know what my schedule will be like, but I have to be willing to put in the work. I gotta be willing to do anything."

"For the belt," I said. *Not for me.*

Manny didn't look up from his plate, where he stabbed at his eggs and corn cakes with his fork.

I thought about how I had almost called him Dad at the cemetery. The truth was genetics couldn't make him a dad. A name couldn't make him a dad. Money couldn't make him a dad. Manny wasn't my dad. He was just the guy that provided some of my genes. I wanted to say all kinds of mean things to him. That I wished I'd never found the photo of him. That I wished I'd never met him.

Before I could say anything, Marlene came over to tell him the meal was on the house. While they talked, I took my angry words and I swallowed them with a gulp of my smoothie. I thought again about how Mom had explained that fossil preparation is like surgery. The fossils are fragile, and you have to be very careful not to damage them when they're being removed from the rock they've lived in for millions of years. And sometimes you just can't remove them without breaking them. Manny was like that, too, a fossil trapped in rock. I didn't know if he'd ever be free.

"Can I give you a ride to school?" Manny asked.

"No," I said. "I have my bike. I'm meeting my friends."

In school, whenever we had to make cards for Father's Day, I'd make one anyway. Even before Alex, when I didn't have a dad. I would imagine what my father might look like. He was always tall, like me, with jet-black hair. I would dig through the container of crayons, looking for the shade of brown that matched our skin.

The dad I drew was always doing brave and exciting things. One year, he was climbing a mountain right toward a mountain goat with its head lowered, horns aimed at him, ready to battle. Another year, he was sailing a pirate ship. He was up in the crow's nest with a telescope to his eye. My favorite was the dad in the hot-air balloon in a sky full of hot-air balloons. I imagined that someday he and I might go up in one at the balloon fiesta in Albuquerque. But at that moment, sitting across from Manny, I knew that this was all I would get from him. Maybe he would change someday. But he wasn't ready yet.

"This is temporary, Addie," Manny said. "I'll be back." He waited for me to say something. Then he stood and wiped his mouth one last time. He dropped the napkin, and it floated down onto his plate like a ghost. "I'll see you at the house? We can talk some more then. And I still want to hear all about the show. Your abuela took some video, you know?"

I didn't respond.

He waited a few more seconds. I didn't look up. Finally, he tugged on my braid and left.

As soon as the door closed behind him, Mom reappeared from the back. She looked at my face and hurried out of the diner. The gust of wind from the door made the paper snowflakes hanging from the ceiling swing and spin like a real snowstorm.

I ran to the window and peered through the blinds as Manny and Mom talked. They didn't touch. Mom's body looked stiff, and she kept her hands on her belly. It was the first time I'd seen my parents together. When they were done talking, Manny waved, got into his vehicle, and drove away.

I walked outside and looked at Mom, who stood in the spot where Manny had left her.

"Are you okay?" she asked, walking over.

"No," I said. I kicked the wheel of my bike, which was propped outside the diner, and knocked it over.

"Come on," Mom said. "Let's go inside."

I followed her into the diner and went back to my booth.

"He's leaving." I couldn't look at her. "You were right."

"I'm so sorry, Addie."

She scooted into the booth next to me, her belly pressed tight against the table, and offered me a rare hug. I leaned into her.

"He broke my heart too," Mom said.

"Will you tell me?" I asked. "Please?"

And she did. Mom told me the story of two childhood sweethearts from Esperanza who had made a pact to get out. She wanted Manny to leave his demanding father, to have a future that was different, one that wouldn't mean being in pain, always traveling and never with his family. One where he didn't have to live in the shadow of a legacy.

They planned to move to Albuquerque together with her bisabuela, where they would go to college and work. Mom went ahead, but Manny kept putting it off because of wrestling. Then, the summer after her first year of college, Mom found out she was pregnant. Manny told Mom that he would move to Albuquerque before I was born. But an opportunity came up, one Manny knew he couldn't pass on, to wrestle in Florida with his dad and Speedy. He said he would quit wrestling after that. Just another year at most. And then Speedy died.

He missed my birth, and when he finally made it to Albuquerque, he said wrestling was all he ever wanted to do and he couldn't give it up. He asked Mom to marry him and move back to Esperanza. But Mom realized that she was tired of waiting and that she didn't want to give up her own dreams for the future.

Time passed, Manny's career got bigger, and we saw less of him. Mom knew how much it had hurt him and his brothers to not have their father around, and she couldn't accept that he would do the same thing to me. He visited until I was about one, when Mom finally told him not to come back unless he planned to stay. She preferred I not know anything about him over knowing that he picked wrestling instead of me.

The story was so simple. There was no pencil heiress given up at birth, no big family cover-up, no one who snitched and ended up in a vat of pencil lead like in the telenovela. There were no zombie Founding Fathers, no Mouse King, no Zeus or Hades, no bad guy you could boo and root against. It was just the stuff of mortals—disappointment and heartbreak and family and two people who were on different paths, and one who wasn't old enough to choose, so the decision was made for her. And in hearing Mom tell me the story, I was able to understand her, or at least I thought I did. We all had our hearts broken. Mom and me, but also Manny.

"Mom," I said. "You should've told me about him. And maybe let me decide if I wanted him to be a part of my life. You were wrong too."

Mom looked taken aback, and for a moment, I thought she was mad.

"You're right," she said. "I'm sorry."

"I'm sorry too. I wanted to know him so badly that I didn't care if I hurt you or Alex or anyone. Just like Manny. He doesn't care who he hurts when he's got his mind set on something. I don't want to be like that, Mom."

"That's up to you," Mom said. "You decide how to be."

"And, Mom," I said. "I love Alex. But I don't want him to adopt me. And it's not because I want Manny to be my dad, or because I don't want Alex to be my dad. I just don't feel ready to make that decision right now. Is that okay?"

"Of course," Mom said.

"Will Alex be sad?"

"Alex will understand."

"You know what one of the cool things about going to Esperanza has been?" I asked.

"What's that?"

"All this time, I was looking for Manny, wanting to know who he was," I said. "But I think I found you too."

"Interesting," Mom said. "I didn't know I was lost."

I felt the backs of my eyes getting warm, and the lump in my throat growing, threatening to burst.

"It's okay to cry," Mom said, looking into my face.

"There's no crying in wrestling," I said, sniffling. "Don't you know?"

Mom rolled her eyes. We both laughed. And then the tears came.

CHAPTER 37

The Friday before winter break was a busy one. I skipped lunch to stuff copies of the invitations I'd printed in all the seventh-grade lockers. In Mrs. Murry's class, I turned in my final mythology project. It was a poster-board collage with pieces of the New Mexican sky and landscape, mountains and tumbleweeds and cacti and piñon trees cut out of nature magazines, glittery purple bubble letters, and the little photos from my instant camera taped across it like the illustration of the pantheon in *D'Aulaires' Book of Greek Myths*.

I'd managed to get a photo of everyone, even Hijo. There were photos of Pancho in the family room, the twins in the squared circle, Rosie in her workspace surrounded by tumbleweeds, Uncle Mateo with his golden scissors and sewing machine and pink bouffant wig, Manny in the gym, and Alex at the diner. Marlene with her order pad. Cy on opening night. Rosie had let me borrow a photo of Speedy to scan and print for the poster. On the back, on index cards, I had written a series of short family myths about powerful fathers who hold their offspring under their spell, strong mothers who raise their children alone, daughters looking for their ghost lineage, a dog that transforms into the greatest fighter when no one is around to see, star goddesses who come to Earth in the form of teenage girls, a best friend whose bond is as strong as that of a sister—stories about heartbreak and loss and found family.

I had placed the Polaroid on the wall in the living room with the other tumbleweed snowman photos, and I had taken my printouts from the historical society out of my closet and put them up in my bedroom. When Mrs. Murry returned my mythology project, I planned to put that up too.

As soon as the afternoon bell rang, dismissing us for the day, I hurried to meet Cy at her locker.

"You're coming, right?" I asked. I'd told Cy about Gus and the worms and my plan.

"Of course," she said. "This whole thing sounds bizarre, and you know I love bizarre. Besides, you saved the show. Twice. I wouldn't leave you hanging."

I was glad she wanted to join us. I needed my best friend there. "Think anyone else will show up?" I asked. Kids ran out of the school like they couldn't escape fast enough.

"I'll be there," Brandon said, limping past us on his air cast. "That's all that matters."

Cy swiped at him with her water bottle, but he moved surprisingly fast.

Outside, Gus waited with the box. He lifted it in greeting.

"The guests of honor are here," he said. "Lead the way."

We walked past the playground behind the school, across the baseball diamond, out beyond the PE field. A handful of seventh graders joined us on the walk. A few more showed up to the meeting spot when we arrived.

"Thanks for coming to the first meeting of the F.A.C.E.S. Club," I said, addressing the group.

"Faces?" Brandon asked.

"Yeah," I said. "Like in wrestling. The good guys? That's us. For Action, Care, and Equality in School. This won't take long. I know everyone is eager to start the break."

"This *is* a pretty inconvenient time to meet," a classmate named Delia admitted.

"Gus said that at his other schools, kids expressed their opinions and challenged things they didn't agree with," I went on. "So we thought it would be good to have something like that, an activism club, at Thorne Middle."

There were murmurs of agreement.

"Our first order of business, and the only order of business today, is a celebration of life."

I motioned to Gus, who knelt on the ground and opened the box. He pulled out ten plastic bags.

"Are those what I think they are?" a girl named Carol asked, moving closer.

"*You?*" Brandon said, looking wide-eyed from the worms to Gus.

341

"We don't know where these worms came from, how they were caught, or if they were killed to be sold to the school for dissection," I said. "But we thought they deserved a more dignified ending."

Gus began to dig a hole in the ground with the small gardening trowel I'd brought.

"Ugh," Cy said, pinching her nose. "I can smell them from here."

"That's the formaldehyde," Gus informed us. "It's what keeps them preserved."

"If you want to learn more about animal cruelty," I said, "including how animals are used for experimentation and dissection, check out Gus's display in the library. And our first action item when we come back from break is to demand more information about where these animals came from and see if the school will work with us on alternatives to dissection of animals."

"There's no alternative to cutting open a dead worm," a boy named Tristan said.

"Sure there is." Gus stood, looking at the hole he'd made. "Some schools use models or computer programs. And another question is, do we need to dissect animals to learn about them?"

"Ready?" I asked.

Gus opened the bags and, one by one, dropped the worms into the hole. "Back to their home," he said, refilling the hole with dirt once all the worms were in. He patted the dirt down.

I placed a rock and a plastic toy worm on top as a head-stone and a token of respect.

"Do we need a moment of silence?" Cy asked, looking around at the group.

Everyone lowered their heads. When I looked up again, I caught Gus's eye, and for once, he didn't look away.

"We'll send out information about our next meeting after the break," Gus said. "Thanks for coming."

Kids began making their way back across the field. Brandon flashed a peace sign and followed the group.

"That wasn't as bizarre as I expected," Cy said. "But I'll be at the next meeting anyway."

"Well?" I said to Gus, who collected the box and empty bags. "Not bad, right?"

"Yeah," he said. "Not bad."

"I know it probably wasn't as cool as the stuff you did at all your other schools," I said. "You've moved around a lot, huh?"

"Yeah," Gus said, looking away. "My dad works for the government. I hate it."

"That sounds tough," I said. "This is the only place I've ever known. Must be hard to make friends."

He shrugged.

"You know what also makes it hard?" Cy asked. "Not letting people be your friends."

Gus didn't say anything. When we reached the bike racks, he stuffed the box in a nearby recycling bin.

"See you in January," he said, mounting his bike.

"Later, Gus." Cy waved.

"Hey," I called to him before he could leave. "I just thought of a good nickname for you. Besides Gus."

"I don't need another nickname," Gus said.

"Of course you do," I insisted. "Friends don't let friends miss out on a great nickname. Wanna hear it?"

"I do," Cy said.

I looked at Gus, waiting.

"Fine," he said. "What is it?"

I started to laugh.

"Not again." Gus covered his face with the palm of his hand.

"Okay," I said, taking a deep breath and trying to keep a straight face. "It's . . . Gusano! Get it? Because you're Gus, and the Spanish word for worm is—"

"Gusano!" Cy shrieked and doubled over laughing.

"I get it," Gus said.

He shook his head, but I was certain I saw something that resembled a real smile before he rode away.

★ CHAPTER 38 ★

After parting ways with Cy, I biked to the historical society. As I locked my bike, I found myself hoping Sleepy Reading Lady would be there and was pleasantly surprised when I opened the front door and she was, at her table, like always. She looked up and smiled in recognition. I smiled back.

"Hi," I said as I passed her table.

"Hello," she greeted me in return.

"Well, look who it is," Rudy said. He put down his pencil and folded his hands on his desk. "Ms. Bravo."

"Huh?" I stopped in my tracks.

"I'm sorry," Rudy said. "I forgot your name. But not your face or what you were researching. I always remember what people research."

"Oh," I said. "It's Adela. And yeah, I was researching the Bravos."

"I knew that," he said, wagging his finger at me. "What brings you back to us? Did you get an email that the Bravo box was ready?"

"Oh, no, I didn't," I said. "I'd like to look at it if it is, but I'm here for another reason."

"Go on, then," Rudy said.

"I wanted to know how people donate their things," I said. "You know, so that you can take care of them here and make them available to others."

"Well, if it fits the scope of what we collect—anything related to the history of Esperanza and Thorne, we collect it," Rudy explained. "People sometimes contact us and ask if we're interested in something they have. And sometimes we reach out to people who we know have something we'd like to keep here."

"Okay," I said, shoving my arm into my backpack. "I have something for the wrestling collection."

I pulled out a wrinkled brown paper bag and a green school folder and placed them on Rudy's desk.

"What's this?" Rudy asked, opening the folder. He held up the photo of Rosie and let out a whistle. "How about that?"

"That's La Rosa Salvaje, the world wrestling champion," I informed him. "She was Rosa Terrones there. Now she's Rosie Bravo."

"This is fantastic," Rudy said, admiring the photo. He placed it back on top of the folder and opened the paper bag. He carefully lifted Rosie's folded red cape, shaking it loose and holding it up with both hands.

"It's the cape she's wearing in the photo," I said.

"Amazing."

"It is, isn't it?" I smiled.

"And how did you come by these?" he asked. "You didn't *borrow* them from someone, did you?"

"Oh, no." I laughed. "Rosie is my abuela."

"Imagine that," Rudy said. "Does she know you brought these here?"

"She let me have them," I said. "And I want you to take care of them. Will you?"

"And how do you think these items fit into our collection?" He looked at me over the top of his glasses as if he was quizzing me.

"Well, you collect items that tell the story of the Dos Pueblos area. That includes the Bravos and the Cactus Wrestling League," I said. "Rosie should be included. She's an important part of those stories. She was a wrestler, too, and without her, a lot of what the Bravos have done wouldn't have been possible. Not to mention, she's part of local culture. She makes the tumbleweed statues."

Rudy sat back and studied me.

"Ever thought about being an archivist?" he asked. "I'd be honored to add these to our collection."

"Good," I said. "I want you to put them out in a display case for everyone who comes in here to see. Rosie had them in a cardboard box in her work shed. That's no place for something valuable like this, right?"

"You are absolutely right," Rudy agreed.

★ CHAPTER 39 ★

On Christmas morning, after opening gifts, Mom and I pulled on our sweaters and headed out together while Alex drove with Marlene.

"It's too bad Cy couldn't be with us," Mom said.

"Yeah," I agreed. "I wish she was coming too." Cy had gone to Philadelphia to visit her family for the holidays.

When we arrived at the tumbleweed snowman, there were a few other people admiring it and taking their own photos. The tumbleweed creation towered above us, at least thirteen feet tall. It was painted white and wore the blue scarf Rosie had made for it. Its hat, face, and buttons were made of scrap metal. The hands were old work gloves attached to the ends of two broomsticks. I felt myself beaming with pride at my abuela's work.

Alex got busy setting up the tripod and camera. A family, a mom and dad and two little kids, asked him if he could take their photo. They stood together, smiling, saying cheese, while Alex snapped several photos on the dad's phone. When he handed it back, they thanked him, and the kids crowded around their father while he swiped through the images. I could hear them laughing at each other's funny smiles or closed eyes.

Alex finished setting up the camera and walked back to where Mom, Marlene, and I leaned against the hood of Mom's car. That's when a couple of vehicles pulled up behind ours. I recognized Rosie's truck.

"Rosie!" I yelled as my abuela climbed out.

She smiled at me before walking around to the passenger side to help Pancho. Behind them, Uncle Mateo and Carter and the twins climbed out of another truck. Maggie held the door open, and Hijo jumped out. They all wore cactus Christmas tree sweaters.

"Seriously, Mom?" I laughed. "Where did you find all these sweaters?"

"I have my ways," Mom said. "Next year I need to remember to get one in dog size." She pointed to Hijo.

Mom wasn't much of a hugger, but that didn't mean I couldn't be one. I put my arms around her, and she squeezed me in turn.

Eva jumped on Maggie's back, and Maggie carried her toward me.

"Merry Christmas!" the twins yelled. They were dressed in their tzitzimime outfits, gold satin skulls-and-stars jackets over their sweaters. Eva wore a reindeer antlers headband on her nest of black-and-gold hair.

"These sweaters are so dorky," she said, clicking the lights on and off.

"Don't say that too loud," I warned, laughing. "My mom might hear you."

But Mom was busy greeting Rosie and Pancho. She took the potted cuetlaxochitl Rosie held out to her. Then she let Rosie hug her too. I looked at her face. It wasn't happy, but it also wasn't sad. It must have been hard for her to invite them to the photo. But maybe Mom was evolving.

Uncle Mateo carried a white gift box under one arm. He let Carter's hand go and took mine, leading me away from the group.

"I have something for you." He held out the box.

"For me?" I said, surprised. "I have gifts for all of you, too, but I was going to bring them over later."

"This one's not from me."

"Oh. Okay. Should I open it now?"

"Sure," he said.

I crouched down and pulled away the white tissue paper that concealed the box's contents. I gasped as I pulled out the mask and held it up. It was shades of green and blue to match the New Mexican landscape and embroidered with a design of stars and tumbleweeds and cacti.

"Manny commissioned it. That means he asked me to make it for you," he explained. "Merry Christmas, Adela."

I slipped the mask on over my head, pulling it down tight around my face, and ran my hand along the soft fabric. It wasn't a poem, but it was poetry.

"Whoa, that's dogdamn sweet," Eva said, walking over to us.

"Eva," Rosie warned from behind her.

"What?" She flashed Rosie a mischievous smile. "I didn't say anything."

"Tzitzi girl gang taking over the world!" Maggie whooped.

"Bdelloidea girl gang taking over the world!" I yelled back.

Maggie and Eva looked at each other, puzzled. I'd have to tell them about the Bdelloidea. Eva came up behind me and put me in a headlock that I struggled to twist out of because I was laughing so hard.

"No wrestling on Christmas, cabezonas!" Rosie called out.

"I'll teach you how to get out of one of those later," Uncle Mateo said, as if reading my mind.

"Okay, everyone," Mom said. "Over by the snowman."

I studied Alex and Mom through the eyeholes of my mask as they danced around each other, moving everyone into place. Rosie and Pancho flanked the snowman on one side. Uncle Mateo and Carter and Marlene stood in front of it. Maggie and Eva and I, the tzitzis, sat on the ground up front with Hijo.

I thought of those science transparency pages in Alex's old encyclopedia again. This time, I imagined myself in layers on top of layers, and all of these people, Manny included, as part of who I was.

Alex set the timer, then ran over to stand by Mom on the snowman's other side. Behind us was that constant backdrop of mountains and sky.

"Say tzitzis!" Maggie said, like she was shooting sparks from between her teeth.

We smiled. We yelled, "Tzitzis!" We made scary faces and goofy faces. Anyone who saw us taking our photos would think we were a family, and we were. Long-lost family, stepfamily, blood family, chosen family. Part myth, part science. We were all those things.

★ ACKNOWLEDGMENTS ★

In the introduction to his classic novel *Bless Me, Ultima*, Rudolfo Anaya wrote: "But a novel is not written to explain a culture, it creates its own." While my stories are a blend of truth and imagination, the creation of a new place with its own culture, I sincerely hope that I was able to do justice to the real places, things, and experiences that inspired this book. I am grateful to everyone who shared with me their expertise and personal knowledge.

Many thanks to all the tag-team partners, both in writing and in life, who helped make this book possible and who have supported me in my writing over the years: Joanna Cárdenas and everyone at Kokila and Penguin; Stefanie Sanchez Von Borstel; Steph C; Delia Cosentino; Jessica Mills; Stephanie Roe and the 2020–2021 sixth and seventh graders of Grant Middle School in Albuquerque, who were generous with their time and responded to my questionnaire; Stephanie Flores-Koulish, Xelena González; Pablo Cartaya; the Perez family; the Zeeb family; all of my dear friends; and the educators, caregivers, booksellers, and readers who keep my stories alive. And, of course, Emiliano, Brett, and Bagel. I am always in your corner.